Book #2

Seduced by the
NIGHT

Seduced by the
NIGHT

Robin T. Popp

WARNER **FOREVER**

NEW YORK   BOSTON

Copyright © 2006 by Robin T. Popp
Excerpt from *Tempted in the Night*
copyright 2006 by Robin T. Popp

Warner Forever and logo are registered trademarks of
Time Warner Book Group Inc.

Cover design by Diane Luger
Cover illustration by Craig White
Book design and text composition by
Stratford Publishing Services

Warner Books
1271 Avenue of the Americas
New York, NY 10020

Printed in the United States of America

ISBN: 978-0-7394-6787-9

ISBN: 0-7394-6787-5

To Dakota, Mihka, and Garrett – if I had all the wealth and fortune of the world, you three would still be my greatest treasures.

Acknowledgments

I would like to thank Marlaine Loftin, Adam Popp, Mary O'Connor, Georgia Ward, Donna Grant, and Corkey Sandman for brainstorming plot ideas, reading various drafts, keeping me on track, and just generally being there for me.

I would like to thank Rod O'Connor for sharing some of his biochemical knowledge and expertise with me. Any errors in the various research techniques, methods, or logic are completely my own.

I would like to thank Karen Kosztolnyik for her continued support and for pushing me to be the best writer I can be.

Also, I would like to thank Michelle Grajkowski for being such a terrific agent and having such enthusiasm for my writing.

Special thanks to Katie Popp and Kevin Nowak who provided my family with a "port in the storm" when we evacuated our home during Hurricane Rita. What could have been a truly miserable experience turned out to be rather pleasant and I was able to finish work on this book and make my deadline.

Seduced by the
NIGHT

Chapter 1

On an otherwise still and silent night, the faint noise and gentle breeze barely registered with Bethany Stavinoski, whose thoughts were focused elsewhere. On her way to the office, she walked another half a block along the deserted Washington D.C. sidewalk before it occurred to her that a woman alone at night should be more cautious—and alert.

Spinning around, she half expected a mugger or vagrant to leap at her. She felt both relieved and a bit foolish when the only other person in sight was a man leaning against the inside wall of a building's doorway, half a block behind her. Strange, she thought. She hadn't noticed him before. The feeble glow of a nearby streetlight only touched the outer half of him, leaving the rest swallowed by the darkened entryway. His features were unclear and a trick of the poor lighting gave his eyes a reddish glow. He wore a long black duster over equally dark clothes. With one leg bent at the knee so he could brace his foot against the wall, he smoked a cigarette, appearing both unhurried and extremely dangerous.

As she watched, he took the cigarette from his mouth to exhale and his lips lifted in a slight smile as he tipped his head in a subtle greeting. Afraid that her staring might be misconstrued as an invitation to approach, she turned and hurried away.

That's right, sweet thing. Be very afraid. Dirk Adams watched the look of apprehension cross the young woman's face just before she turned and walked off. He raised his hand, bringing the cigarette to his mouth, and took a long drag before slowly exhaling the smoke.

He waited until she disappeared around the corner before flicking the cigarette to the street, where he watched the tip flare briefly as it bounced and rolled away. It wasn't even his; Dirk didn't smoke—not anymore.

"Thanks for the loaner," he said conversationally, turning to the creature he held pinned to the door by the neck. "But you know? They just don't taste as good as they used to. Probably just as well. Those things'll kill you." He smiled at his own joke as he studied the creature, more monster now than the twenty-something man it used to be. "I don't suppose that matters to you, though."

"I'm . . . going . . . to . . . kill . . . you," the creature choked out past the constriction of its throat, sounding harsh and wild. "You can't . . . stop me."

Sharp clawlike nails raked across Dirk's hand and he winced at the pain. It hurt like a son of a bitch and he felt his anger rise, but didn't loosen his grip. Instead, he let his lips curl back in a snarl.

The creature's eyes widened in surprise, then it renewed its struggles. Dirk hesitated to do what had to be done, hoping to get some useful bit of information while there was a modicum of coherent thought left in his captive. "Where are Harris and Patterson? Where is the lair?"

"Go to hell," it spat back.

"Right." Dirk pulled a small dagger from its sheath beneath his duster and drove it into the vampire's heart. "Save me a seat."

Bethany anxiously glanced up and, seeing the familiar shape of the Van Horne Technologies building ahead, breathed a sigh of relief. It wasn't a large building, only four stories in height, but it was home—more so than her apartment, lately. She'd worked there as a research biochemist for almost five years and enjoyed what she did. There was an inherent order to doing research that appealed to her. She liked her life neat, organized, and most important, uneventful.

She reached the door of the building and swiped her ID tag. The doors immediately opened and she crossed the lobby to the security desk, her footsteps ringing loudly in the silence. Bethany found it curious that the guard was not at his post, but assumed he was making his rounds. She signed the after-hours register, noticing her assistant's signature on the line above, and couldn't help worrying what havoc Stuart was wreaking in her absence. The thought sent her hurrying for the elevators.

Stepping inside, she pushed the button to the fourth floor, and as the elevator began its ascent, she thought about her latest project. It had her baffled, but she was determined to rise to the challenge even if it meant running a battery of timed tests that dragged her into the lab at all hours of the night.

She'd questioned Miles Van Horne about who had commissioned the project, but he'd remained stubbornly closemouthed. It wasn't that she expected the CEO to divulge that information to just anyone, but she was not only the researcher in charge of the project, she was his . . . fiancée.

The word rolled around awkwardly in her mind and she tried to view the very recent change in their status from a strictly analytical perspective. She had been dating Miles for almost a year now and although she'd considered it unwise to date the boss, he had been charmingly persistent.

Miles was quite a bit older than she and their physical relationship was more PG-13 than R, but that seemed to suit them both. They never mixed business with their personal lives and she thought it unlikely that she'd find anyone else as supportive of her research and the crazy work schedule she kept. Add to the equation Miles's wealth and status and the end result was that she could do a whole lot worse.

She'd made the right decision in accepting his proposal, she told herself, running her thumb over the band of the two-carat, emerald-cut diamond solitaire perched on her ring finger. All in all, theirs was the perfect relationship. So when he'd suggested they get married, why had she hesitated?

A soft voice whispered the answer in the back of her head and she silently scoffed at herself. *Love? Please.* She was far too realistic to believe in that fairy tale. The score of disastrous relationships before Miles flickered through her mind. No, this was a good, practical match.

As the elevator stopped, Bethany forced herself to mentally switch gears and glanced at her watch. *Damn.* She was running late and knowing Stuart, he'd started without her. She wondered, not for the first time, if she should talk to Miles about the man. Maybe if Miles understood how incompetent Stuart really was, he'd . . . he'd what? Fire Stuart? Bethany sighed. She didn't want to be responsible for someone losing his or her job.

Resigned to working with the man for now, she opened the door to her office and saw the light on in the lab beyond—Stuart hard at work, no doubt. Yeah, that was a laugh. Please don't let him have started the next phase of the experiment, she silently prayed.

She stashed her purse in her desk drawer, grabbed her lab coat off the nearby rack, and shrugging into it, hurried through the connecting doorway.

"Stuart—?" She came to an abrupt halt and felt her heart lurch.

Beakers lay shattered on the countertop while reagents ran off the edge, dripping onto the floor where puddles already formed. Stands that had held flasks and tubing in place now lay strewn about in broken pieces. Everything was ruined—all of her hard work, flushed down the proverbial toilet.

And Stuart was conspicuously absent.

She walked farther into the room to assess the damage. "Stuart. Damn it! Where the hell are you?"

She felt anger burning inside and fought to control it. Had he done this? There was no question that the man hated her. He'd practically accused her of sleeping her

way to the department manager position. This destruction
was yet another childish act of professional jealousy. Well,
this time, he'd gone too far.

Hurrying back to her office, she grabbed the phone and
dialed the front desk. There was no answer so she hung
up, her irritation growing to include the absent guard as
she next punched in Miles's cell number. He picked up on
the second ring but she didn't give him time to say a word,
launching immediately into her tirade.

"Everything is ruined, absolutely ruined. I can't believe he'd do such a thing—"

"Who?"

"Stuart! He destroyed everything. All of my work on
this project is now strewn across the floor. I still have my
notes, of course, but now I have to start all over. Is this his
idea of working together? How could he—?"

"Bethany!" Miles's raised voice stemmed the flow of
angry words. "Slow down and tell me what's going on.
Are you all right?"

She took a deep breath, trying to bring herself under
control, and then, speaking more slowly, told him what
she'd found.

"Are you positive Stuart did this?" he asked when she
finished.

"Yes . . . no," she admitted reluctantly. "But who else
could it have been?"

"We'll find out, okay?" Without waiting for her response, he continued. "I'm on my way. Don't touch anything. I'll be there shortly and then we'll decide if we
need to call the authorities or not. If Stuart is responsible,
he'll be dealt with. Just in case whoever did this is still

around, though, I'd feel better if you called Frank to come wait with you."

She felt another stab of annoyance at the mention of the missing guard. "I tried. He's not at his desk."

"He's probably making his rounds. Go down to the lobby and see if he's back, but first call me back on your cell phone. I want to be in touch with you the entire time."

Bethany hung up, grabbed her cell phone from her purse, and headed for the elevator. She knew the phone wouldn't work once the doors closed, so she waited until after she reached the ground floor to place the call. Though she'd grown accustomed to the silence of the office after hours, now the quiet took on an ominous quality.

"Okay, I'm downstairs," she told Miles when he answered. She crossed to the front desk and looked around. "Frank's still not here." Frustrated, she headed to the far corridor, thinking he might be in the men's room. She'd just passed the open door to the conference room when something she saw caused her to stop and take a closer look.

Frank was in the corner, lying with his legs bent at an angle too awkward to be natural. He didn't appear to be breathing. "Oh, God."

"Bethany, what is it?" Miles's concerned voice sounded in her ear.

She fought to overcome her squeamishness long enough to bend over the guard's body and place her fingers against his throat. "I found Frank."

"Good. Tell him to get his ass back to the desk where he belongs."

"I can't. He's dead."

Dirk hauled the body of the dead vampire from the back of his SUV and slung it over his shoulder. He didn't have to carry it far, only about ten yards to the "dump" pile. He threw it on top of the bodies already there and then studied the sight. Six vampire corpses—and he'd been responsible for bringing in four of them. The numbers bothered him because he knew that tomorrow there'd be more. It almost seemed that lately, Harris and Patterson, the two dominant or Prime vampires, had been engaging in some orgiastic feed-fest.

Dirk gritted his teeth and searched the pockets of the latest victim, looking for some form of ID.

His hand closed around the vampire's wallet and pulled it out. In among the credit cards and driver's license was a photo of the man beside an attractive young woman and a little girl. Dirk shoved the wallet into the pocket of his duster and glanced toward the back of the mansion he called home. The admiral would be making another anonymous donation to a grieving family.

With one final task remaining, Dirk returned to the SUV and retrieved the rolled blanket in the backseat. Holding it carefully, he placed his hand against one end. There was a brief hum of energy and then a pommel hit his palm. He wrapped his fingers around it and pulled the long, gleaming sword from the scabbard inside the blanket, then placed the blanket and scabbard back in the car as he held up the sword, admiring how the blade glinted in the moonlight. It was the Death Rider sword, used to slay vampires, and only a changeling—half vampire, half human—could wield it and command its full power. There were only two changelings in the entire D.C. area, hell, in the entire United States. Dirk was one of them. As he held the sword, the pommel grew warm in his hand and the ruby eyes of the vampire's head etched in the side gleamed a bright red.

He went to stand before the pile of bodies and not for the first time wondered what would happen if he pulled the dagger out of a vampire's heart. Would the body rise again? His cell phone picked that moment to start buzzing and he glanced at the caller ID before answering it. "Yes, Admiral?"

"John Boehler called. There's been another killing. He thought we'd want to take a look. I saw you drive by the house—are you almost done?"

"Yeah. I'll be right there." Dirk put away the phone and stared at the sight before him. Tomorrow, the sun would turn the pile of corpses into a stone mass that the first stiff wind would then reduce to dust. There was only one final task to perform.

Raising the sword high, he brought it down in one swift, smooth stroke. There was no blood as the head hit the ground with the muted thud that Dirk had grown accustomed to. With a grim countenance, he tossed the head back on the pile and cleaned the blade of his sword on the dead man's clothes.

There were moments when he liked being a Night Slayer—this was not one of them.

Elsewhere in the city, Kent Patterson wiped the blood from his mouth as his meal slumped to the ground, already forgotten. Patterson had fed until he could consume no more, yet the hunger would not abate. It clawed at him until anger and irritation rode him relentlessly. He silently berated himself for not going out with Harris tonight. He would have enjoyed a good hunt.

The silent admission caused him to sigh. It was probably just as well that he remained at the lair. Lately, he and Harris hadn't been seeing eye to eye on things, and that troubled him. He considered tasting one of the other humans chained to the wall, their fear a cloying scent in the otherwise rancid atmosphere of his lair, but a sound from the outer chamber distracted him.

His converts had returned and Patterson was eager for the prize they'd brought him. Patterson, ever resourceful, had a plan—one that included personal wealth and power. The success of this plan, however, depended on having a biochemist; one who would do work for him, either willingly or coerced, it made no difference to Patterson.

Stepping through the door, he gazed upon the frightened young man in a white lab coat, held suspended by his arms between the two underlings. Patterson suspected they retained their grip on the young man more to support him than to keep him from bolting. The irony here was that it was not the young man who should be the most frightened.

"What the hell is this?" Patterson bellowed, causing the two lesser vampires to stumble back.

"It . . . it's the biochemist you wanted," the braver of the two responded.

"No," Patterson said, his voice sounding deceptively calm. "This is not the biochemist *I* wanted. This biochemist is a *man*." He raised an eyebrow as he looked first at one underling and then the other as if daring them to refute the obvious truth. "Where is the *woman*?" If it was possible for the two vampires to grow paler, they did.

"We went to the lab as instructed, but he was the only one there."

"Then. You. Failed." Patterson spit out the words, making sure the converts fully appreciated the extent of his displeasure. Their hold on the prisoner grew tentative as if they would leave him there and return immediately to the lab. *Imbeciles*. "You can't go back now. Your incompetence has put me in a difficult situation. I'll have to find another way to get what I want." He turned to go back into his chamber.

"What do we do with this one?"

Without turning, Patterson waved his hand in a dismissive gesture. "I don't care. Drain him if you like."

"Wait!"

Patterson stopped and looked back at the young man who was either braver or more foolish than Patterson had expected. "You wish to say something?"

The young man swallowed visibly and took a deep breath. "You want Bethany Stavinoski, right? I can help you get her."

Chapter
2

Dirk nodded to the uniformed officer guarding the entrance to Van Horne Technologies as he walked past the man. He took in the expensive tiled floors, the opulent reception station, the high-tech security desk, the vaulted ceiling, and the expensive artwork hanging on the walls. Everything reeked of money and nearly untouchable sophistication, with no thought to real functionality or security.

A place like this would be child's play to breach and nearly impossible to defend. That's how Dirk viewed everything—in military terms. Ten years as a Navy SEAL followed by six months of hunting vampires did that to a man.

"There's John," Admiral Charles Winslow said, leading his small group across the foyer to the security desk where the detective stood waiting for them.

Besides the admiral and Dirk, there was Mac and Lanie Knight. Dirk had known Mac for years, having first met him in boot camp and then later serving in the SEALs with him. Their paths had split a year and a half ago, following an ambush that took the lives of half their unit and left Mac's femur shattered when a sniper's bullet hit his leg. That was when Mac left the Navy and, after months of rehab, started flying private charters, which is how he'd met his wife.

A librarian by day and EMT/firefighter by night, Lanie had hired Mac to fly her to South America as soon as she learned of her father's death. Dr. Weber had been working at one of the government's research facilities and had supposedly died after being attacked by a wild animal.

"Charles, glad you could come." Detective John Boehler's words broke Dirk from his thoughts and he watched the detective shake hands with the admiral. "The body's back here."

He led them down a corridor to the right and stopped at the first doorway, taking them into what appeared to be a conference room.

With his overdeveloped senses, Dirk picked up the smell of blood immediately and looked past the long dark conference table and chairs to the body lying at the far end of the room. The crime scene investigators had already taped the outline and presumably collected all the evidence they could, in hopes of finding the murderer, but Dirk knew they never would. That was no reflection on the Metropolitan police department. They simply didn't understand what they were looking for.

The deceased appeared to be in his mid-fifties, with dark hair heavily streaked with gray. Dirk thought the man would have been about five feet ten in height and had the wider girth that comes from years of bodybuilding. In other words, a hard man to bring down, had he been fighting humans.

Lanie removed a glove from her pocket and pulled it on. Then, kneeling beside the body, she stretched out a hand to touch it, stopping short to glance up at John. "Is it okay?"

John nodded. "Yeah, we're done."

Lanie gripped the guard's head and twisted it to the side, exposing the neck. "There." She pointed to the puncture wounds. Against the unnaturally pale color of the skin, the two dark holes stood out in stark contrast, each approximately the size of a cotton swab and filled with partially congealed blood.

"Is this the only victim?" Dirk asked the detective. It didn't make sense to him that a vampire would go to the trouble of breaking into a corporate building to feed off one guard when there were other food sources more easily available out on the streets.

"It's the only body we found," John replied. Dirk wasn't the only one to notice his choice of words, because Mac pinned the detective with a questioning look. "Meaning?"

John shrugged. "Meaning we have a missing research assistant. According to the security log, he signed in a couple of hours ago, but he's not in the building. What's more, the lab he works in looks like it's been torn apart and we found a small amount of blood on the floor. Everything points to an abduction, but what I don't have is a motive or suspects."

"What kind of research was he doing?" Dirk asked.

"I don't know," John admitted, leading them out of the conference room. "This is a small-scale biochemical research facility. Let's go upstairs," he suggested. "You can take a look at the lab and meet the CEO and department manager. I'll introduce you."

The police were not obligated to show them anything and it was only because of John that they were allowed into what would otherwise be a restricted site.

"Miles Van Horne, of *the* Van Hornes, owns this place," John explained, leading them to the elevators. They stepped into the waiting car and he pressed the button for the fourth floor. "The department manager, Bethany Stavinoski, is his fiancée." He sighed. "She's involved in this somehow. Not only did she find the guard, but it's her lab and research that were destroyed and the guy missing is *her* assistant."

When the elevator stopped, they followed the detective down the hallway past several closed doors until they reached one standing open. This time, when Dirk stepped into the room, the blood scent was not as easy to detect—first, because there wasn't as much, and second, because the smell of chemical reagents filled the air, masking the odor. Nevertheless, he moved past the lab tables to the very back of the room, Mac close by his side.

"There." Dirk pointed at the bloodstains on the floor and the top of the counter. The small droplets were more in keeping with a cut from broken glass than from a mortal wound.

Dirk did a slow visual inspection of the destruction inside the lab. "Sloppy," he commented softly, for Mac's ears only, not referring to the debris but rather the method of attack.

"Definitely wasn't Harris or Patterson," Mac agreed. "They would have been in and out a lot cleaner than this."

"Agreed, but they must be involved. The lesser vamps

couldn't have planned this by themselves." Dirk moved about the room, studying the broken glassware and equipment. "Be nice to know what type of research was being done here."

"Mac? Dirk?" Lanie called to them from the front of the lab and the two men went to join her. She stood slightly behind the admiral and John, who were talking to a distinguished-looking man in a business suit. He appeared to be older, about the admiral's age. The woman standing beside him wore a white lab coat but Dirk couldn't see her face with the detective's body blocking his view.

At a break in the conversation, the admiral motioned the two men forward. "Mac Knight and Dirk Adams, this is Miles Van Horne and his fiancée, Bethany Stavinoski."

"Mr. Van Horne; Ms. Stavinoski." Mac shook hands with both of them and then moved to one side so Dirk could step forward.

Dirk held out his hand to the man first and thought Van Horne's stance reeked with a confidence born of having an excess of money. Old childhood resentments stirred and he had to resist the almost uncontrollable urge to squeeze the man's hand just a little harder than necessary when they shook. Next, he turned to meet the fiancée and felt the impact of recognition hit him as their hands touched and a jolt of awareness shot through him.

Bethany stared at the man before her and the rest of the room faded. She was almost positive that she'd seen him before and tried hard to remember where. Almost as if he knew she was trying to guess, he smiled—a slight lifting of his lips—and in her mind, she was suddenly back on the darkened street, staring at that same smile.

He wore the same black duster, dark, collarless shirt, black jeans, and boots. With piercing blue eyes and sandy blond hair that looked like it hadn't been cut in a while, there was a James Dean wildness to his appearance.

"Bethany?" Miles's voice cut into her thoughts and she turned to him guiltily.

"I'm sorry?" She was horrified to realize that, for a moment, she'd forgotten that he was there.

"Admiral Winslow asked if you knew why anyone might wish to harm Stuart?"

"No, I'm afraid I don't. As I told Detective Boehler, Stuart and I weren't that close. He didn't confide in me."

The admiral nodded and turned to discuss something with the detective, allowing her a chance to study him. He was about the same age as Miles, putting him in his mid-to-late fifties. His gray hair, combed straight back, and darker-colored, neatly trimmed beard and mustache gave him a Sean Connery appearance. She couldn't hear what he was saying to the detective, but soon lost interest in trying to listen when the feeling of being watched distracted her.

"What type of work were you doing here?" Dirk asked her, his voice filled with a natural male assurance that caused her to focus more on the man than the question.

"I was trying to produce a synthetic duplicate of a plant extract." His intense scrutiny unnerved her and she had to work to focus her thoughts. "I'm told it's a plant found only in the thickest part of the Amazon jungle. One of the local tribes uses it for medicinal purposes with miraculous results. Van Horne Technologies was hired to see if it's possible to duplicate it."

"Who hired you?" Dirk asked Miles in a tone that indicated he expected an answer. Bethany tried not to show her own interest in hearing the response to a question that she, herself, had asked Miles countless times.

"I'm afraid that information is confidential—for now," Miles replied. It was the same line he'd given her each time she'd asked. Frustrated, she looked away and found Lanie giving her an interested look.

"How long have you been working on this project?" Dirk asked.

"About a month," Bethany replied, turning back to look at him. She was struck again by the intensity of his gaze.

"Does it usually take that long to duplicate something?" he asked.

It does when I intentionally drag my feet. "This extract is not like anything I've come across before," she offered by way of explanation, hoping that none of them knew enough about biochemistry to challenge her statement.

There was a pause in conversation and Bethany watched as the group exchanged meaningful looks with one another. She didn't have to wait long to find out what it meant.

"Here's the situation," the admiral began, sounding like he was about to deliver bad news. "Based on the method by which the guard was murdered, we believe a small underground terrorist faction is responsible. Until we can determine that their interest in Mr. Meyers is personal and not related to the project he and Ms. Stavinoski were working on, we have to assume that Ms. Stavinoski is also in danger."

"No, you must be mistaken," Miles insisted. "Stuart is behind this. I'm sure of it."

"Ms. Stavinoski's assistant didn't kill the guard," Dirk replied. "More likely, he's been taken by the group that did. If so, the odds of seeing him alive again are remote."

Bethany felt a shiver run down her spine at his words. She was horrified to think that Stuart might have been kidnapped by the guard's murderers, might even now be dead. Worse still, it had never occurred to her that her own life might be in jeopardy. She folded her arms in front of her, feeling suddenly unsure and exposed.

"No." Miles shook his head as he shifted his weight from one foot to the other, drawing her attention to him. "Given the type of person Stuart Meyers is, I feel confident that his abduction is personal. Frank died because he got in the way. That's all."

"Are you willing to bet your fiancée's life on that?" Dirk pinned Miles with a cold, hard look.

Bethany saw the muscles of Miles's cheek work as he clenched and unclenched his jaw, trying to control his anger. He had opened his mouth to respond when the detective cut him off.

"Mr. Van Horne, with all due respect, I'm afraid that in this instance, I have to agree with Admiral Winslow. This is not the first time I've come across this particular terrorist group, we call them the Exsanguinators, and if there's the slightest possibility that Ms. Stavinoski's life is in danger, she'll need protection." He paused and proceeded hesitantly. "I think it would be best if I placed her in protective custody. It's the only way to ensure her safety."

The suggestion stunned Bethany. She had no idea if the detective could actually do that, but she didn't like the sound of it. She opened her mouth to voice her objection when she was cut short.

"There is another option." Dirk's voice was cool steel slicing through a thick silence. "Hire a bodyguard."

"It can't be just anyone," Mac Knight pointed out, joining the discussion. "It has to be someone who understands the unique nature of this particular threat. It'd have to be one of us."

Dirk stared at Bethany, making her uneasy. "I'll do it."

His announcement caught her off guard and she studied the unreadable expression on his face, trying to figure out what he was thinking.

"That won't be necessary." Miles's tone was chilly. "If Bethany needs protection, I'll make the necessary arrangements for a bodyguard." His tone brooked no argument.

The expression on Dirk's face darkened, but it was the admiral who spoke. "In that case, we should be on our way. It was very nice meeting you both." He shook hands with each of them. "If there's anything we can do to help, please don't hesitate to contact us. John," he said, turning to the detective, "may I have a word?"

As the two walked out of the lab, Bethany shot Miles a questioning look that he ignored. Instead, he turned his attention to Mac and Lanie, who were waiting to shake hands and say their farewells. The woman, Lanie, gave her a sympathetic smile as she shook Bethany's hand.

"It was very nice meeting you," she said. "And congratulations on winning the Rod O'Connor Award. That's quite an achievement and well deserved, I'm sure." Bethany's surprise must have shown on her face because the other woman smiled and shrugged. "I read it in the paper."

"Thank you." Bethany wouldn't have thought anyone

outside the field would have noticed the article, much less read it. It wasn't what most considered exciting news.

"She was in the paper?" Dirk's voice dragged her from her musings as he looked first at her and then at Lanie. It was the latter who answered.

"Yes. I think it was a week ago, wasn't it?" She glanced at Bethany who could only nod in the face of Dirk's clear interest.

"What was the award for?" Mac asked in such a way that Bethany thought he sounded nearly as intimidating as Dirk.

"The award was for biochemical excellence," Miles announced proudly, draping an arm around Bethany's shoulders and briefly pulling her close. "Bethany is one of the leading researchers in her field." She blushed at Miles's praise and show of affection, trying not to let the condemnation that flashed across Dirk's eyes bother her. She'd seen it time and again since she and Miles first started dating, from people who thought she was a young gold digger after a rich man's money—or that Miles was an old lecher robbing the cradle in hopes of reclaiming his youth.

"It's time to go," Dirk announced suddenly. Everyone said their good-byes and as Mac and Lanie went to join the admiral and Detective Boehler, Bethany found herself waiting breathlessly for a second touch of Dirk's hand against hers, wondering if it would cause the same spark of awareness to shoot through her as it had the first time. Unfortunately, she wasn't given a chance to find out.

"Mr. Van Horne. Ms. Stavinoski." Dirk nodded his head once in farewell and then strode from the room, leaving her to feel irrationally disappointed and more than a little baffled at his abruptness.

"Are you all right?"

Miles's question caught her off guard and it took a second to realize that he was referring to the break-in and murder, not Dirk's behavior. She nodded slowly.

Glancing around to make sure she and Miles were alone in the lab, she gave him a hard shove. "Do you think that maybe *now* you can tell me more about where you got the extract?"

Though there was no obvious change in his expression, suddenly her warm fiancé was replaced by the cool, efficient businessman. "Not tonight, Bethany. It's almost morning and neither of us has had any sleep. Let's go back to my place. You can relax in a nice hot bath while I make arrangements for the bodyguard and then—"

"—we'll talk?"

"We'll go to bed."

His suggestion distracted her from the topic at hand. "Miles, I . . . um . . . I'm pretty tired. I don't know if I feel like . . . you know."

Smiling down at her, he was the warm fiancé once more. "I only meant that we should sleep, my dear—but at my place. I don't think it's a good idea for you to return to your apartment tonight."

So much relief swept through her that she felt guilty. Miles had practically been her best friend—her only friend—for the last couple of years. In many respects, he was more her family than her parents and siblings. She didn't think there was anything wrong with marrying her best friend, but wasn't she supposed to *want* to "sleep" with the man she'd promised to marry? She shoved the thought aside, telling herself that with all that had happened tonight, it was only natural to feel uncomfortable with . . . everything.

"I don't have any clothes at your place," she objected in a feeble attempt to justify going back to her apartment.

Miles merely chuckled and guided them into her office so she could retrieve her purse. "Not a problem. I'll simply call one of the stores and have an outfit delivered."

She rolled her eyes. "That'll cost a fortune."

He smiled. "What's the point of having all this money if I can't spend it on the woman I love."

Two hours later, Bethany was soaking in the oversized tub in Miles's penthouse suite, letting warm vanilla-scented bubbles soothe her nerves as the hot water worked to relax her muscles. Lit candles around the tub provided enough light to see without the harshness of the overhead lights, giving the room a quiet, peaceful atmosphere. She could almost forget the night's traumatic events or that Miles was, this minute, on the phone in the living room making arrangements for a bodyguard.

In her mind, she replayed the evening, from the moment she first saw Dirk on the street, to when she found Frank dead, to the memory of Dirk in the lab, standing before her. It was all like a strange, disturbed dream that made no sense and Bethany finally closed her eyes, willing everything to go back to normal. She wanted her structured, uneventful life restored.

When the water grew tepid, she climbed out of the tub and dried off before slipping into the extra set of pajamas Miles had provided for her. When she walked into the bedroom, the sun was beginning to peek over the horizon.

She went to the window and looked out, a sense of hopeful anticipation filling her at the thought of the day that awaited and the opportunities that lay ahead. It was the way she felt every time she witnessed a new dawn.

Then her thoughts turned to the chaos that awaited her at the lab, and heaving a sigh, she pulled the drapes closed and plunged the room into darkness.

Dirk sat in the admiral's Humvee as their small group drove back to the mansion and felt the clawing weight of fatigue spread over him as the sun rose on the horizon. He hated the dawn and the sooner he went to bed, the better off he'd be. It had been a strange night. Not that killing vampires or finding dead bodies was unusual. That was becoming all too familiar.

Six months ago, Mac and Lanie had gone to the research facility in South America expecting to identify the bodies of Lanie's father, Dr. Weber, and that of Lance Burton, a former SEAL teammate of Mac's and Dirk's. Both men had been killed in a wild animal attack. However, when Mac and Lanie got there, they found everyone at the research facility was dead. The only marks on their bodies had been two puncture wounds in the neck through which the bodies had been drained of blood. To make matters worse, the bodies of Weber and Burton were nowhere to be found.

A search resulted in Lanie finding her father's journal and from it, they learned that the mysterious creature her father had been brought in to study was the legendary El Chupacabra. It didn't take a detective to figure out the wild animal that had attacked Weber and Burton was none other than the chupacabra and that, in killing them, the creature had turned Weber and Burton into vampires. They, in turn, had killed the researchers at the lab.

Then, to make matters worse, Burton escaped with the chupacabra to Washington, D.C., where he forced the creature to kill his friends in order to create his own special ops vampire team, which in turn targeted the President of the United States for assassination. Stopping him had almost cost Mac, Lanie, and Dirk their lives and in the end, two of his team got away—Patterson and Harris.

For the last six months, Dirk and Mac had been searching for Patterson and Harris—without success, but they had hunted plenty of the creatures Harris and Patterson created when they fed off humans—so much so that Lanie had affectionately dubbed them "night slayers."

Kidnapping was something new, though, and Dirk had to wonder why, suddenly, Harris and Patterson had targeted a biochemist.

Given their military background and their mercenary tendencies, the first answer that came to mind was that they had decided to continue with Lance Burton's original plan.

Not liking the direction of his thoughts, he turned in his seat so he could face Mac and Lanie in the back. "How hard would it be for a biochemist to make a biotoxin that could, say, take out the entire D.C. area?"

"It couldn't be just anyone," Mac replied thoughtfully. "It would have to be someone who really knew what they were doing."

"Like someone who'd just won the Rod O'Connor Award for Biochemical Excellence?" the admiral put in from the driver's seat.

"Oh, no," Lanie breathed out, expressing how they all felt.

They fell silent and Dirk let his mind wander back to the lab; back to the image of a woman with shoulder-length ash-blond hair and features so delicate and fine, it was little wonder Miles Van Horne wanted her for a wife. He did his best to push that thought to the back of his mind, where it refused to stay.

Almost a foot taller than Bethany, he'd lost himself staring down into her emerald-green gaze. He relived the memory of their hands touching when they first met and the spark of electricity that sizzled between them. His mental image shifted to include Miles Van Horne and he frowned. The man was clearly wrong for her.

Glancing back at Lanie and Mac, it was hard to miss the look of affection Mac gave his wife. Not for the first time, Dirk felt there should be something more to his life.

He silently scoffed at himself. The kind of peace and fulfillment he longed for came to others—it didn't come to people like him. He slammed the door on emotions leaking past the mental barrier he'd erected long ago.

When they reached the mansion, Dirk and Mac climbed from the vehicle with obvious effort.

"You boys should go on to bed," Lanie said as they went inside. "I can see you're both dragging."

"What about you?" Mac asked.

"I'll be there shortly." She smiled as she gave her husband a kiss. "I want to be here when the new assistant arrives—help her get settled."

"You're kidding?" Dirk said, surprised. "He refuses to hire a maid or housekeeper for security reasons, but now he's hired an assistant?" Confusion and concern overrode

Dirk's fatigue as the group automatically headed for the kitchen. "Why?"

"Oops, what are you doing here?" Lanie walked over to the large gargoyle-shaped statue sitting on the kitchen counter and picked it up. Then she turned to Dirk. "Our security work is starting to take up more of my time so Uncle Charles thought it would be a good idea to hire someone to help out."

"Where'd he get this person?" Mac asked. "It's not like he can just hire anyone off the street."

"Don't worry," she assured them. "He went through a special agency. This woman has cleared all the background checks."

"If he's already checked her out, then I guess there's nothing for us to worry about," Dirk mumbled around a yawn. "I'm going to bed."

"Yeah, me, too," Mac added.

The two walked in silence up the stairs to their respective rooms. Being half vampire came with a cost—one of which was they had a hard time functioning during the day. Although Dirk missed the sunshine, he didn't mind sleeping during the day and being up all night. After all, he was a vampire slayer and night was when he hunted.

Bethany left for the lab the next evening dressed in the outfit Miles purchased for her. She'd almost refused to wear it, afraid of what an errant drop of acid might do to the fine linen. He'd dismissed her concerns and sent her to work, accompanied by her new bodyguard, Mr. Yarbro, a huge, beastly-looking, bald man who was nearly as broad in the shoulders as she was tall. It didn't take much time in his company, however, to realize that while he might be effective at protecting her from outside dangers, she was at risk of dying from boredom. Not used to having someone with her constantly, she'd tried engaging the man in conversation only to discover that he had the wit and personality of a rock.

On a lighter note, however, Miles had ordered the lab to be cleaned and the broken equipment replaced, so everything was ready for her to begin work when she arrived. She went to the refrigerated safe and keyed in the combination to open it. Inside was the original vial of plant extract that Miles had given her. She used a dropper to siphon off a small amount that she then placed in another tube before setting to work.

After studying her notes, she realized that there were only a few tests she needed to run to be caught up to where she was before the break-in. By eleven P.M., neck and back muscles aching from bending over the counter for hours and a nauseous hollow feeling eating away at her stomach, Bethany finally decided it was time to quit. "Mr. Yarbro, I think I'm ready to call it a night."

The bodyguard nodded and together they left the building. As she walked to the parking garage several blocks away, Bethany felt like she was being watched. A flash of something across the street caught her eye and she looked to see what it was.

A couple of men, their backs to her, stumbled into the open alleyway, at least one of them too drunk to stand on his own. She thought the dark coat of the man supporting him looked familiar and felt her heart lurch in hopeful anticipation.

A touch at her elbow dragged her attention away. "Ms. Stavinoski, we really should keep moving."

Bethany glanced at Mr. Yarbro's profile as his eyes kept a constant surveillance of their surroundings. His caution reminded her of just how surreal her situation was. She glanced back down the alley and, seeing that the men were gone, allowed Mr. Yarbro to steer her toward the garage. She silently chided herself for silly daydreams that conjured up images of Dirk Adams everywhere she looked.

Dirk held the dead vampire up against the building behind the trash Dumpster where they were well hidden from view. He counted to ten and then to twenty, resisting the temptation to lean out far enough to catch one more glimpse of Bethany Stavinoski.

Letting her see him wouldn't do any good and might even prove disastrous. She might wonder why he was following her and he didn't want to tell her that her human bodyguard couldn't keep her safe. Neither could he tell her that she was being stalked by vampires—she'd think he was a nutcase.

She was observant, though, which was more than he could say for her bodyguard. At least, he assumed that's who the joker in the monkey suit was. The man had been totally unaware of the vampire shadowing them for half a block. If Dirk hadn't been there to eliminate the threat, there was no telling what might have happened.

He let the body of the creature slide to the ground, the small wood stake barely visible in the vampire's chest. Pushing the body out of sight behind the Dumpster, he left the alley and headed for his Expedition. With luck, he'd have the body loaded and be waiting to follow Bethany and her bodyguard when they pulled out of the garage. After tonight, there was no doubt in Dirk's mind that he needed to keep an eye on her—even if he did it from afar.

Bethany went into the lab late the next afternoon to run her experiments. Miles had offered to pull a couple of college students off another project to assist her, but she wasn't sure she wanted to involve anyone new on the project, even if it meant having to spend a little more time in the lab herself. At least this way, she knew the experiments would be done correctly. *Not* that she was a control freak, as Miles liked to imply.

As they had the night before, she and Mr. Yarbro parked in the garage and walked to the research building. Bethany again felt as if she was being watched and fought the urge to turn around for as long as she could. When she did finally glance behind her, she noticed one man in particular among the other pedestrians.

He wore a familiar black duster over dark clothes and had shaggy blond hair. His dark sunglasses prevented her from seeing his face well enough to tell if it really was Dirk Adams, but she felt almost positive it was.

"Is there a problem?"

She glanced up at her bodyguard and considered pointing out the man she thought might be Dirk, but then changed her mind. "No, no problem."

She allowed him to lead her away, but after walking about ten yards, she glanced back again. The man was gone and for some reason she found that even more disturbing.

Her thoughts remained on him all the way to the Van Horne building and as soon as she entered the lab, she crossed to the window looking down on the street below. The sun had completely set and a streetlight lit patches of the sidewalk while leaving the rest in shadow. It was enough, though, that she was able to make out the form of a man standing against the building across the street. Though she couldn't see him clearly enough to make out his features, from his stance she knew he was the man she'd seen earlier. Logic told her that it could be anyone, but intuition told her it wasn't.

It was almost one in the morning when Bethany recorded the last test results. The next set of experiments she wanted to run would keep her at the lab until dawn if she started them now and she didn't feel like being there that long. She cleaned up, and then, accompanied by the ever-present Mr. Yarbro, left the building. Though she looked around outside for the familiar figure, it appeared that she and the bodyguard were the only ones on the street.

When they reached the garage, they rode the elevator to the third floor. The garage seemed unusually quiet and the sound of their footsteps echoed loudly as they started toward her car. They had gone about halfway when a scrape and muffled cry stopped them in their tracks.

Mr. Yarbro stepped closer to her as he pulled a gun from inside his jacket. A flicker of movement to one side caught Bethany's attention and before she could figure out what was happening, the bodyguard was off and running.

Wondering exactly what she should do, she spun around several times, realizing just how alone she was in the darkened garage. A tremor of fear shot through her as she imagined bogeymen lurking behind every car and in every shadow.

Her own vehicle was parked about twenty yards away and the overhead lights that should have kept the spot well lit were mysteriously dark. The safety of the elevator loomed a good thirty yards behind her, leaving her feeling trapped in the open. Only the stairwell, dark and ominous off to the side, lay close enough to provide an escape, yet it could just as easily be another source of danger.

As she focused her attention on it, she became aware of a shuffling noise coming from out of the shadowy depths. Frozen in place, she strained to see beyond the blackness as the sound of metal scraping metal caused the hairs on the back of her neck to stand up.

Heart racing, Bethany stared helplessly as the shadows swirled and took form. Then, a dark figure appeared, looming larger than life, exuding danger. It was the devil incarnate and he was coming for her. Somewhere inside her head, a voice screamed for her to run.

Chapter
3

I won't hurt you."

"You!" Her voice came out sounding breathless as she found herself staring at a familiar face.

"You shouldn't be standing out here in the open," Dirk chastised her.

Less afraid now, she reacted to his tone. "Well, no, but on the other hand, you shouldn't be jumping out of dark places and scaring me half to death either, should you?"

He was closer now and held her gaze for a moment before looking around the empty garage. "You'd think as rich as your boyfriend is, he could afford to hire a real bodyguard for you." The disgust in his voice was hard to miss.

Bethany opened her mouth to defend both Miles and the errant bodyguard, but Dirk cut her off.

"Save your breath. Any bodyguard worth his salt would have made sure you were safe before leaving you. I've got a good mind to . . ." He let the threat trail off as he scanned the area once more. "Where's your car?"

"Over there." She pointed to it.

"Come on." He placed a hand at her back and though his touch was light, her skin tingled from the contact, even through the layer of clothing. She glanced up at him, wondering if he'd noticed the frisson of electricity that snapped between them, but he wasn't looking at her. His eyes were in constant motion, looking everywhere except at her.

"Do you have the key?" he asked as they drew near her vehicle.

She nodded, glad she'd made a duplicate key for the bodyguard and kept her original. She pulled the key ring from her purse and handed it to Dirk. As they got close, he unlocked the driver's side door. "Get in. I'm going to see what happened to your *protector*. If I don't come back in five minutes, or you see anyone that you don't know, start the car and get the hell out of here." He reached into the pocket of his coat, pulled out a business card, and handed it to her, along with her keys. "If you do have to leave, don't go home. Call this number and talk to either Admiral Winslow or Mac Knight. They'll know what to do."

She climbed inside the car and then took the card from him, gazing at it skeptically. "I really don't think this will be necessary. I'm sure Mr. Yarbro is around here somewhere."

"I'm sure he is, but is he dead or alive?"

When she started to protest, he held up his hand. "Look, I'm not going to argue about this. Do I have your promise that you'll leave?" He gave her a stern look.

"Okay, okay. I promise."

He started to shut the door but she stopped him. "That was you I saw the other day, wasn't it? In the alley?"

It seemed to her that a gleam lit his eyes, but he neither admitted nor denied it. All he said was, "Lock the door." Then he slammed it shut, ending any further conversation.

For a long second, he stared at her and she held his gaze, expecting him to tell her something more. Then he tapped on the window and she belatedly realized what he was waiting for.

As soon as she locked the door, he raised his hand, fingers spread wide. "Five minutes," he mouthed, then turned and walked off between the parked cars until Bethany lost sight of him. She was alone—again.

Only this time was different. This time she wasn't standing out in the open, midway between her car and the elevator. Before he left, Dirk had seen that she was safely tucked away, with a means of escape. It was more than her own bodyguard had done and that realization irritated her. Then Dirk's words echoed in her head, *Is he dead or alive?* And she immediately felt guilty.

Dirk crossed to the far side of the garage, moving silently and staying hidden from sight. There had been two vampires lurking in the stairwell when Bethany and her bodyguard had stepped out of the elevator. The one had made enough noise to catch the bodyguard's attention and then led him on a merry chase, no doubt with the intent of leaving Bethany alone—an easy target for the remaining vampire. Neither had counted on Dirk being there.

He'd entered the stairwell, drawn his sword, and dispatched the vampire lurking there before it could attack, but in doing so, he'd made noise and Bethany had heard him. It was good that she was wary, he told himself, but seeing the frightened look in her eyes as she'd stared into the stairwell, he'd felt compelled to go to her. To reassure her, he'd argued to himself, not wanting to pursue the thought that there might have been another motive.

She had seemed so lost and vulnerable standing there, he'd had to fight the urge to pull her into his arms and comfort her, but the harder feat had been to leave her. She was safer in the car than standing in the middle of the garage and Dirk was pretty sure that he'd removed the most immediate threat to her, but the bodyguard's continued absence bothered him.

As if his thoughts had summoned him, Dirk heard the sound of running footsteps long before he caught sight of the missing man. Ducking behind a parked car, Dirk watched him come into view, appearing unharmed, and Dirk briefly wondered what happened to the vampire he'd been chasing. Finding that creature, however, was a secondary concern. The first priority was to see that the bodyguard returned to Bethany and the two left, unharmed.

Between his SEAL training and enhanced changeling abilities, it took little effort for Dirk to trail the bodyguard back to Bethany without the other man knowing he was there. He watched the man climb into the car and remained hidden until the two drove out of the garage. As soon as he was sure they were safely gone, he returned to the unfinished business in the stairwell. It was a good thing no one else had come this way. Finding a decapitated body would have been quite a shock for most people.

The corpse was where he had left it on the top landing—a body with a head lying nearby. Dirk stared at it, wishing that the vampires would just vanish in a burst of exploding dust like in the movies. It would make cleanup so much easier. Now he had to haul the damn thing to his Expedition and hope he didn't run into anyone.

Stepping back into the garage, he looked around and spotted a large trash canister. Hauling it into the stairwell, he bent over to pick up the body, feeling the duster pull tight over the sword at his back. He was grateful once again for his increased strength because this vampire had been almost as tall as he was and would have been difficult to pick up otherwise.

He stuffed the body into the trash bin and then pulled the edges of the plastic liner together to hide the body. Then, leaving it there, he raced down the steps to the lower level where his SUV was parked and drove it up, coming to a stop beside the stairwell. From there, it was a simple matter of loading the body into the back of his vehicle. At least vampires didn't bleed a lot.

He left the garage and drove to Bethany's apartment. He parked along an empty stretch of street and then walked the short distance to the spot he'd been using lately to stand sentry. It gave him a clear view of the street in both directions, the front entrance to her apartment building, and the front and side windows of her corner apartment on the third floor.

She was home now and the lights were on. He saw the shadow of a figure pass in front of the curtained windows and knew from the stance and height that it was the bodyguard. A second later, another shadow appeared in the corner window. This one was smaller and he knew it had to be Bethany. He wondered if she was in her bedroom and as she disappeared from view, his mind conjured an image of her getting ready for bed. A small growl rumbled low in his throat when he thought of the bodyguard there with her and he had to remind himself that it was none of his business.

A second later, the lights in both rooms went out, but Dirk continued to stand there. He wouldn't leave until the first rays of sunlight shone over the horizon. Only when he knew the vampires were fast asleep would he leave his post.

A flutter of movement at the corner window caught his attention and as he watched, the curtain pulled to one side and Bethany's face appeared. With his improved night vision, Dirk had no trouble making out her troubled expression or the way her light blue camisole hugged her upper body.

He saw her eyes peruse the street below as if she was searching for something and it finally occurred to him that she was looking for him. He knew she couldn't see him standing in the unlit entryway where he stood and it would be smarter to leave it that way, but he stepped forward anyway, into the glow of the streetlamp.

The moment she spotted him, her eyes lit up and a small smile touched her lips. Or maybe that was his imagination. He raised his hand in acknowledgment and couldn't stop the warm feeling that filled him when he saw her hand lift in a small wave. Then the curtain closed and she was gone, but the warm feeling stayed with him the rest of the night.

Bethany woke late the next morning feeling more rested than she had in several days. It took her a moment to realize why. It was because, for the first time since this ordeal started, she felt truly safe. She knew nothing about Dirk Adams and on the surface his dark looks and mysterious habits of lurking in the shadows should have scared her. Instead, he made her feel safe.

She decided not to try to figure out why that was and climbed out of bed. She was having lunch with Miles to go over the announcement of their engagement for the paper. She was also secretly hoping to worm more information from him on who had commissioned the project she was working on.

There were several aspects of the plant extract that bothered her. For instance, the way human cells absorbed it so readily suggested it could be addictive. It also created an unnatural increase in molecular activity, which might give anyone taking it a sense of being stronger or faster than normal. She'd even discovered a by-product resulting from a reaction with some of the body's natural enzymes that was similar to dopamine. In moderation, it might leave the user with a pleasant buzz, but if taken in excess, it might result in psychotic episodes.

To Bethany, the extract had all the earmarks of a designer drug. The question in her mind, which never would have been a question in the first place if Miles would just be honest with her, was whether this drug was really slated for medical, FDA-approved distribution as Miles led her to believe—or for illegal street distribution.

She would not be a party to something illegal. Even if she succeeded in creating the perfect synthetic duplicate, she'd destroy it before she let it be used for illicit purposes.

Lunch proved to be as uneventful as it was frustrating. All Miles would talk about was their upcoming wedding and how to word the announcement for the paper. Regardless of how many times she tried to steer the conversation to work, he brought them right back again. They finally parted company with Bethany no more knowledgeable about their client than she had been before.

Going directly to the lab, Bethany tried to push lunch from her mind and for the next two hours focused on her work. She was heavily immersed in thought when one of the techs from the second floor popped in to visit, carrying a shoebox-sized package wrapped in brown paper.

"This is for you, Bethany. Delivery guy dropped it off downstairs and since I was coming up anyway, I said I'd bring it to you."

"Thanks, Laura, I appreciate it." Baffled, she put down her instruments and then carefully peeled off the rubber gloves she wore. "Here, I'll take it." She waited until the young woman left and then glanced at the bodyguard. He seemed uninterested in it and Dirk's assessment of him flashed through her mind, quickly forgotten when she saw the name on the return address. It said, simply, *Adams*.

A thrill of excitement raced through her and she took the package into her office where she would have some privacy.

Ripping off the brown paper, she saw that it really was an old shoe box. Curious, she lifted the lid. Inside was a small hairspray-sized canister with an easy spray nozzle. She lifted it out and turned it over, but there was no writing or label on the can. Beneath it, though, she found a folded note.

Bethany laid the canister aside and read.

> *Bethany—This canister contains a mixture of Mace and pepper spray. Do me a favor and keep it with you at all times—especially at night. Dirk.*

Bethany wasn't sure how she felt about Dirk's gift, but she placed the canister in her purse. It never hurt to be cautious, she thought, returning to her work.

Several hours later, she and Mr. Yarbro left the lab. They arrived at her apartment building and though she looked for him, Bethany couldn't see Dirk anywhere. Feeling irrationally let down, she silently scoffed at herself. A man like Dirk had more important things to do than watch over her all the time.

And yet, she couldn't dismiss the feeling that she was being watched.

After taking the elevator to the third floor, Bethany stood patiently in the hallway while Mr. Yarbro checked out her apartment. Still thinking about Dirk, a grunt from inside drew her attention and she was instantly alert.

"Mr. Yarbro? Are you all right?" She imagined the big muscular man running into the small corner table or plant stand next to the window. When no quick response came, a chill ran down her spine. Digging in her purse, she pulled out the canister of Mace, grateful that she had kept it, and held it in front of her as she moved slowly through her front door.

The sight that met her was straight out of a nightmare. Mr. Yarbro lay on the floor, a man bent over him with his mouth pressed to the bodyguard's neck.

Blood seeped from the seam of the man's lips against the bodyguard's neck and dripped onto the carpet. When the man tilted his head up, she found herself staring into a pair of red glowing eyes.

Transfixed with terror, she nearly missed the movement off to the side.

This time, she didn't hesitate to act. Pulling the trigger

on the canister, she turned to her right and sprayed the Mace blindly in the direction of the second man before racing from her apartment.

Heart pounding, she stabbed the elevator button several times, praying for the doors to open. She looked back down the hall and saw the man stumbling after her, his hand over his eyes. About to bolt for the stairs, the elevator doors opened and she jumped in, slamming her hand against the button to shut them again.

Seemingly in slow motion, the man charged forward, his image framed by the closing doors. They were almost shut when his arm shot through the opening. Screaming, Bethany stumbled against the back wall of the elevator, barely escaping his reaching fingers. She raised the can of Mace and fired a steady stream. The man fell back and the doors slid closed.

Unable to remain still, heart racing, Bethany shifted from one foot to the other while the elevator descended, the lights over the door flashing on and off as they counted down the floors. As soon as she reached the bottom, the doors opened and she raced out, not stopping until she reached the street. Then, she hesitated. Feeling at a loss for what to do, she glanced at the darkened entryway on the opposite side, praying Dirk would be there as he'd been the night before.

He wasn't.

The tenuous grip she'd had on the reins of her fear slipped and pure, unadulterated panic filled her. She spun around, searching the night, afraid that whatever manner of monster it was that had just killed her bodyguard and chased after her might also be lurking out here, waiting to spring on her and rip out her throat.

Just then, the front door of her apartment building burst open and a man ran out. Bethany immediately backed away, never taking her eyes off him. She was about to bolt when she heard him call her name.

"Dirk . . . Mr. Adams? Is that you?" Her heart pounded in her chest as the figure slowly moved toward her. Uncertainty gripped her and she stood, frozen in place, straining to make out his features, but he kept his face tilted down and the light shining behind him cast his features into shadow.

"Dirk?" she asked again. "Is that you?"

Now, only a few feet away, he finally looked up. Her heart plunged to her toes at the sight of the unfamiliar face with eyes that glowed with an unnatural red light. Just like the eyes of the man upstairs had glowed. Suddenly every horror movie she'd ever seen flashed through her mind. Clutching the Mace, she raised her arm to spray him, but before her finger could pull the trigger, he closed the last few feet of distance and grabbed her wrists, tearing the canister from her hand and tossing it to the ground.

"No . . . no . . . please." She barely had the breath to force the words past her trembling lips. Never in her life had she been so terrified.

"I hear your heart racing. Are you frightened, little rabbit?" He spoke in an almost conversational tone, despite the manic gleam in his red eyes. When his lips curled back farther, she saw the sharp fangs in his mouth. "The blood, pulsing through your veins, calls to me. I can't help but wonder what it will taste like."

Instinctively, she tried to pull away, but he held her easily. When he stepped closer, her paralysis broke and she tried to break free. He only laughed at her as he drove her backward until she was pinned against the opposite building, with no means of escape. She was going to die— and there was nothing she could do to stop it. She stared in horror as he bared his fangs and lowered his head toward her neck.

She screamed.

Chapter
4

Held in his viselike grip, Bethany fought for her life, expecting at any moment to feel the sharp stab of pain when he bit her. Suddenly her attacker jerked ramrod-stiff and a strange expression came over his face. He looked down, and following the direction of his gaze, Bethany saw the glistening tip of a sword sticking out of his chest. As her mind struggled to make sense of it, his grip on her relaxed and he crumpled to the ground at her feet.

She stared at him in stunned surprise for several seconds, and when she dared to look up, Dirk stood there, sword in hand and a cold, feral expression on his face.

With a sob of relief, she threw herself into his arms. He embraced her, pulling her close. "Please tell me that you're all right," he said softly, his chest rumbling against her cheek.

"I couldn't find you . . ." A shudder ran through her.

"It's okay, Beth."

"You weren't in the doorway."

"I'm here now. I won't let anything happen to you."

She almost sobbed with relief, because she knew that he would protect her, unlike . . . "Oh, God! Mr. Yarbro—there's another one upstairs."

Dirk jerked his sword from the body and, taking her hand in his, started for the building. "Come on."

She pulled back and shook her head. "I can't go up there." She felt her lips tremble as she pleaded with him to go without her.

"Beth, I can't leave you out here alone. You have to come with me." He stared deep into her eyes, willing her to trust him. "I won't let them hurt you."

Slowly, she nodded.

They went inside and as they rode the elevator to the third floor, Dirk kept an eye on Beth. Several times, he saw her gaze drift to the bloodied blade of his sword and then to him. She wasn't stupid. Even now, as terrified as she was, he knew her mind was putting together all the pieces. He prayed she waited to ask questions until later, when he had time to answer them.

The elevator slowed to a stop and when the doors opened, he tensed for an attack, but none came. From where he stood, the hall loomed long and empty before him.

Pressing the button that would hold the elevator there until released, he stepped out. He suspected that the vampires were gone, but it paid to be cautious.

Bethany's apartment was at the far end and when they reached it, they found the door standing ajar. Dirk paused to listen for any sounds from within. Then, hearing nothing, he pushed the door open farther and peered through the crack to make sure no one hid behind it.

Moving into the foyer, he paused at the entrance to the

living room. There, lying in the middle of the floor, was the bodyguard.

It was obvious the man was dead, and even from several feet away, Dirk could see the two holes in the side of his neck. Behind him, he heard Beth's gasp, so he steered her past the scene, needing to check the rest of the apartment.

He had to stay alert to the possibility that more vampires lay in wait. It would be unusual for them to stick around, but nothing about what he'd witnessed over the last several nights had been "usual." Hell, he'd already killed more in this one night than was normal. There had been the three he'd dispatched in the alley before he heard Beth's scream and then the one who'd tried to kill her. Four in the last hour alone. If Harris and Patterson were behind this assault, they must be growing desperate.

With Bethany right behind him, Dirk slowly worked his way through the entire apartment. In the bedroom, he found the window open and a bloodstained handprint on the curtain where it had been pushed aside. He didn't know if this was how they'd gotten in, but it was definitely how the one had escaped.

Dirk stepped out on the fire escape and looked around, but saw nothing. He contemplated going to the roof, but there was no point. The vampires wouldn't be returning tonight.

Climbing back inside, he sheathed his sword and turned to Beth, who still stared at him through haunted eyes. She was in shock.

"They're gone." Going to her because he couldn't seem to stay away, he slowly rubbed his hands up and down her arms in what he hoped was a reassuring caress. "Are you all right?"

She nodded, and then shook her head. "No, I'm not all right. I don't understand what's going on. It's like something out of a bad Vincent Price movie." Her voice rose with her excitement and she paused to catch her breath. "I know this sounds crazy, but they looked like vampires . . ." Her words trailed off into a desperate kind of laugh as she raised a hand to rub her head. "You probably think I'm losing it. I don't know; maybe I am."

He knew he should tell her that it was her imagination playing tricks; that the killers were human. Yet, when he opened his mouth to spin the lie, he found himself telling her the truth instead. "They *were* vampires."

He waited for her reaction, but all she did was nod her head.

"Okay. That's what I thought." Her voice sounded too matter of fact and Dirk again recognized the symptoms of shock. It was buffering her reactions—letting few emotions in and none out. Studying her face, he wondered when the dam would break, knowing it would be soon.

"I need to make a couple of phone calls," he said, hoping he had time.

She nodded. "I should call Miles. He'll want to know about Mr. Yarbro."

Dirk found her statement revealing, but didn't point out that Miles's first concern would most likely be for *her* safety. The mention of the man's name, however, raised an issue that needed to be addressed. "Let's not mention the vampires to Miles, all right? In fact, let's not mention them to anyone."

A quizzical look penetrated through an otherwise glassy, distant gaze. Then she shrugged. "He probably wouldn't believe me anyway." Still sounding unnaturally calm, she walked over to the bedside table where a cordless phone sat next to a book.

When she began to dial, Dirk pulled out his cell phone and punched in Mac's phone number. As he listened to the rings, his eyes scanned the room, taking in details that helped paint a picture of the woman who lived here. The furniture was elegant but simple in design, consistent with the soothing neutral tones of the bedspread and curtains. Bookshelves lined the walls and except for one shelf dedicated to photos of what Dirk assumed to be family, they were filled past capacity with various paperback and hardback volumes. Scanning the titles, he saw everything from scientific reference books to popular fiction. He took all this in at a glance and it didn't tell him much about Bethany Stavinoski except that she was neat and liked to read. Only the little cloth clown doll, perched on her dresser, seemed out of place.

Its little purple velveteen outfit was stained, the ruffled collar had become detached at one side, and the once white color had faded to gray. The clown's hat sat precariously on its head, above the once-golden strands of hair, and one eye was missing from the face. To anyone else, the doll might appear to be junk, but Dirk suspected it had been the object of a young girl's love, so much so that the grown woman couldn't bring herself to throw it away. A man would be lucky to earn the love of a woman like that.

A click on the other end of the line caught his attention. "Mac here."

"I'm at Bethany's apartment. There was another attempt. I've got three bodies in the back alley, one on the sidewalk out in front of the building, and a dead bodyguard inside." He kept his words clipped and to the point.

"And the woman?"

Dirk cast a glance at her and, seeing her hang up the phone, he turned his back so she wouldn't hear him. "She's in shock, but otherwise okay." Dirk paused. "I told her."

There was a moment of silence, but when Mac spoke, he didn't pretend to misunderstand. "Everything?"

This time, Dirk felt embarrassed. "Only about the vampires. She saw them and I . . . didn't want to lie."

"Okay. You were there so it was your call. I'm on my way. I can get the bodies outside, but what about the bodyguard?"

"I think we'll have to call John."

"I'll do it."

"Thanks." Dirk hung up the phone and turned to check on Bethany, only to find her walking past him to the living room. Worried, he followed after her as she walked over to the dead man's body and stared down at it.

"He died because of me." Her voice cracked with emotion. "I don't understand." She looked up at Dirk, her eyes pleading for him to explain it, and a single tear slipped from the corner of her eye. He barely heard her next words, they were so softly spoken. "I'm scared."

Dirk sensed the dam break and pulled her into his arms, gathering her close. "You're not responsible for these attacks, Bethany. It's not your fault. And I won't let them hurt you, I promise." He heard her muffled sobs and vowed that he'd keep that promise, even if it killed him.

In the protected safety of Dirk's embrace, Bethany's defenses fell. She burrowed closer, needing the feel of his solid, wide chest and the strength of his arms wrapped around her to block out the horrors of the night's events. She knew she should have felt embarrassed, crying as she was in a stranger's arms, but at that particular moment, he didn't feel like a stranger.

How long they stood there, Bethany had no idea, but when she finally stopped crying, she expected Dirk to release her. Surprisingly, he didn't, nor did she make any effort to step away from him. It felt right and she never wanted the moment to end.

"Bethany—are you all right?"

She jumped at the sound of Miles's voice and stepped away from Dirk quickly, as if she'd been caught doing something wrong. Giving Dirk a last, longing look, she went to Miles and let him hug her. If his arms felt small and spindly compared to Dirk's, or his chest cadaverous compared to the firm, muscled tone of Dirk's, she tried not to notice. After all, their relationship wasn't about physical attraction, she reminded herself. His looks were not why she was marrying him.

"What happened?" Miles asked. "Who did this?"

Vampires! I came home and they were waiting for me. They killed Mr. Yarbro and almost killed me. Even in her mind, it sounded too far-fetched to be true. She eased herself out of his embrace. "I don't know."

"Do you think you could give the police a description?"

She knew she'd remember the glowing red eyes, the sharp, gleaming fangs, and the pale, translucent faces of the vampires for the rest of her life. "I'm sorry, Miles. It all happened so fast." She rubbed her temple, knowing that Miles would believe her too frazzled to remember any details of her attackers.

A commotion at the front door drew their attention and seconds later Mac walked into the room. His glance took in everything, touching briefly on her and Miles before coming to rest on Dirk.

"Any problems?" Dirk asked.

"Maybe." Mac glanced over at the couple before turning back to Dirk. "John's on his way."

Dirk nodded. Then Bethany saw him glance at the bodyguard's body. "Let's step into the other room," he suggested.

Momentarily confused until she saw his subtle nod toward Miles, she took Miles by the hand and led him into the bedroom.

Dirk watched them go and as soon as they were out of hearing distance, he turned to Mac. "What?"

"I found the three bodies in the back alley, but there was nothing across the street."

Dirk crossed the room and pulled back the curtain. He had been running on pure adrenaline and fear since he'd heard Beth's screams from half a block away. He was in no mood to put up with crap like a missing corpse. Looking out the window, his improved night vision allowed him to pick out the darkened entryway across the street. "Son of a bitch."

Mac moved behind him and looked over his shoulder. "What?"

"He's not there."

"Like I said."

"I watched him die. How could he have simply disappeared?"

"Maybe you missed the heart?"

Dirk let the curtain fall back in place. "Shit."

"I guess you were distracted."

Scared shitless was more like it, Dirk thought, wondering what the price would be for his mistake.

From the other room, Bethany strained to hear what Mac and Dirk were saying, but couldn't make out their words. Then Detective Boehler arrived and she and Miles went out to join the others in the foyer.

"Mr. Van Horne. Ms. Stavinoski. I'm sorry to see you again under these circumstances," the detective said, coming over to them. "Neither of you was injured?"

"No," Miles replied. "However, Mr. Yarbro, the bodyguard I hired, wasn't as lucky."

Detective Boehler nodded. "I'd like to look at the body."

"This way, John," Dirk said.

The detective started to follow him into the living room, but then stopped to look at Bethany. "I'm afraid you'll need to move out of the apartment for a few days."

She nodded. "I don't want to stay here anyway."

As the detective, Dirk, and Mac continued on to the living room, Bethany and Miles returned to her bedroom. He stood off to the side as she pulled a suitcase from her closet and set it on the bed. Sifting through her clothes, she had no trouble deciding what to take with her. The sooner she was out of this apartment, the better. She only wished she could take everything now and never have to return.

Focusing on packing, she almost forgot Miles was there until he spoke.

"I'm so sorry, Bethany. I never meant for you to get hurt."

"Well, of course not." She stopped packing long enough

to go to him and lay her hand comfortingly on his arm. "You hired the best bodyguard you could find. It's just these . . . people . . . are more dangerous than we realized. Luckily, Dirk was around."

The minute she said it, she knew it was a mistake. Instantly, his eyes narrowed. "And how, exactly, did Mr. Adams come to be here at this particular time, anyway? Awfully convenient if you ask me."

"No one asked you," Dirk answered abruptly, walking into the room.

"You just *happened* to be in the neighborhood?"

"No, I made it a point to be in the neighborhood. You see, I had some concerns about what you thought would be adequate security."

Miles's chin rose in indignation. "I'll have you know that I hired the finest agency in town."

"Then you should get your money back. And don't bother hiring someone else. From now on, I'll protect Beth."

Beth? It sounded like a pet name and Bethany didn't know if Dirk had used it without thinking—or if he'd done it on purpose to annoy Miles. Either way, Miles was irritated.

"*I* will see to *Bethany's* protection, thank you."

"How? They've broken into both your lab and her home. The bodyguard you hired couldn't fight them off. So tell me, exactly, how do *you* plan to protect her?"

"I will hire an army of bodyguards to be with her around the clock and I'll increase the security at the lab. When she's not at work, she'll stay with me. I live in a well-guarded penthouse suite and my place is close to the lab, so she won't have far to commute."

The announcement caught Bethany off guard and she stared at Miles in surprise. She was not ready to move in with him and was wondering how to break the news to him when Dirk beat her to it.

"First of all, *Beth* should stay as far from the lab as she can until this is over. Second, these terrorists are highly skilled and dangerous. Your high security penthouse suite will be nothing more than a minor obstacle to them."

"Really?" Miles asked sardonically.

"We've already seen the quality of protection you hire," Dirk continued. "Hiring new guards will only get more people killed—possibly even Beth. I won't allow that."

"When it comes to Bethany, you have no say in anything that concerns her."

"I do now. She's coming with me to Admiral Winslow's estate. We have plenty of room and it's the last place anyone will look for her."

Miles gasped. "Are you suggesting that *my* fiancée move in with *you*? I refuse."

A dark gleam came into Dirk's eyes as he moved closer to Miles, causing the older man to instinctively step back. "You misunderstand—I'm not asking permission. I'm telling you how it's going to be. She's coming with me because I *can* protect her. You had your chance and fucked it up."

Chapter
5

Bethany watched Miles's face grow so red with anger that she worried he might have a stroke. The two men were standing toe to toe and Bethany wanted to bash their heads together. As they continued to glare at each other, she took advantage of their silence.

"First of all, both of you can stop acting like I'm not here. I don't appreciate it. Second, nobody tells me what I will and will not do, understood?" She raised her chin defiantly as two sets of eyes, one blue and one brown, turned to her.

"Miles, you're right. I need to keep working on the project and I fully intend to do so. And your place *is* closer to the lab." She ignored the look of triumph that spread across his face and put a hand up to stop Dirk when he opened his mouth to protest. "But it's not safe, so I'm going to move into the admiral's place until this is over."

"Bethany, there's no need for this," Miles hurriedly protested. "I'll hire a dozen bodyguards. Hell, I'll hire two dozen, but you will not live with this man, do you understand me?"

She shook her head. "No, Miles. I don't need two dozen bodyguards—I only need Dirk." Her cheeks began to burn the second she realized what she'd said. Hurrying on, she tried to explain to Miles what she meant. "You may not realize it, but Dirk has been acting as my bodyguard for the last several days. Haven't you?" She pinned him with a look. "I didn't realize it at the time, but there have been other attempts. Last night in the parking garage, for instance. And how many others?"

Dirk clenched his jaw shut and refused to answer.

"That's okay. I know there were other attempts." She turned back to Miles. "In trying to respect your wishes, he only stepped in when Mr. Yarbro failed to do his job, which was happening a lot." She took a step closer to Miles and laid her hand on his chest. "I know you only want what's best for me and if that means living at the admiral's, then that's what I should do."

She counted on Miles's intelligence to see past his jealousy to the bigger picture. She wasn't wrong. "Very well, Bethany. If that's what you want." His petulant tone let her know how much he didn't like the idea.

"It's not about what I *want*, Miles. It's about doing the smart thing." She smiled up at him and placed a kiss on his cheek, which seemed to make him feel better. When she glanced at Dirk and saw his scowl, she couldn't help but wonder what, exactly, she was getting herself into.

"Pack enough to stay for several days," he told her. "If you need something from the other room, I'll get it for you."

Hoping she wasn't making a huge mistake, she packed

the clothes she'd laid out and turned back to the dresser. Practical in every other aspect of her life, Bethany had a penchant for lacy, barely there matching bras and panties. Stuck wearing a unisex lab coat all day, they were the only things that allowed her to feel feminine.

Having a set for almost every outfit, she riffled through her collection of undergarments to find the ones that went with the outfits she was taking and tossed them on the bed. Down to selecting the final set, she pulled her brand-new deep purple see-through demi-bra and panties from the drawer. With them dangling from her hand, she turned to the suitcase and stopped. Heat suffused her cheeks when she saw both Miles and Dirk staring at her.

Miles looked outraged that she would dare display her undergarments so publicly, especially with another man in the room. The intensity of his gaze, however, was nothing compared to that of Dirk's. Sheer raw, animal hunger burned there, sending a thrill of excitement racing through her, leaving her feeling terribly confused because she wasn't the kind of woman to feel strong passions; it was a flaw in her genetic makeup.

Frowning at both men, she shoved the clothing into her suitcase and closed it. Grabbing a second, smaller case, she packed her toiletries.

"Ms. Stavinoski," Detective Boehler said, walking into the room with Mac. "Where can I reach you?"

"She'll be staying with us," Dirk answered.

If the detective seemed surprised, he didn't show it. "Fine. I'll contact you there if I have any questions."

"Is that it?" Dirk asked, nodding to the two suitcases as he took a step toward them.

She looked around the room, giving it a final inspection. When her gaze fell on her little clown sitting on the bookcase, she grabbed it. The doll had been a gift from her grandmother many years ago and was a memento of happier times. She wasn't about to leave it behind. Refusing to meet either man's gaze, she placed the doll in her purse. "That's everything," she said, finally risking a glance at Dirk. Instead of the amusement she expected to see at her show of sentimentality, there was an unexpected flash of warmth and understanding. Then, gesturing with his head that she should precede him from the room, he picked up both of her suitcases and followed.

Thirty minutes later, Bethany sat in the front seat of Miles's car, staring at the taillights of the gold-tone Humvee Mac was driving, without really seeing them. Lost in her thoughts, she didn't at first notice Miles's silence or the glaring looks he shot her. "I'm sorry, did you say something?"

"As a matter of fact, I said quite a few things, until I realized you weren't listening."

"I'm sorry," she apologized again. "This evening was traumatic. I keep seeing Mr. Yarbro's body in my mind and wondering if I could have done something to save him."

Miles sighed, the anger draining from him as he reached across the seat and took her hand in his. "I'm an insensitive jerk. Of course you're upset about what happened this evening, but don't worry, I won't let anything happen to you."

His words were an eerie echo of Dirk's, but they left her feeling far less reassured. She knew he meant well, so she gave him a grateful smile and then turned to gaze out the window.

They were out in the country and the sun was beginning to rise. Bethany felt as if she were in a different world. She watched the open pasturelands pass by and was just beginning to wonder how far out in the country Admiral Winslow lived when the brakes of the Humvee lit up. It turned onto a drive partially hidden behind a line of trees edging the road.

The mansion, for that's truly what it was, loomed before them. Two rows of huge, ancient oaks trees graced the front drive, reminding Bethany of Oak Alley in Louisiana.

All three cars pulled to a stop in front and Bethany, feeling suddenly awkward, hesitated before getting out. Was she doing the right thing in staying with these people when she didn't even know them?

Miles came around and opened the door for her, helping her out. She held his hand, grateful to have him with her, and he seemed to like her show of attention, laying his other hand on top of hers before turning to face Mac and Dirk who joined them, each carrying one of Bethany's suitcases.

"This way," Mac said, walking to the front door. He opened it and, looking back once to make sure they followed, led the way inside.

As soon as Bethany stepped into the foyer, she was overwhelmed by the old-world charm that greeted her. Admiral Winslow and Lanie walked up to greet them, offering warm smiles and words of welcome. Mac set the suitcase he carried by the door and gave his wife a kiss.

Bethany saw the tender way Lanie gazed at him and how his eyes burned possessively when he looked at her. They were clearly in love and Bethany felt a small stab of jealousy, which she quickly suppressed.

"Good morning, everyone," the admiral said pleasantly, shaking hands with Miles and Bethany. "Please, come in. Can I interest anyone in breakfast or a cup of coffee?" He showed them into the kitchen. Bethany wasn't hungry, so she politely refused—as did Miles—but the coffee sounded good and after she took a seat at the table, she gratefully accepted the cup offered her.

Bethany noticed that Dirk, silent and sullen as he leaned against the counter, refused the coffee and she found it odd, considering how tired he looked.

As if he felt her gaze on him, Dirk turned and she saw a flash of something cross his eyes, but it was gone too quickly for her to know what it was.

"How are you?" Lanie asked, drawing Bethany's attention by the warmth in her voice. "It must have been horrible."

"It was frightening," she admitted, not wanting to relive the whole thing again so soon.

Lanie must have sensed her reluctance because she didn't push. "I'm glad you've come to stay with us," she said. "We have plenty of room and it will be nice to have another woman staying here."

"Thank you." Bethany took a sip of the coffee and let its warmth seep through her. Beside her, Miles had struck up a conversation with the admiral. Both of them men of wealth and means, it turned out they had many of the same acquaintances. For fifteen minutes, while they talked, Bethany remained quiet and did her best to keep her attention focused on their conversation. The entire time, however, she felt Dirk watching her and couldn't resist sneaking a peek at him every now and then.

The intensity of his gaze was unsettling. She didn't

know how to react, so she turned her attention back to the conversation, but high society had never interested her much and it wasn't long before the night's events caught up to her. Placing her cup on the table, she fought to keep her eyes open.

Suddenly a warm hand was at her elbow, pulling her to her feet.

"If you all will excuse us," Dirk's voice filled the room, interrupting the conversation, "Beth is exhausted. Lanie, if you'll lead the way, we can show Beth to her room."

"Of course." Lanie jumped to her feet.

Miles and the admiral also stood up. Bethany saw the irritation return to Miles's eyes as he looked to where Dirk's hand supported her elbow and rather than watch the two men get into another round of adolescent posturing, she politely pulled her elbow free from Dirk's grip. Almost immediately, she wished she hadn't because she was apparently more tired than she thought and for a moment the room swayed before her.

"I think I'd better help you." Instantly Dirk's hand was back and this time she let it stay.

"Thank you."

Miles, maybe sensing that any effort on his part to help her would draw undue attention to the situation, let it go and followed along quietly.

Feeling like a VIP surrounded by her entourage, Bethany was led up the main stairs and down a long corridor. When Lanie finally stopped and opened the door, Bethany was sure there'd been some mistake. The room was huge and luxurious.

"Oh, this is beautiful," she exclaimed breathlessly, looking around. "Really, this is much too nice."

Lanie laughed. "Nonsense. We have more than enough room and, as I said before, it will be nice to have another woman staying here. I get lonely sometimes. Now, do you have everything you need?"

"I think so." Bethany eyed the large queen-sized bed. It looked like heaven and she wanted nothing more than to collapse across it and fall fast asleep.

"Well, I guess it's time for me to leave." Miles sounded reluctant. He took her hands in his and gave her a warm smile. "What time do you want me to pick you up tonight? I assume you'll want to sleep, but we have that gallery reception at eight."

"She'll have to pass," Dirk said. "Going to a public function is too dangerous."

Miles started to protest, but Bethany put a hand on his arm to quiet him.

"He's right," she said. "Besides, I have plenty of work to do at the lab. All those tests have to be rerun."

Miles sighed, but didn't push her. "All right. I'll pick you up at six, then, and drop you at the lab."

Bethany thought through her schedule and slowly nodded. "Okay, that will be—"

"Unnecessary," Dirk's voice interrupted. "I'll take her to the lab whenever she needs to go. There's no reason for you to pick her up."

"Now see here." Miles sounded indignant. "I will not have you telling me when I can and cannot see my own fiancée."

"I'm not telling you when you can or cannot see Beth," Dirk bit out. "But since I'm now her bodyguard until this thing is over, I'm going to be her shadow whenever she leaves this house. So that means if she goes to the lab, I go to the lab. If you want to ride in with us, then by all means, drive out here first."

Beth gave him a quelling look as she laid a pacifying hand on the older man's arm. "He's right, Miles. There's no need for you to come all the way out here when he can just as easily bring me into town."

"Okay," Miles finally agreed. "If you're sure."

At that moment, Admiral Winslow and Mac joined them.

"Are you leaving, Miles?" the admiral asked.

"I'm afraid so. Bethany is tired and there are things at the office that must be attended to." The two men shook hands. "It was very nice seeing you again. Thank you for allowing Bethany to stay with you. She and I are most grateful."

Dirk watched as Miles pulled Bethany into his arms and gave her what Dirk guessed was supposed to be a deep passionate kiss. He thought Bethany looked more embarrassed by the display than anything else. Then Miles stepped out into the hallway and, accompanied by the admiral, Mac, and Lanie, headed for the front door, allowing Dirk to breathe his first easy breath in almost twelve hours.

Finally alone, Dirk turned to Beth and found her looking at him expectantly. Suddenly, feeling self-conscious, he cleared his throat. "What time do you want to go into town?"

Dirk silently prayed that it wouldn't be too much earlier than the time Miles had originally suggested. Winters were proving to be tough. The days were short and the nights were long and hard, which didn't allow for much downtime. As it was, he was using the last of his strength just to remain upright.

"I should read the test results about two this afternoon," she said, "but I think I'll call one of the lab students to do that for me. Would six be all right with you?"

He sighed with relief. "You bet. I'll meet you in the great room then." He started to step through the door when she stopped him.

"Dirk, about the vampires—"

"Not right now, okay? I know you have questions and I'll be glad to answer them—after we've both had some sleep."

She nodded. "Okay." She paused. "Thank you—for everything." There was such sincerity in her tone, he knew it was heartfelt.

He gave her a slight smile and nodded his head once. "You're welcome."

He shut the door then and headed to his room where he found Mac waiting for him.

"You look like shit."

Dirk cocked an eyebrow but continued to his bed so he could sit on the edge. "And your point?"

Mac gave him a serious look. "Are you all right?"

Dirk rubbed his face before looking up to meet Mac's gaze. "I almost let her get killed."

"But you didn't. Don't beat yourself up over what might have happened. Take it from me, it'll eat you alive."

"But next time . . ."

Mac held up his hand. "Next time, you'll do what needs to be done, just like you did tonight."

"I pray you're right." He stood up and started for the door.

"Where are you going?"

"I forgot about the bodies."

Mac stood and waved him back. "Go to bed. I'll take care of them. Your night was tougher than mine."

Dirk didn't need to be convinced. "Thanks."

"No problem. I know you're tired, but sometime soon, we need to talk about Harris and Patterson."

Dirk nodded. "Come to the lab tonight. We can talk then."

Harris licked the last drops of blood from his fangs and lips as he lowered the body of the drug dealer to the ground. Reaching into his jacket pocket, he pulled out the wood stake and drove it through the dead man's heart, ensuring he wouldn't rise again. He felt no remorse at killing a drug dealer. In fact, in his own way, he considered it a service to the community. He'd spotted this one trying to sell drugs to a group of teenagers. It hadn't taken much to scare the kids away and he knew they'd think twice before buying drugs again. The thought caused him to smile as he rolled the body behind a Dumpster where, eventually, someone would find it.

Then he slipped back down the alley, moving faster than any human could, and made his way along the back streets of the city until he reached the entrance to the lair. With a last look around, he descended into the lower levels, winding his way through oversized pipes that reeked of human waste. The smell was offensive, but an effective deterrent to curious humans.

Reaching the old abandoned underground workstation, he let himself into the room, his eyes going immediately to the humans chained to the wall. They were young, healthy males, in their early twenties if he had to guess.

They cowered in fear when they saw him, but he ignored them and continued down the short hallway to the back room and without knocking walked in.

The first thing he noticed was the man chained to the wall. This was not a food source, as the others were. This was a vampire, or had been several nights ago. Now it was nothing more than a depraved creature straining at its chains, trying to break free.

"Another remission?" he asked Patterson, who lounged in a nearby chair. "This one only lasted a week."

The other Prime gave him an irritated look. "I know how long he lasted." Rising from his seat, a stake clutched in one hand, Patterson attacked the creature before it could react, driving the stake into its heart. "We'll have to rely on the vampires we convert ourselves for now. Third generation and below are too unstable."

Harris swore under his breath. "We're never going to get anywhere like this. We need a biochemist."

"Look," Patterson snapped. "If you think you can do better, then feel free to try."

Harris's sight bled red as he glared at Patterson. He'd never particularly liked the man when they'd been alive. How ironic that they would be thrown together in death. He tried to remember skills learned in life and tamped down his anger and frustration. "What happened tonight?"

"Adams was there. As we thought, putting the three in the alley distracted him, but not long enough. The woman got away and we lost our team, such as it was, except for that newest one. Another inch and we would've lost him, too." He rubbed his jaw. "Maybe we should try converting some of our former SEAL teammates, like Burton did?"

Harris shook his head. "No. Once they start to regress, these civilians are hard enough to control. I'd hate to try and control a SEAL in that state." He paused. "Maybe we should go after a different biochemist—one that's not so well protected." Harris was growing desperate. He'd lived as a vampire for over six months now and hated every minute of it.

If Lance Burton wasn't already dead, Harris would kill him. He hadn't asked for this. His life had finally started looking up. He'd met a girl, Cynthia. They'd started dating and he'd thought she might be the one. Six months ago, when he'd looked to his future, it had included marriage, kids—the whole "happily-ever-after" story. Now all he saw was an endless road of death and destruction, mostly by his own hand if he hoped to survive. And he did, but not like this.

"You want to risk letting a second-rate biochemist use our last vial of chupacabra venom?" Patterson snarled at him.

Harris shot him a look. "As opposed to the assistant you currently have working on it? Yeah."

"That assistant worked with the Stavinoski woman. He can't exactly be an idiot."

Harris studied Patterson's face and knew his former teammate wasn't any more convinced than he was, but decided not to press the issue. "I'm going to rest." The sun would be up soon and Harris needed time alone to think.

He left the room and walked down the tunnel for another hundred yards, coming to a stop at a seemingly random spot. Glancing both ways to make sure no errant vampires were nearby, he activated a lever and a part of the pipe slid back, revealing the small hole he'd tunneled out to be his resting place. It had taken almost a month of hard labor, but had been worth it. At least now when he slept, he didn't have to worry about someone staking him in his sleep.

Climbing inside, he closed the door and lay back. He opened his mind and reached out, moving past Patterson, to the city beyond, feeling for a presence he hoped—he prayed—would be out there. He'd felt her once before—the adult chupacabra. Dr. Weber, the biochemist who'd been coerced into working for Lance Burton, had told them she'd died, but if she truly had, the link they all shared would have died with her. That hadn't happened.

He conducted his search systematically, covering each inch of the psychic plane until he felt the first pull of fatigue. The sun would rise soon and he could add another failed attempt to his list of achievements.

Then he touched something. He was so shocked that he almost let the link dissolve and had to scramble to hold on to it. It was her, the adult chupacabra. He recognized her "feel." Stretching his awareness, he tried to get an impression of where in the city she was—if she was even *in* the city. He had no idea how far the mind link stretched.

As the sun came up, the link shuttered and collapsed, but at least now he had hope. If he could find her, then he could secure more venom. Then all he needed was a biochemist to unlock the venom's secret—and make him human again.

Chapter
6

Good evening." Miles's voice came from the doorway. "I brought you a cup of your favorite gourmet
coffee . . ." His words trailed off as Bethany swiveled
around on the lab stool to face him, a cup similar to the
one he held suspended halfway to her mouth. "Oh. I see
you already have some." His gaze shot past her to the
other side of the lab table where Dirk sat and his expression turned cold and resentful.

Hoping to stave off another argument between the two
men, Bethany placed her cup on the table, hopped off the
stool, and hurried to Miles. "That was so sweet of you.
You must have read my mind. I told Dirk when we
stopped on the way in that one wouldn't be enough to get
me through the evening. You saved us a trip back out."
She planted a kiss on his cheek as she took the cup from
his hand. "Thank you for being so thoughtful."

Miles pulled his attention away from Dirk and the expression in his eyes softened, but not by much. Grabbing

her elbow with his free hand, he steered her out of the lab, into her office. "Are you sure you won't come with me tonight?" he implored her. "I could have a dress delivered here in no time."

Bethany couldn't think of anything she'd like less than attending the boring social affair, but she didn't say that to Miles. "No. I really do have a lot of work to make up."

He glared past her into the lab. "How long, Bethany? How long are you planning to stay out at that place?"

"I don't know, Miles. Until it's safe to leave, I guess."

"I don't like it—and I don't like that man. I know you trust him and it seems he's good at what he does, but . . . it's just not right."

Miles was usually a very patient man, but even he had his limits. "The award ceremony is coming up," he ventured on. "You'll want to accept the Rod O'Connor Award in person, won't you?"

It was a cheap shot. He knew how much receiving that award meant to her. She struggled to control her irritation and was saved from answering him when a buzzer went off in the lab. "Miles, I have to go. I'll talk to you tomorrow."

She started to walk away, the extra cup of coffee in her hand, but Miles put a hand on her arm to stop her. "I'm sorry, Bethany. I miss you." He kissed her then, but it wasn't their usual gentle exchange. She wondered if he was trying to overwhelm her with the intensity of his passion. Whatever his intentions, the kiss smacked of desperation and was almost painful in its forcefulness. Only because she understood how threatened he felt by Dirk's presence did she manage to endure his "show of affection" and not push him away. Finally, the kiss ended and she took a step back. Not knowing what to say, she mumbled a simple "Good night, Miles," and walked back into the lab.

As she returned to her workstation, she felt Dirk watching her. Setting the cup of coffee on the counter, she glanced up and saw the dark expression on his face.

"What?" she asked irritably.

"So that guy really does it for you?"

"Brings me coffee? Yes, on occasion, when he knows I'm working late."

Dirk narrowed his eyes. "That's not what I meant. Does he rev your engine? Get your juices flowing?"

She turned to gape at him. "I beg your pardon. That is disgusting."

"Yeah, I think so, too, but I'm not the one kissing a man old enough to be my father."

"He's not old. He's"—she searched for the right word—"mature."

Dirk gave a bark of laughter. "Is that what you call it? Out of curiosity, what's the age difference? Twenty? Thirty years?"

She gave an exasperated sigh. "Twenty years, and that's not that big of a difference."

Dirk shrugged. "So, again, what's the attraction?"

Bethany forced herself to get back to work. "I don't expect someone like you to understand."

"Someone like me?"

"Yes. Someone who thinks that sweaty bodies, rolling around in bed, having marathon sex is the signpost of a strong relationship."

He got off his stool and Bethany hoped he was leaving her alone to work. She didn't even bother to watch him go, focusing her attention instead on pouring the exact amount of reagent into the flask before her. That is, until she felt him come up to stand behind her, the heat from his body warming her back. His hands came up to caress her shoulders and his touch rattled her so much that she had to set the beaker of reagent back on the counter before she dropped it.

She knew she should step away from him, yet he held her trapped between his body and the table and his hands on her shoulders felt strong and his soothing strokes rendered her incapable of moving. He closed the last small distance between them until their bodies touched and her heart pounded with anticipation. Then he lowered his head so that his cheek brushed Bethany's ear.

His breath fanned across her neck in warm moist puffs of air. "When you're with *him,* " he said, his voice rumbling low in his chest, "is *he* all you think about? Does he fill you with a need so great you're afraid that if he touches you, you'll explode, but if he doesn't, you'll die?" His lips grazed her neck as he spoke, sending shivers down her spine. "Do his kisses rob you of every thought?" His hand slipped around her waist and he roughly pulled her tightly against him. "Can you feel the longing for him all the way down to that sweet spot between your legs?"

Bethany couldn't have responded if her life depended on it. His words, his touch, had reduced her to a mass of quivering emotions. She closed her eyes, lost in the sensations he stirred deep inside her; feelings that scared and tempted her at the same time. She knew he should stop, but prayed that he wouldn't.

Abruptly he released her and stepped away. Her body chilled in the sudden absence of his heat and as she tried to pull herself together, he crossed the room, only to stop when he reached the door. She dared to look at him and his hungry, burning gaze raked over her body before meeting her eyes. "You wouldn't be so quick to dismiss the physical aspect of a relationship if you'd ever experienced it done right. Maybe Miles isn't the right man for you, Beth. Not if he can't unlock that passionate nature you try to keep hidden inside. What you need . . . is a real man."

Like me. The unspoken words echoed in her head long after he walked out the door. She reached out, blindly, for the lab stool and pulled it closer so she could collapse onto it. She was in trouble, she thought over and over. How could she react like that to one man when she was engaged to another? More surprising to her was how she could react at all? She'd never felt like that. No one had elicited those feelings from her—ever. All her life, she'd thought the problem lay with her; that she was genetically incapable of feeling passion. Yet here she stood, breathless, hot, and aroused—and all he'd done was rub her shoulders and whisper in her ear.

Inside her chest, her heart still raced. Taking a deep breath, she tried to be rational. Dirk was a good-looking man and had probably been with hundreds of women. He was a master seducer and she, with her handful of pathetic past relationships, was no match for his mechanisms.

Miles, on the other hand, while not ruggedly masculine, was nevertheless warm, sensitive, intelligent, and refined. He might not be manly by Dirk's standards, but he was still a good man. And the fact that Miles had never, *ever* aroused in her even a modicum of the feelings Dirk just had, meant nothing. Nothing at all.

Dirk stormed out of the lab. He had to get out of there before he did something he'd regret later. Or worse, that he wouldn't regret at all.

Walking through the outer lab doors, he stopped short when Mac blocked his way. From the expression on his friend's face, Dirk knew that he'd witnessed most, if not all, of what had just taken place. Dirk saw the condemnation in his friend's eyes—it mirrored what he felt for himself—but Dirk wasn't prepared to deal with it. He started to push past Mac, but the latter grabbed his arm.

Dirk glared into the hard gaze of his friend before turning his attention to the offending hand until Mac removed it. Without a word, Dirk continued down the hallway to the elevators and then out the building's front doors before Mac caught up to him.

"What the hell's the matter with you? She's engaged."

"Stay out of this, Mac. It doesn't concern you."

"It does if you're letting your emotions distract you. These are vampires we're dealing with, or had you forgotten?"

"No. I haven't forgotten."

Dirk heard Mac sigh. "Then what's gotten into you?"

Dirk paced a short distance away and dragged a hand down his face before turning to Mac, his anger and hostility fading. "She has."

Mac studied him for several minutes and then slowly nodded. "You've got it bad, don't you?" He came over and clapped a hand against Dirk's back in a gesture of sympathy. "Yeah. Happened the same way to me."

"With one glaring difference. Lanie wasn't married.

Beth is . . . She's not mine—never will be. She belongs to someone else."

Dirk would have loved to have Mac tell him he was wrong, that Beth could be his, but his friend remained quiet. They both knew the way things had to be.

"Watch her for me, will you? I need to get away from here for a while."

Bethany looked up from her work and was surprised to see Mac walk into the lab. "Where's Dirk?"

"He . . . had something he needed to do."

She tried to ignore his all too knowing look. "When will he be back?"

"I don't know."

She nodded, feeling the hurt and anger squeeze her chest. Maybe it was just as well that he was gone, she argued to herself. She found his presence all too unsettling and that was not a good thing for a woman to feel when she was engaged to another man.

Inside the lair, Patterson stared at the withered, dying form of the latest experiment. "I can't sell this crap on the black market," he shouted. "No one's going to buy it if it doesn't work." He turned away from the sight and pinned Stuart with a glare. "I should have killed you the day you arrived."

"What you're asking for is virtually impossible," the cocky young biochemist shot back.

"Is that right?" Patterson snarled, turning back to the body chained to the wall. The subject's life had finally expired. "Then tell me, Stuart," he said, affecting a calm he didn't feel, "why should I keep *you* alive?"

Stuart's eyes widened slightly. "Because you still need me."

"Really? I don't know. I feel like you're wasting my time. Are you wasting my time, Stuart?" He moved closer to the young man, but stopped when he felt the familiar tingling along the psychic link of Harris's presence. It was followed seconds later by the vampire's appearance.

"What's going on?"

"Where have you been?" Patterson snarled.

"Out." Harris didn't offer any further explanation but Patterson knew already. He knew about the adult chupacabra. It was a testament to his higher intellect, he thought, that he allowed Harris to operate in ignorance. Let Harris find the creature and when he had, Patterson would move in and use it, much as Burton had.

Still, even with the adult chupacabra, there was a need to have a supply of synthetic venom. Burton's experience taught him that much. The adult was unreliable.

"I need the Stavinoski woman," he muttered to no one in particular. "My source tells me that she's been working nights at the lab. Maybe we should try to take her again."

Harris shook his head. "Building security will be tighter than ever. We'd have a hell of a time getting in undetected."

"Not if you had an ID badge."

Patterson and Harris turned together to stare at Stuart, who smiled back at them. In his hand he held his Van Horne Technologies security card.

Bethany woke up the next morning feeling tired and out of sorts. Dirk hadn't come back to the lab last night and Miles hadn't bothered to call her after the reception.

She'd done her best to shove both men from her thoughts as she worked and Mac had finally brought her back to the mansion around two in the morning.

The kitchen was empty by the time she'd dressed and gone downstairs, but a fresh pot of much needed coffee sat on the counter. Pouring herself a cup, she searched for sweetener and creamer and met with limited success. She didn't care, though, and after mixing in a packet of sweetener, she took a drink. Closing her eyes, she let the sweet hot essence slide down her throat and tried to imagine the liquid energy coursing through her veins, spreading throughout her body, reviving her. It was enough to make her sigh.

"I don't suppose you have any more of whatever it is you're drinking?"

Startled, Bethany opened her eyes to see an unfamiliar forty-something woman standing at the kitchen entryway, holding a large gargoyle statue in one hand and a small collection of notebooks in the other. She had dark chestnut hair that fell to about chin length. It was perfectly coiffed and the silk navy-blue suit she wore probably cost as much as Bethany's monthly apartment rental.

The woman smiled and moved confidently toward the table. "I'm Julia Penrose," she said, setting the notebooks down before carefully placing the gargoyle in the middle of the table, where it was less likely to fall. "I'm Admiral Winslow's new personal assistant."

She held out her hand and Bethany finally remembered her manners. "I'm sorry. Bethany Stavinoski. I'm . . . staying here." She cringed at the vagueness of her words, but Julia smiled.

"The admiral explained that in addition to his philanthropic pursuits he also runs a security agency and that a client was currently in residence. I assume that would be you."

Bethany opened her mouth to offer some explanation, but Julia stopped her. "He also explained that much of the security work was on a need-to-know basis. If he wants me to know, he'll tell me."

Relieved, Bethany took another drink of her coffee and then abruptly set down the cup. "I'm sorry. You wanted coffee." She took another cup from the cabinet. "How do you take it?"

"Sweetener and cream, please."

"Well, I found the sweetener, but I haven't had much luck finding creamer."

"I think I can help there." Julia walked over to the pantry beside the oven and opened the door. "I seem to remember seeing it in here yesterday. Oh, yes, here it is." She handed Bethany the nondairy creamer and Bethany caught a whiff of the woman's perfume. It was a warm, rich scent of cloves and cinnamon that seemed to somehow fit her. Spooning creamer into the cup, she glanced at Julia.

"One will be fine, thank you," the woman answered her unspoken question.

Bethany poured the coffee and then handed the woman her cup. Fixing herself another, she resumed her spot leaning against the counter.

At that moment, Mac's voice drifted in from the other room. "Are you telling me you didn't feel it?" He sounded tired and incredulous.

"What? The 'disturbance in the force'?" Dirk asked in a mock movie-announcer voice. Then, sounding like himself again, he went on. "Okay, seriously. Yes, I did, but that doesn't prove anything. It certainly doesn't mean she's still alive."

"But it might."

The two men appeared in the kitchen doorway and when Bethany looked up, her gaze locked with Dirk's. Her cheeks heated at the memory of his body pressed close to hers and she found herself incapable of speech.

When she finally tore her gaze away, she found Mac staring at Julia.

"Who are you?" he asked.

In her cultured tone, she introduced herself. "My name is Julia Penrose. I'm Admiral Winslow's new assistant. And you are?"

Surprisingly, a small smile touched Mac's lips. "Mac Knight. It's very nice to meet you." He shook hands with her and then turned to gesture toward Dirk. "This is Dirk Adams. We run the security end of the business, which means we usually work nights."

Julia held her hand out to Dirk, who hesitated a moment before taking it. "Nice to meet you, ma'am," he said gruffly.

"Are you just coming in?" Julia asked the two men.

"As a matter of fact, we are," Mac replied.

"There's plenty of coffee," Julia offered. "Would you care for any?"

"No, thank you. I think we'll just get some shut-eye."

"I thought I heard your voice," Lanie said, walking in and going straight to her husband, who pulled her close for a thorough good-morning kiss. When she broke away seconds later, she looked flushed and happy. "I see you've had a chance to meet Julia."

"Yes," Mac said. "We were just introducing ourselves."

"Good morning, everyone." Admiral Winslow's deep booming voice filled the room as he joined them. "I trust everyone had a good night?" The way he asked the question, his gaze lingering on Mac and Dirk, Bethany knew he was asking if they'd encountered any more vampires.

The two men nodded solemnly. "Nothing we couldn't handle," Dirk said.

"Good, good. Glad to hear it," the admiral continued. He turned his attention to the women. "Lanie, Bethany. Good morning to you. I trust all is well."

They each nodded.

Then he turned his full attention on Julia. "Good morning, Julia."

Bethany noticed the subtle change in his tone and gaze when he addressed his new assistant. It seemed warmer, more personal.

"Good morning, Admiral," Julia replied and for the first time all morning sounded a little flustered.

"Call me Charles, please. I'm retired now and Admiral Winslow sounds too . . . formal." He smiled and Bethany found herself thinking that the admiral's interest in his new assistant might be more than professional. Judging from the pleased expression on Julia's face, she didn't think the interest was one-sided.

"What's this doing here?"

Lanie's question distracted her and Bethany noticed she was looking at the statue.

"Oh, I brought that in here," Julia said. "It was sitting in the middle of the desk, making it terribly difficult to work. I wondered if we might find a new home for it?"

"Of course," Lanie said. "In fact, I'll put it away right

now." She picked up the statue and walked out of the kitchen.

"Julia, it was nice meeting you," Mac said. "If you'll excuse me?" She nodded and he turned to Dirk. "We'll finish this later."

Dirk also pushed away from the counter. "Julia, it was nice meeting you. Beth." He dipped his head in farewell, gave the admiral a curious look, and then followed Mac out of the kitchen.

"Shall we get started?" the admiral asked Julia.

"Yes." She turned to Bethany. "Thank you for the coffee. I do hope we'll have a chance to talk again soon."

"I'd like that," Bethany agreed. She watched the two leave and was alone once more. Fighting an inexplicable sense of disappointment, she refilled her cup and went back to her room, where her thoughts turned to Dirk Adams, as they tended to do all too often.

Thinking of that man was not doing her relationship with Miles much good. What she needed was a chance to spend more time with her fiancé. Struck with an idea, she picked up her cell phone, as there wasn't a phone in the room, and punched in a number.

"I can't believe it," Miles teased when he answered and heard her voice. "Your warden is actually allowing you to make a social call?"

Remembering the violent way Mr. Yarbro had died and the look in the eyes of the vampire that almost killed her, Bethany had a hard time laughing off his joke. "I know Dirk seems rather strict, but he *has* kept me safe."

"Has he really?" He sounded doubtful. "Or have the attacks stopped and that's why you've been safe?"

Not wanting to continue this line of conversation,

which could only lead to a fight, she counted to ten, slowly. "The reason I called is because I thought maybe we could get together for lunch."

She heard the sound of typing as he accessed his on-line schedule. "I'm sorry, Bethany. I've got back-to-back meetings all afternoon. My last one starts at six-thirty tonight."

Bethany forced herself to swallow her disappointment. "Okay. Some other time, then."

She was seconds from disconnecting the call when she heard him sigh. "No, wait. I do want to see you. How about dinner—say seven-thirty? I'll make reservations at Nicolette's—a cozy little table for two."

Seven-thirty meant it would be after dark. "Maybe we could go someplace else?"

"Why? I thought you liked Nicolette's."

Frustrated, Bethany shook the phone in her hand like she wanted to shake Miles. Then she calmly placed it back to her ear. "I do, but it's going to be hard to have a cozy dinner for two when there will be three of us. Dirk's not going to let me go anywhere without a bodyguard."

"I'm sure Mr. Adams won't mind letting us have a table to ourselves while he sits nearby. After all, his job is to watch over you, not have dinner with you."

Bethany had to bite her tongue to keep from pointing out that it wasn't Dirk's job to do anything—he wasn't getting paid. He was protecting her—at no little risk to himself—because . . . well, she wasn't sure exactly why. Maybe it was out of a sense of obligation or duty. Maybe it was something more.

Accurately interpreting her silence, Miles tried again. "Bethany, I promise that I'll be on my best behavior.

Please, let's get together for dinner. I feel like I haven't seen you in days. I miss you."

Though she couldn't help feeling like she was making a mistake, she agreed. "All right. Make the reservations. We'll meet you there."

Miles hung up his phone and a part of him seethed. Bethany might be blind to it, but he knew Dirk Adams's attention went beyond simply keeping her safe. It was almost as if he thought Bethany belonged to *him*. Miles's temper flared at the other man's audacity. Dirk Adams, by his very actions, had issued a challenge and while Miles might not be able to hold his own in the physical arena, he was not without means.

He picked up the phone again and within minutes he was connected with the manager of Nicolette's. It didn't take him long to make reservations and when he hung up the phone, he couldn't stop the smile that lit his face. He felt like rubbing his hands together in gleeful anticipation.

Chapter
7

When the sun went down shortly after six, Dirk was already awake and dressed. He knew that sooner or later, he'd have to face Beth again. He didn't worry about whether she'd try to avoid him; he wasn't going to give her the chance, but he *had* embarrassed and humiliated her, and for that he was sorry. Yet, he couldn't quite bring himself to regret what he'd done. Even now, the memory of her body pressed against his tormented him.

He forced her from his thoughts and glanced at the Death Rider sword, hanging in its sheath from his bedpost. He wouldn't take it tonight to the lab. Instead, he'd take his smaller dagger and let Mac carry the sword. He made a mental note to ask the admiral if he'd had a chance to contact his relatives living in England. That branch of the family was descended from the original blacksmith who'd forged the Death Rider sword and there had been some discussion about another being made now that there were two changelings to wield them.

Dirk wondered how easy it would be to make another sword—or if it was even possible. There was something about the Death Rider sword that made it unique. Dirk didn't believe in magic, but he wasn't sure how else to explain why the eyes of the vampire emblem etched in the side of the pommel glowed when a vampire was around. Or why the ordinary blade remained eternally sharp and could easily sever the head of a vampire. Or why he and Mac, who had never used a sword before, could wield this one with the skill of master swordsmen.

He looked at the sheathed dagger in his hand. There was nothing magical about it, but in a close fight with a vampire, it was more than adequate. He slipped it onto his belt, pulled on his duster, grabbed the Death Rider sword, and headed for the study.

There, he found Beth sitting in one of the admiral's large oversized leather chairs, reading. She looked up when he walked in and their eyes met. The intense awareness that surged between them was almost physical and Dirk wondered, again, what it was about this woman that had him acting so unlike himself. Even a simple greeting eluded him.

Beth recovered first, closing the book she'd been reading. "Hi. Were you looking for me?"

"No."

"Oh."

He wanted to kick himself for sounding abrupt. "What I meant was that I didn't come to the study looking for you—I didn't know you were here." He paused and realized that he wasn't making the situation better. Finally, he held up the sword. "I came to put this back."

He continued across the room to the display case at the

back, aware of Beth rising from her chair to follow him. He worked the combination to the lock on the case and opened the heavy glass lid. With special care and reverence, he set the sword on the stand inside, admiring the way the display light reflected off the silver and onyx sheath.

"It's beautiful."

Dirk glanced down at the woman beside him. "Yes, she is."

A touch of pink stained Beth's cheeks as she glanced up at him and then quickly looked around the room. "Are all these weapons yours?"

Dirk followed the direction of both her gaze and the graceful sweep of her hand as she waved to the contents of the room. "No. All of this belongs to the admiral."

Her gaze returned to the Death Rider sword. "That's the sword you used the other night, isn't it?"

"Yes, it is."

"And where do you keep the silver crosses, wooden stakes, and supply of holy water?"

He smiled. If she was joking with him, then she must not be too mad at him. "You know, I've never tried using a cross or holy water before. I have no idea if they would work. As for the stakes, well, I do carry a few with me, but I find the sword is a much more environmentally safe weapon."

She fought her own smile. "You don't exactly strike me as the environmentally conscientious type."

"I have hidden depths," he said with feigned seriousness. This time, she smiled in earnest before changing the subject.

"How long have you lived here?"

"Almost six months."

"What about Mac and Lanie?"

"The same." He paused, trying to think of it from her perspective. "I guess that seems strange to you, that we all work and live together."

She shrugged. "Given your particular line of work, not really. I think it's nice. You're kind of like your own little family."

Family. Dirk had never thought of it that way before, but she was right. It'd been so long since he'd had a family, he'd forgotten what it felt like. "Yeah, I guess we are." Afraid this line of conversation would lead to places he'd rather not go, he glanced at his watch. "It's almost dinnertime—are you hungry? We could see what's in the kitchen to eat. Or grab something on the way to the lab."

"Oh, no. What time is it?" She grabbed his wrist and turned it so she could read his watch while he stared at her in amusement.

"What's the matter? You late for a hot date or something?"

"As a matter of fact." She released him as if she suddenly realized that she was touching him. "We're meeting Miles for dinner."

He was shaking his head before she even finished the sentence. "No." She scowled, but he refused to cave. "Not just no, but *hell* no."

"Fine. I'll ask Mac to take me."

The idea that she would even consider asking Mac irritated him. "Mac's busy."

"Then I'll go by myself." She spun around and strode out of the study, leaving him to stand with his hands clenched into fists.

He wanted to punch a hole in something—the door, the wall . . . Miles's face. "Come back here," he shouted after her. "We're not through discussing this."

She didn't answer and Dirk cursed loudly. Knowing he had no choice, he left the study and headed back upstairs to change clothes. It was going to be a long, long night.

When Beth came down twenty minutes later, Dirk was waiting for her in the foyer. Silently, he groaned and prayed that years of harsh discipline would be enough to see him through the evening.

She wore a tailored dress, the same emerald-green as her eyes, and it fit so perfectly that little of her figure was left to the imagination. The line of her cleavage above the plunging neckline led one's gaze down an enticing trail until it disappeared beneath the fabric of the dress. His gaze lingered on the breasts that were fuller than he expected, having seen her in just the lab coat and oversized shirts up to this point. Her waist and hips were narrow and despite her being almost a foot shorter, from what he could see of her legs below the hem of her dress, they were long, slim, and shapely.

Dirk's pulse sped up. "You look stunning," he told her when she reached the foot of the steps and stood before him.

She gave him a nervous smile, like she hadn't expected the compliment but was grateful for it. "You look very nice as well."

While she'd been getting dressed, he'd gone back to his room and replaced the black jeans, T-shirt, and duster with a monotone charcoal suit. The dagger was still strapped to his belt, but the jacket hid it from view.

He moved toward the door and held it open for her. "Shall we go?"

Across town, Miles finished the last of his paperwork and checked the clock on his desk. He needed to leave in a few minutes in order to meet Bethany. Tonight Miles would take extra pleasure from his dining experience. Nicolette's wasn't the type of place one expected to see a tough, unrefined man such as Dirk Adams. The contrast between Adams and himself would be stark and Miles felt sure that whatever attraction Bethany might feel toward Adams would vanish in the face of it.

Miles signed the document before him, closed the manila folder, and placed it on the corner of his desk where his secretary would find it the next morning. He was about to stand up when the door suddenly opened and a man walked in.

"What are you doing here?" Miles asked as equal parts of fear and annoyance coursed through him.

"I thought it might be good if we talked." His visitor closed the door before crossing the room to sit in one of the chairs in front of the desk.

"What about?" Miles asked, even though he thought he knew the answer.

"I'd like to discuss the progress you've made on the work you're doing for me—or rather the *lack* of progress."

Not normally one to be easily intimidated, Miles, nevertheless, found himself feeling nervous. He was playing outside his league and he knew it. "As I already told your errand boy, there have been a few delays, but we should be back on schedule shortly."

"What kind of delays?"

"There have been several attacks on my fiancée, the lab was broken into, and one of the assistants is missing. Every time something like this occurs, naturally, it disrupts the work and puts us behind schedule." He paused, eyeing the man across from him carefully. "I don't suppose you'd know anything about these attacks?"

"Me? No. Why would I know anything?"

Miles let it go. This client was not the usual pharmaceutical representative or law enforcement agent that he was used to dealing with and he had no idea what the man was capable of. Wanting to bring an end to the conversation, he stood up. "If that's all, I'm late for an important engagement. You see, I'm meeting my fiancée at Nicolette's for dinner tonight."

"Is that right?" The other man smiled politely as he pulled out a cell phone, but otherwise made no move to leave. "I'm afraid you'll have to miss it. But please, feel free to call her with your regrets. And if you'll excuse me, while you do that, I have a call of my own to make."

Bethany couldn't keep her eyes off Dirk, walking beside her. He really did look spectacular in his dress clothes. Miles always said that clothes made a man, but he'd never looked like this, no matter how expensive his clothes. There was even a fluid grace to Dirk's movements that Bethany knew had nothing to do with clothing and everything to do with the finely honed athlete beneath.

As they moved across the parking lot, she risked another glance, only to snap her gaze away when she found him watching her. Grateful for the darkness that helped to hide her blush, she focused her attention on the building ahead.

Nicolette's was an old house that had been converted into a restaurant. It was located in Georgetown, situated some distance from the road and surrounded by trees that gave it a feeling of privacy. And intimacy. Her traitorous thoughts returned to the man beside her and she grew all too aware of Dirk's hand at the small of her back, guiding her along as they walked. By the time they reached the entrance to the restaurant, her nerves were wound tight.

The maître d' looked up when they stepped inside. "Miss Stavinoski, how nice to see you again," he gushed. "Mr. Van Horne called earlier and your tables are ready. If you'll follow me, please?"

They were led to a cozy booth in a private corner of the restaurant.

"I'm sorry," Bethany said. "There must be some mistake. This table doesn't look big enough for three."

The maître d' merely smiled and gestured to another table a short distance away. "Mr. Van Horne also had this one reserved."

Bethany felt a flash of annoyance as she realized what Miles was trying to do. "This is unaccept—" Dirk's hand on her arm stopped her words in mid-protest.

"This will be fine," he said. He ushered her into the side of the booth facing the back of the room while he sat opposite her, a gleam in his eyes.

"I believe Mr. Van Horne reserved this table for you," the maître d' said curtly.

"I'm sure he did, but I've decided to sit here. Is that a problem?"

His tone made it clear that the only problem would be if the man tried to argue with him, and the maître d', looking fretful but intelligent, offered a pained smile and called over the waiter, who took their drink orders.

Left alone, Bethany stared at Dirk, trying to figure him out. "You don't like him, do you?" she asked.

"Who? The waiter?"

She gave him a look. "Miles."

He picked up a menu and made a show of studying it, but she refused to let him ignore her. "Miles is a warm, caring man. He's smart, sophisticated—"

"Look." Dirk folded the menu and set it aside to look at her. "We've already had this conversation. The bottom line is—no, I don't like the guy. The Van Hornes are old money. Growing up, I doubt the guy wanted for a single thing."

Something in the way he said the words told her that his childhood hadn't been the happiest. She wanted to ask him about it when her cell phone rang. Digging in her purse, she pulled out her phone.

"Hello?"

"Bethany, it's Miles. I'm sorry, my dear. I'm not going to make dinner tonight. Something unexpected has come up. Business. I hope you'll forgive me."

"Oh. Can't you get out of it? Please?"

"I'm afraid not. There's just no way. Are you already at the restaurant?"

"Yes."

"Did you come alone?" He sounded worried.

She glanced over at Dirk. "No."

There was a pause and she heard him sigh. "I need to go. We'll talk later, okay?"

"All right." She disconnected the call and put away her cell phone. "Miles won't be joining us," she told Dirk as she looked around. "Do you see our waiter? We should try to cancel our order."

"Why?"

His question surprised her. "Well, you don't want to really stay here and eat—do you?"

"Have you eaten here before?"

"Yes, Miles likes it, so we come here often."

"Is the food any good?"

"Well, yes."

"Great, then I don't see a problem. We have to eat anyway and we're already here. Why leave and go someplace else?"

She gave him a doubtful look. "This is a fondue restaurant. You don't strike me as the kind of man who eats a lot of fondue."

He shrugged. "Food's food. I'll give it a try and if we don't get enough to eat, we'll stop off and grab a burger on the way home. How's that?"

"Actually, that sounds really good."

That caused him to raise an eyebrow. "You a burger and fries girl?"

"I can't tell you how long it's been since I had a really great burger and hot, crisp French fries. Miles refuses to eat such 'common fare,' as he puts it." She shrugged, a little embarrassed to have shared that. "You know what they say—simple pleasures for simple minds."

He gave her an intense look. "There's nothing simple about you, Beth."

At that moment, the waiter appeared with their drinks and Dirk ordered a selection of meats and vegetables for two. When they were alone again, Bethany glanced around to make sure no one was within listening range before leaning forward slightly. "Tell me about vampires. We didn't get a chance to talk yesterday."

Dirk raised an eyebrow. "What do you want to know?"

"Everything. Start at the beginning. Where'd they come from? How'd you get involved? Is fighting vampires something you do for the police? How long have you been doing it? What—?"

"Whoa, slow down," he said, chuckling. "First things first. I don't know how long vampires have been around, exactly, but the sword you saw earlier today was forged centuries ago to slay them, so they must have been around for at least that long. Here in the United States, though, I don't think any existed until six months ago."

"I don't understand. Isn't it a chicken and egg scenario? You have to have at least one vampire to create another."

"Not necessarily. Have you ever heard of El Chupacabra?"

"No, what's that?"

"It's the name of the creature that created the vampires we're dealing with today."

She waited for him to go on.

"A year ago, I hadn't heard of it either. The name, El Chupacabra, is Spanish for the goatsucker. Goats are the creatures' preferred food source—or rather the blood of the goats, because chupacabras live off blood. Until a year ago, they were considered to be like Bigfoot. Nothing more than the product of folklore—tales told at night around the campfire. There have even been sightings, but nothing that could ever be proven."

He glanced at her, maybe to see how she was reacting

to his story, but she kept her face blank, waiting for him to continue.

"About a year ago, the U.S. government found two creatures in the Amazon that they believed to be El Chupacabras. They called in a scientist to study them—a cryptozoologist, Dr. Clinton Weber. Lanie's father."

He took a swallow of his drink before continuing. "Weber studied them for several months and discovered that these creatures have hollow fangs and they inject their prey with venom while they are feeding—like a snake does. Weber thought the venom might prevent the blood from clotting while the chupacabra is feeding. Anyway, once the animal dies, end of story. Not so with humans. The venom has a strange effect on people and when the human dies, the venom somehow restores life to the corpse, and two nights later the victim rises as a vampire."

Bethany sat very still, willing herself not to reject, out of hand, what he was telling her. He obviously took her silence as acceptance and went on.

"Of the two creatures found, one was an adult and the other was much younger. About six months ago, the adult chupacabra attacked and killed Dr. Weber and another man, Lance Burton. At that time, no one knew about the chupacabra-vampire connection. Two days later, Dr. Weber and Burton literally rose from the dead and killed the remaining members of their research team."

Bethany gasped. "How awful." In her mind's eye, she saw an image of Mr. Yarbro, clutched close to the vampire's chest as it leaned forward, fangs buried in his neck. "Is that who's been after me? Lanie's father and this Lance Burton?"

"No. Dr. Weber was never a threat. Burton, on the other

hand, was." He paused and for a moment Bethany thought he might not continue. "Burton was a former SEAL, along with me and Mac. In life, he was psychotic, but when he became a vampire, he was much worse. He came up with a plan to assassinate the President and to do that, he needed help. So he kidnapped the adult chupacabra and forced it to kill several other members of our former SEAL team—men who had been his close friends. In that way, he created his own special ops team of vampires. Mac and I killed all but two of them six months ago, including Burton, but I believe it's the two who escaped who are responsible for the attacks on you."

It was almost more information than Bethany could process, but there was one question above all others that she still wanted answered. "Why do they want me?"

"I'm not sure. I think they want to continue where Burton left off—only there aren't enough of them to wage an all-out physical assault. So instead, they're going for a biochemical assault. Germ warfare. And they need a biochemist."

Bethany gasped. "What? That's unbelievable."

"It's the best theory I have right now," Dirk said.

"And, of all the biochemists in the area, they randomly selected me?"

Dirk's pointed silence caused a shudder to run through her. "I wasn't randomly selected?"

His features were grim when he spoke. "I did some checking. Van Horne wasn't just bragging when he said you were the best in your field—and trust me, they'll need the best. Your being a woman was an added benefit. They probably thought you'd be easy to intimidate."

While Bethany digested this, the waiter arrived with

their food. As soon as he left, Dirk reached over and took her hand in his. "I won't let anything happen to you, okay? Now, let's try to enjoy the meal."

He gave her hand a gentle squeeze before releasing it. The gesture was meant to be reassuring and shouldn't have sent warm shivers up and down her arms. She wondered if the contact had affected him, too, but his attention was focused on the array of bite-sized food and pots of cheese. He viewed them with obvious skepticism.

She used the opportunity to study him as he tentatively pierced a cube of bread and dipped it into the nearest fondue pot. Then he popped it into his mouth.

"Not bad," he said after he swallowed it. Bethany smiled. She'd always thought there was something inherently feminine about eating fondue, but Dirk pulled it off with such smooth, masculine confidence, it left her wondering what those hands could do under different circumstances.

She picked up her skewer and stabbed a vegetable piece, then dunked it into the cheese. As she lifted the food to her mouth, she felt Dirk's gaze on her. He made her feel self-conscious and she worried that she had cheese stuck to the corner of her mouth, or something equally ludicrous. She picked up her napkin and pressed it to her lips, just in case.

Across from her, Dirk was, once again, spearing another piece of steak and her attention was drawn to the hand holding the skewer. It was a strong hand, square and wide, with veins running across the back. She knew from the few times he'd touched her that his hands were slightly rough, with calluses, not smooth and soft, like Miles's hands were. Her gaze wandered to his thumb and she wondered if there was any truth to the old wives' tale about the size of a man's thumb and the size of his—

"You want my meat?"

Her eyes flew up to his face as she tried to decide if she'd heard him correctly? "Excuse me?"

There was a devilish twinkle in his eyes as he waved his skewer in the air, the piece of steak on the end coming close to dripping cheese all over the place. "You were staring at my steak here, so I thought maybe you wanted it."

"No, thank you." Bethany mumbled, trying to decide if his comments were deliberately suggestive or whether it was her own depraved imagination running wild. The meal that was supposed to help focus her thoughts and attention on her fiancé was doing just the opposite.

Lost in speculation, she pierced a piece of steak and placed it in her mouth, pulling it from the skewer slowly as she savored the flavor. Across from her, she thought she heard a groan and when she glanced up, Dirk was watching her with an intensity that fairly sizzled across the open space between them. It gave her a guilty thrill to think that he might be as affected by the innuendos as she.

"Does it taste good?" The low rumble of his voice washed over her, teasing her senses.

Feeling daring, she gave him a seductive smile. "Yes. Juicy and thick." She enunciated the words slowly, another maneuver in a dangerous game of enticement.

He held up his skewer with a piece of steak on it and brought it close to her mouth. "Let me feed you *my* meat," he said, touching the steak to her lips and then pulling it away slightly just as she opened her mouth to take it. In the darkness of the room, his eyes seemed to take on a strange reddish glow.

Tightness started building deep in the pit of her stomach and her breathing grew shallow. Warning sirens
screeched in her head that this game had gone too far.
They were close to crossing that invisible line dividing
flirting from something far more dangerous, and yet she
couldn't resist edging just a little closer.

Wrapping both her hands around his, she brought the
steak to her mouth and gently sucked on it, taking her
time. Then she pushed the skewer well into her mouth,
drawing it out slowly before pushing it in again.

Across from her, Dirk's eyes were glued to her mouth,
mesmerized by her movements. He groaned, released the
skewer, slid out of the booth, and disappeared into the
back, leaving Bethany to savor her moment of triumph.

He was in so much trouble. Dirk knew that he should
never have pushed the game that far. He walked into the
bathroom and, seeing it empty, turned on the faucet closest to him and splashed cold water across his face. Then
he placed his hands against the edge of the sink and leaned
forward, staring deep into his reflection, where glowing
red eyes gazed back at him.

When his breathing returned to something more normal and his eyes faded back to blue, he wiped his face
with a paper towel and walked back to the booth. Bethany
looked up when he sat down, but didn't say a word. They
continued to eat in silence, only occasionally asking for
something on the table to be passed. When they were
done, Dirk paid the bill, feeling that the sooner they were
out of this place, the better.

He held the door open for her and they made their way
across the quiet parking area. It wasn't until they were al-

most to his SUV that Dirk realized that the edgy feeling he had was more than discomfort from what had happened inside. He looked around, noticing the empty lot and the unnatural silence.

He reacted as the first rush of wind hit him, shoving Bethany to one side. "Run!"

The impact of the vampire slamming into him knocked Dirk to the ground and he didn't have time to reach for his dagger. He landed on his side and ignored the jolt of pain that shot through his hip. He didn't give his attacker time to settle on top of him, but immediately threw him off. He used the momentum of the effort to roll to his side and then jumped to his feet just as a second vampire leaped on his back. The two were not as experienced in fighting as Dirk, but their superhuman strength made up for their lack of skill.

Dirk took several punches before he could pull his dagger free and plunge it deep into the first attacker's heart. Before the vampire hit the ground, Dirk turned toward the second. His own emotions, already on edge, raged out of control. He curled his lips back to give the vampire a savage grin and saw the creature's eyes widen in surprise. The decision to run flashed across the vampire's face as clearly as if it were written on a page.

"Too late, asshole." Dirk took the stride that would close the distance between them, grabbed the creature about the neck, and jerked him forward, onto the blade of his dagger, held at the exact angle needed to pierce its heart.

Bethany's scream ripped through the night air and sent him racing to where he'd seen her disappear around the side of the old house.

Bethany fought her attacker with all her might, kicking her feet and bucking her body as he dragged her farther and farther away from Dirk—and safety. Something wet ran down her arms and she suspected it was blood from where his fingernails bit into her flesh.

Desperation and terror consumed her, leaving a bitter taste in her mouth. She didn't want to die like this. She screamed again and was vaguely aware of Dirk, racing around the corner of the house, before her attacker shifted and blocked him from her view. "Dirk!" she shouted, hoping he'd hear her. They'd just passed the Dumpster when suddenly the vampire released her, staggered, and fell back.

Then Dirk was there, between her and the vampire, a towering wall of protection as he faced the enemy. Bethany wanted to grab his arm and flee before the creature could kill them, but she was frozen by fear. When Dirk moved toward the vampire, she cried out for him to stop, but he didn't listen. He hauled the creature up by the scruff of his shirt and plowed a hand into the creature's face, knocking it back several more feet.

"Dirk, let's go," Bethany pleaded from where she stood. She took an involuntary step toward him and he must have heard her, because he hesitated. At that moment, the creature lunged to its feet and attacked. Snarling, its lips curled to reveal fangs glowing pearly white in the moonlight, it thrust its mouth against Dirk's neck.

Roaring in anger, he swiveled and grabbed the creature, plucking it off as if it were a bug and tossing the vampire so far that it landed behind the Dumpster, out of sight. This time, when Dirk went after the creature, she didn't call him back. She waited, listening to the sounds of fighting that filled the night air. Frantic, her mind conjured images of more vampires lurking in the shadows, waiting to jump out at her.

She considered running for help, but then remembered the can of Mace in her purse. She pulled it out and held it before her as she moved slowly toward the Dumpster. Cautiously, she rounded the corner and all hopes of a clear shot vanished.

The vampire was between her and Dirk. She started to edge around, hoping to come at the creature from a different angle. At that moment, she heard the sound a knife makes when it's thrust into a melon. It was accompanied by a grunt. Then, in slow motion, the vampire crumpled to the ground and she watched it fall in morbid fascination.

Was it over? she wondered. Was it dead? She looked up, needing to see the reassurance in Dirk's face, needing to know that she was safe.

Chest heaving from the effort of fighting, a bloodied dagger still clutched in his hand, Dirk stared at her with eyes that glowed with an unnatural red light and lips curled up in a feral snarl, revealing two sharp, pearly white fangs.

Chapter
8

Still caught up in the adrenaline rush of the fight, it took Dirk a moment to realize Bethany was staring at him in horror. He knew how she must see him—no different from the vampires who'd attacked her.

He closed his mouth, once more hiding his fangs from sight, willing the vampire half of his changeling nature into submission. For several long seconds, he thought he might be able to save the situation, because while he'd been fighting to control his temper, Bethany hadn't moved.

Not knowing exactly how to reassure her that everything was okay, he took a step toward her. In that instant, she screamed and pulled the trigger.

The spray hit him in the face, burning his eyes and temporarily blinding him. He roared in pain and frustration, wiping his eyes as he stumbled after her, using the sound of her running footsteps, more than sight, to guide him. It didn't take long to catch her and by the time he grabbed her arms and pulled her to a stop, he'd managed to sheath the dagger.

"Bethany, stop fighting me and let me explain."

"Please don't hurt me," she whimpered as she tried to pull away from him.

"Oh, Beth, honey. You're breaking my heart. I would never hurt you." She thought him a monster, like the ones who had killed her bodyguard, and the knowledge sliced through him more effectively than any knife's blade. Still, he couldn't let her run off without making sure no other vampires were around.

Though she resisted, he pulled her up against him and locked her in his embrace so she couldn't move. Instead of kicking at him now, she trembled helplessly in his arms, small whimpers continuing to tear him apart.

His eyes hurt like hell, so he closed them while he rested his head against hers. "Beth, hush now. No one's going to hurt you."

"You're a vampire." The accusation came out in a choked voice.

"No, I'm not. I'm a changeling—half vampire, that's true, but also half human. I'm not the undead. I have a conscience and a soul." He waited for his words to sink in, hoping she believed him, knowing she didn't. "Beth, how can I prove to you that I won't hurt you?"

She stilled in his arms. "You can let me go."

"And if I let you go, you promise not to run away?"

She started to nod her head and then stopped. "No."

He felt a smile tug at his lips, despite how worried he was. Keeping his tone steady and even, he tried to reason with her. "We have several problems here. First, I don't want anyone coming out and seeing dead bodies all over the parking lot. They might call the police and things could get complicated until I can get hold of John. Second, I don't know if those vampires I killed are really dead, so the sooner I get the bodies out of here and dispose of them properly, the better. Finally, while I think we've seen the last of the vampires for tonight, I don't know that for a fact, so I need to get you somewhere safe ASAP."

He waited to see if she reacted to anything he said, but she remained quiet and still in his arms. Deciding he had no other choice, he slowly let her go. To her credit, she took a very purposeful step back, but didn't bolt. Up until now, she hadn't looked at him—not really—and he tensed, waiting for that moment. Finally, she raised her eyes and he knew that despite the fact that his fangs were covered and his eyes had returned to their normal blue, she still saw the vampire.

After tonight, she'd never see him any other way. She'd probably want to move out of the mansion, away from him, but it didn't mean he wouldn't still be there, in the shadows, doing his best to protect her from Harris and Patterson—at least until this whole thing was over. After that—he didn't know. Maybe he'd still be there, trying to catch glimpses of her, hoping that would be enough for him, but knowing it wouldn't be.

Moving slowly, so as not to alarm her further, he reached into his pocket and pulled out the keys to his SUV. Then he held them out to her. "Take these. Drive yourself home, or wherever you want to go, but for God's sake, be careful. This isn't over yet and there will probably be other attacks."

"How . . . how do you know?"

"Because you're still here. Beth, they're not going to stop until they have you—or until I kill them all." When she still didn't move, he jangled the keys in front of her. "Go."

Hesitantly, she reached out and took them. "What about the bodies?"

"I'll call Mac and ask him to meet me here."

She nodded and backed away from him in the direction of his SUV. Minutes later, she pulled out of the parking lot and drove away.

The sound of the restaurant door opening tore Dirk from his thoughts and he hurriedly ducked out of sight, behind the Dumpster where the one body lay. He dragged it farther out of sight and waited for the latest patrons to drive off before recovering the other two bodies.

Then, reluctantly, he pulled out his cell phone and called Mac.

Hands gripping the wheel, Bethany drove, not caring where she headed as long as it was away from the restaurant, away from Dirk, and away from vampires. Right now, all she felt was numb, but she knew that fear and confusion lurked just beneath the surface. She wanted to scream and the temptation to head out of town and keep on driving, leave all of it—Dirk, Miles, the research project, and the vampires—behind was great.

"Get hold of yourself, Bethany." Her voice sounded unusually loud in the too quiet vehicle and she reached over to flip on the radio. A rock tune came on and its familiar melody soothed her, chasing away the numbness and fear, letting the cogwheels of her brain turn once again.

It occurred to her that while she had tried to adjust to the reality of vampires, there had been a part of her still in denial. Seeing the three tonight had shattered that tiny illusion. She'd never seen anything like them. Their strength and speed so far exceeded human capabilities that she wondered how anyone could possibly defeat them.

It was little wonder that Mr. Yarbro had failed, despite being strong and, presumably, well trained in the art of hand-to-hand combat. The image of Frank, the security guard, rose in her mind. Even Frank hadn't stood a chance against them. No human could.

Bethany stopped at a traffic light, and staring into its red glow, she once again saw Dirk's eyes staring at her—worried and uncertain—but not with malice. Never with malice—because Dirk would never hurt her. She knew that with an unshakable certainty. Since the moment she'd first met him, he had done nothing but protect her.

She thought back to the way he'd fought the vampires—his strength and speed equal to theirs. It made sense, didn't it? It would take someone not quite human to defeat them. Not quite human—or maybe half human and half something else?

By the time the light changed, Bethany had made up her mind. She pulled off on the side of the road and turned around. As she neared the restaurant, her pulse began to pound. She hoped she wasn't making the biggest mistake of her life. If so, she'd find out soon enough.

At first, she didn't see Dirk and the beginnings of panic set in. Had he already left? Or maybe gone inside? She considered parking the SUV, but the memory of vampires springing out of thin air was too fresh. Instead, she slowly drove around the lot, finally going behind the restaurant. There she spotted him standing near the line of trees.

She pulled even with him and put the SUV in park, letting the engine idle. He was on the phone.

As she stepped out to face him, he lowered the phone from his ear, but didn't disconnect the call. He gave her a curious look, equal parts of confusion, concern, and, she thought, hope.

"I don't understand everything that's going on," she told him. "That scares me—a lot. I've seen things that I would have said were impossible, and that scares me, too. The only time I've felt safe lately was when I was with you—but tonight, for the first time, I was afraid of you."

"Beth, I—"

She held up her hand to silence him. "I did some thinking while I drove around. You could have killed me any number of times over the last couple of days, but you didn't. So, I'm back." She walked around to the other side of the SUV and opened the passenger door. She looked at him from behind the V formed by the door and the windshield. "Like I said before, I don't understand all of it, but I think I'm safer *with* you than *without* you." She glanced at the trees behind him. "Do you need help with the bodies?"

"No."

She nodded but couldn't think of anything else to say, so she silently climbed into the SUV and closed the door.

Dirk stared at her, both amazed and more than a little relieved. Remembering the phone, he lifted it to his ear. "Forget the ride. I'm good. I'll be there shortly."

He glanced back at Bethany, half afraid he'd imagined her return, but she continued to sit in the SUV, waiting for him to join her. He hoped she wouldn't change her mind when he started hauling out the bodies and dumping them in the back.

Working quickly, he carried each one from where he'd placed it just behind the line of trees. To her credit, Bethany didn't bolt. She sat there, a stoic look on her face, eyes forward, never once turning her head until he finally finished and climbed in beside her.

Their eyes met briefly and it pained him to see the flicker of fear that passed through hers. He wanted to say something, but wasn't sure what, so he merely put the car in drive and pulled out of the parking lot.

They'd driven for about five minutes in silence when she finally broke it. "Are those things dead? I mean, I know they're dead or rather undead, isn't that how they refer to it in the movies? But back at the restaurant, you said you didn't know if they were really dead, so . . ." As if she realized she was rambling, she stopped and took a breath. "Is there any chance they'll climb over the back-seat and come after us?"

"They're as dead as I can make them—for now." Which he hoped was dead enough—at least until he could get to his sword and cut off their heads. As far as he knew, that was the only guarantee.

Bethany rubbed her forehead, but Dirk knew from ex perience that no amount of massaging would make the pain go away. The most he could do to help was wait until she was ready and then answer her questions when they started. He didn't have to wait long.

"You said you're half vampire. Were you born that way? Is one of your parents . . ."

"A vampire?" he finished for her when she seemed to hesitate. "No. I was born human, but back when all this started, I was attacked by the adult chupacabra."

He heard her gasp. "How horrible."

"Yeah, it was." He thought back to that night so long ago. "Mac got there before the creature could finish me off, but by then it had injected so much venom into my bloodstream that my body reacted. It *changed* me." He hesitated for the length of a heartbeat and then went on. "That's what they call those that are like me—*changelings.*"

"There are more of you?"

"Just one, that I know of. Mac."

"Did the same thing happen to him, too? He was attacked by the chupacabra?"

"Yeah. In fact, Lanie's the one who saved him."

"Is she . . . ?"

"No. She's still human."

She nodded slowly like she was processing the information. "What's the admiral's involvement in all of this?"

"From what I understand, his ancestors used to find the changelings, help them adapt, and make sure they had the training and equipment to hunt the vampires."

"By equipment, you mean that sword you showed me?"

He nodded.

"But you didn't have the sword tonight?" She cast a nervous glance into the back of the SUV. "Are you sure they're dead?"

"I think we'll be okay. Using the sword to cut off their

heads is the best way to make sure the vampires stay dead, but it's not the only way."

She glanced to the back of the SUV again, but Dirk could tell she didn't look as nervous as she had before. "So if the admiral's family has been doing this for centuries, how come there aren't more changelings? Or fewer vampires?"

"Supposedly, all the vampires had been killed—at least over here in the states. Thanks to Burton bringing the chupacabra from the Amazon to D.C., all that changed."

She fell silent again, so that the only noise heard inside the car was the steady hum of the tires on the road. Finally, she glanced at him, the expression in her eyes nervous. "Do you drink blood?"

He wanted to smile, but was afraid she might misinterpret his expression.

"No. A changeling doesn't normally crave blood and we don't need it to survive. There are certain circumstances, however, when blood can heal us or give us unusual strength and vitality." She looked confused, so he hurried to explain. "You see, blood that is freely given is like the sweetest nectar. It's the gift of life and fills us with so much energy and strength, it's like being supercharged or something—at least, that's what Mac tells me. He's taken Lanie's blood a number of times."

"What kind of circumstances?" Anyone else and he would have thought the person was asking so they could specifically avoid finding themselves in such a circumstance, but Beth just sounded curious. Beneath it all, she was a scientist.

"Well, for instance, there was the time that Mac had been captured by Burton. He was severely beaten, virtually dead. Lanie let him drink her blood so he could get his strength back and rescue them."

She looked frightened again. "That happens often?"

"As far as I know, he's only taken her blood once out of necessity." He couldn't resist giving her a lascivious smile. "The other times were when they made love. Apparently, it's quite the aphrodisiac."

The shock in her eyes made his daring remark worth it. She quickly recovered. "That doesn't turn her into a vampire? Or a . . . a changeling?"

"No. A changeling's bite doesn't seem to affect humans. And vampires only turn humans into vampires if they kill them."

Dirk cast another glance at her and saw that instead of looking scared, she merely looked dazed. He guessed that was an improvement.

"What else is different about you?" she asked.

"Well"—he pretended to think—"I do cast a reflection in a mirror, garlic won't kill me, although I find the odor offensive. I don't burst into flames when I go out into the sun, but I do need sunglasses because bright light hurts my eyes. I also have great night vision."

She remained quiet, as if waiting to see if there was more, so he went on. "I don't 'die' during the day, but the daylight makes me unusually tired, so much so that I have a hard time functioning while the sun is up. Otherwise, I'm much stronger than I was as a human and I can run ungodly fast. I can't fly or leap tall buildings in a single bound and I can't change into a bat or any other creature."

They had finally reached the mansion and Dirk pulled into the driveway. He drove them to the front door and stopped, but didn't shut off the engine. Instead, he honked the horn three times. "Go inside, Beth. Mac and I know what we're doing. You'll be safe here at the mansion. You have my word."

She reached for the door handle, but then paused. "Aren't you coming inside?"

He shook his head. "Not just yet."

At that moment, the front door opened and Mac strolled out, sword clutched in his hand. Seeing it, Bethany nodded and climbed out of the vehicle.

"Lanie's inside, waiting for you," Mac told her as he took her place.

Bethany turned and headed for the front door, very much aware of two sets of male eyes watching her. As soon as she was inside, she heard the SUV drive off.

Ahead of her, the great room looked warm and friendly.

"Bethany!" Lanie rounded the corner and came toward her. "Are you all right?" She didn't give Bethany a chance to answer but pulled her into the living room where they sat on the couch together. "Dirk phoned and told us all about the attack." She gave Bethany a sympathetic look. "And he told us that you found out about him, as well."

Bethany shook her head. "I don't know why I never saw it before, unless—are the fangs retractable?"

"No," Lanie said with a chuckle. "You should have seen Mac and Dirk when their fangs first grew in. They had a hard time just opening their mouths without the fangs being obvious, much less trying to talk. Even now, they don't smile a lot."

Bethany nodded because she had noticed that. "What about the eyes?"

"You mean, the way they glow red? I haven't figured

out what causes that, but it usually happens when they feel extreme emotions."

Bethany remembered the strange appearance of Dirk's eyes at the dinner table earlier that evening and it made her wonder. She shut off the thought before she jumped to any wrong conclusions. Instead, she turned back to Lanie. "I'm sorry about your father."

Lanie gave a sad smile. "Thanks."

"Is he still . . ." She stopped, afraid her curiosity was making her insensitive.

Lanie didn't seem to mind, though. "He's still alive— or rather still undead, as far as I know. There's an old legend about a village inhabited by vampires somewhere in the Amazon. He decided to go look for it."

"When was the last time you saw him?"

"Back when all this first started."

"And you've not heard from him since?"

Lanie smiled. "No, but he's been pulsing money from his bank account. I left it open for him. Still, I miss him."

Bethany's heart went out to her. She knew the other woman must miss her father a great deal and it made her realize how lucky she was that her folks were both still alive. Just then, a flicker of movement off to the side caught her attention and she turned to see something gray huddled by the desk. "I didn't know you had a dog," she commented, wondering why she hadn't seen it around the house before.

"We don't." Lanie stood up and walked over to the desk where she picked up the small animal and brought it back to the sofa.

Bethany stared in amazement. She'd never seen anything like it. It was gray-skinned with a round head and a slightly elongated muzzle. It stood on two larger hind legs and stared at her through enormous red glowing eyes. It could almost be considered cute, except for its two fangs, sharp talonlike claws, and the row of fins running down its back.

"This is Gem," Lanie said. "She's a chupacabra."

Bethany stared at the creature thinking that despite its strange appearance, she'd seen it before. Then she remembered. "She looks like that statue I saw Julia with earlier today."

Lanie stroked the creature's back. "Actually, she *is* the statue."

"I beg your pardon."

Lanie's smile grew broader. "During the day, chupacabras turn to stone."

Bethany stared at her, aghast. "*This* is the stone gargoyle that's always on Julia's desk?"

Lanie looked troubled. "Yes. No matter how many times I chase Gem away from that desk, she keeps going back. There's something about Julia that she likes. I try to lock her in my room before the sun comes up, but she has a tendency to escape when Mac comes home from hunting because I get sidetracked and forget about her." She blushed, reminding Bethany that she and Mac were still newlyweds. She'd seen them together enough to know they were very much in love and a part of her envied them that. She couldn't see her and Miles ever being like that.

At that very moment, she heard the sounds of Mac and Dirk talking and knew they'd finished the task they'd driven off to do.

"I knew something was going on," Mac was saying. "It had to be the link."

"Maybe so. I'm just not sure what it means."

"Yes, you do."

When the men appeared, they wore equally grave expressions on their faces. Dirk's eyes immediately sought out Bethany and she offered him a tentative smile to let him know she wasn't going to bolt. Seeing it, Dirk's face relaxed and though his lips didn't part, he smiled back.

Lanie got up off the sofa and went to Mac. "What are you two talking about?"

"Tonight, Dirk and I felt the link," Mac said.

"You did?" Lanie looked surprised and quickly explained to Bethany. "One of the side effects of the chupacabra's venom is that everyone attacked by the same creature shares some type of psychic connection that allows them to feel one another's emotions and thoughts. When the adult was dying, the link grew so weak that it became more or less nonexistent. We assumed that meant the adult chupa had died."

Lanie glanced at both men and as each nodded Bethany saw the stunned look on her face grow. "But if you were able to feel one another's emotions and thoughts, if the link is still active . . ." She moved closer to Mac and he wrapped his arm around her. "Then she's still alive."

"Who's still alive?" Bethany ventured to ask. Mac and Lanie seemed preoccupied, so Bethany turned to Dirk, who answered the question for her.

"The adult chupacabra. The one we thought was dead."

"The one that attacked you?"

"Yeah."

Bethany studied Gem prowling around the room. It was hard for her to be frightened of the small creature when the others weren't. Yet, when she tried to imagine a creature that looked like Gem, but bigger, she felt the blood rush from her head.

"Do you know where it is?" She didn't like to think of a creature like that wandering loose and killing people.

"We think so," Dirk said.

"Where?"

"Right here in Washington, D.C."

Chapter
9

Late the next morning, Bethany woke feeling drained and exhausted. She hadn't slept much, despite the hot soothing bath she'd taken. Her thoughts had whirled around in her head like a maelstrom until she'd wanted to scream. Nothing seemed normal to her anymore and she desperately longed to have her previous uneventful life back.

Going downstairs to the kitchen, she found Julia at the coffeepot, pouring herself a cup.

"Good morning," Bethany said, walking in.

Julia's face lit up when she saw her, making Bethany feel welcome. "Good morning. Would you like some coffee?"

"Sounds wonderful." Bethany sat at the table and waited for Julia to pour her a cup.

"I'm surprised to see you up so early."

"I had trouble sleeping," she admitted, taking the cup Julia offered her. She took a sip, praying the caffeine kicked in quickly. "Thank you. I need this."

Julia's expression turned sympathetic. "I spoke to Charles when I first came in this morning. He mentioned there had been some sort of attack on you last night. It sounded absolutely frightening."

"It was," she admitted. "But Dirk was with me." Bethany heard the reverent tone in her voice and prayed that Julia wouldn't notice. Unfortunately, she did and for several seconds she studied Bethany's face.

"He seems like a very capable young man," she finally said.

Bethany couldn't help but smile at the understatement. "That he is."

"He and Mac are rather intimidating," Julia admitted. "I'm not sure they want me here."

The statement caught Bethany by surprise. "No, I'm sure you're mistaken. Everyone is very fond of you."

"Perhaps. However, I can't help feeling as if someone is purposely trying to make things difficult for me. For instance, I've asked repeatedly to have that statue moved from my desk, yet every morning, there it is." Julia looked away, shaking her head. "It's silly, I know. I should stop complaining and simply move the darn thing. It's not that it weighs all that much, but it's the principle, you know?"

"I'm sorry, Julia. I can't tell you why the statue is always there. I wish I could, but I do know that everyone here likes you and I don't think anyone's trying to be malicious."

Julia smiled. "I hope you're right."

Bethany took another sip of her coffee. "I need to go into the lab early today."

Julia looked around. "Oh, are the others up? Perhaps I should make breakfast."

"No, don't bother. They're still asleep and I'll get something on the way."

She gave Bethany a concerned look. "You're going by yourself?"

"I'll be okay," Bethany assured her, taking a last drink of her coffee before setting the empty cup in the sink. There was no way to explain to the woman why daytime was possibly *the only* time it was safe for her to be alone, so she walked out of the kitchen before Julia could say another word.

Forty-five minutes later, Bethany's taxi pulled up in front of the Van Horne Technologies building. She paid the driver, climbed out of the car, and strode purposefully through the front doors. She nodded to the new security guard, unable to block the image of his predecessor from her mind, and hurried to the elevators. It felt good to be doing something routine again.

She spent the morning working on the plant extract and the more tests she ran, the more concerned she became. Too many aspects of the substance resembled illegal street narcotics and Miles's continued secrecy bothered her.

The one thing she refused to be was a party to something illegal.

Afraid that Miles might try to put her off if he knew why she wanted to see him, she didn't bother to call. Instead, she took the elevator to the second floor where his office was located. His secretary was not at her desk and when Bethany glanced at the clock, she saw it was after six. Having been so hard at work, she hadn't realized what time it was. For most, the workday was over. She wondered if Miles would still be around.

Hurrying to his office, she raised her hand to knock, but then stopped short when she found the door standing slightly ajar. Voices could be heard coming from inside and she realized that Miles was not alone.

About to walk away, curiosity got the better of her. She glanced around to make sure no one was watching and then edged closer to the door.

". . . my best researcher on it and if anyone can analyze it, she can," Miles was saying to a man Bethany didn't recognize. She couldn't see his face, but he was wearing an expensive olive-green suit. The conservative look of his short-cut hair was ruined only by its bright orange-red color.

"We have a schedule to meet," the man said, speaking with an accent that sounded rough. When he waved his hand in the air for emphasis, Bethany caught sight of several gold rings on his fingers. "I have buyers lined up, but if I can't deliver the product, they're going to turn ugly."

"Don't threaten me, Santi," Miles said in a harsh, cold tone that Bethany had never heard him use before. "I'll deliver the product, just as I said I would, but I don't need you or your boss harassing me. Now, if you'll excuse me, I have work to do."

The two men rose and Bethany, afraid of getting caught eavesdropping, scurried down the hall, not stopping until she was safely on the elevator, headed back to her lab. As she rode the car up, she played the conversation over in her head. Most of Van Horne's clients fell into one of two groups—drug companies and the Department of Justice. Miles's visitor didn't look like he belonged to either group. In fact, Bethany thought he looked like a drug dealer and she struggled to convince herself otherwise, but couldn't.

The last thing she wanted to believe was that Miles was involved with drug dealers.

Harris woke from his dreamless slumber as he usually did. One moment, he was dead; unaware. The next he was fully conscious. He did not immediately rise, but waited patiently.

It came finally, a gentle probing along the link, the barest whisper in his mind. It was the adult chupacabra and that she sought him out this time was no small victory.

He opened his mind to her and her hunger hit him with an unexpected force that ripped through his body. If there'd been room in his safe hole, he would have doubled over from the pain. She was starving but her fear of humans—of being caught—kept her from seeking food.

Harris knew he had to help her and he formed a mental image of a ranch he'd found not far from the city. He'd seen both cattle and goats there, running unattended in large numbers in the pastures. He sent the image to the chupacabra as clearly as he could, envisioning the creature feeding off the livestock.

He knew the minute she received the image because the link grew faint as the creature turned her thoughts to finding the farm. Briefly, Harris considered going there himself in order to capture her, but dismissed the idea almost as quickly as it formed. Not this time, he thought. He wanted the creature to trust him and that had to be built slowly, over time. He just hoped he had that kind of time.

Bethany's breathing had almost returned to normal by the time she reached her lab, but her thoughts were still in turmoil. She was so upset that she didn't see Dirk until she ran into him.

"Don't you ever go off on your own again," he said, gripping her by the arms and shaking her. "Do you hear me?"

"The whole building can hear you." She glared at him. "Do you mind?" She tried to pull herself free, furious with the way he manhandled her, yet inexplicably glad to see him.

"I'm not kidding, Beth. Just because it's daylight doesn't mean you're safe. These Primes we're dealing with aren't stupid—and they've been known to hire daytime help; humans who'll do anything for money." The light in his eyes started to glow softly. "You have to be smarter than this, Beth. And you have to do what I say."

Defiance burned inside her and she longed to defend her actions but the truth was that it hadn't occurred to her that the vampires might hire humans. Staring up at Dirk, she realized how serious he was; how concerned for her. She became all too aware of him looming so close she felt the heat from his body. The clean, woodsy scent of his soap or aftershave surrounded her until every breath she took was filled with his scent. Her arms burned where he held her. Not from pain, but from the hundreds of thousands of nerves suddenly awakened by his touch. Dirk—and everything about him—was an assault on her senses.

Her tongue darted out to moisten lips suddenly gone dry. Dirk's sharp intake of breath caused her to look up into his eyes and then her own breath caught. Twin pools of molten lava gazed down at her, searing her, causing her pulse to race.

Dirk slid one hand up her arm, to the back of her head where he buried his fingers in her hair. With excruciating slowness, he leaned toward her until his breath fanned her lips. Something deep inside her coiled with hunger and anticipation.

It seemed an eternity that they stood so close, yet without really touching. Then his lips broke the thin barrier of air separating them.

It wasn't the chaste, closed-mouthed kisses that Miles usually gave her. This one was both possessive and demanding. It breached all her defenses and took no prisoners. She leaned into him and forgot everything except the feel of his warm hard body as he held her to him.

She'd never experienced anything like it before and though a part of her argued that she shouldn't be doing this, the voice was too faint to be heard over the rushing of her pulse.

A buzzing noise finally permeated her dazed state, an unwelcome intrusion. At first, she tried to ignore it but when it wouldn't go away, enough of her conscious mind surfaced and she recognized the sound of the lab timer, sitting on the table where she'd placed it earlier.

"Oh, no." Bethany tore her lips from Dirk's and in a flash, reality came crashing down about her. She stared at him in horror and this time, when she tried to pull away, he let her go.

"Beth—"

"No." She held up a hand to silence him as she backed away and tried to think. What had she done? She'd cheated on Miles. It was only a kiss, and yet, had the timer not gone off, what might she have done?

She felt Dirk watching her, his concern obvious, but she couldn't look at him. When her back came up against the lab table, she turned around and fumbled with the flasks and beakers, trying to focus on the newly finished test even though her thoughts were far too jumbled and confused for coherent thought.

"Look, Beth—" Dirk tried again, but she interrupted him.

"Let's not read more into this than there is, okay? It was a kiss. It didn't mean anything."

She couldn't look at him for fear he'd see her eyes and know she lied. It *had* meant something to her. Keeping her back to him, she went back to work. Only long after he walked away did she begin to relax.

Dirk watched Beth struggle to work, fighting the urge to gather her back into his arms and kiss her again. Kiss her until she forgot about work, forgot about vampires— and forgot about Miles. Walking away from her was one of the hardest things he'd ever done, but he did it.

He hadn't meant to kiss her, but had known it would happen eventually. The temptation had been eating at him since the moment he'd first seen her and it had finally worn him down. But if he'd thought that one taste of her would assuage his appetite, he'd been gravely mistaken. What he should do now—the right thing to do—would be to ask Mac to replace him as Beth's bodyguard.

Like hell he would. Not that he expected a repeat of what had just happened. In fact, he'd be lucky if she ever spoke to him again. There was a decided frost in the atmosphere of the lab. Wondering if he should try to talk to her or let the silence continue, a faint popping noise suddenly caught his attention.

"What was that?"

Beth looked at him, her brows furrowed. "What? I didn't hear anything."

He crossed the room so he could stand by the door. When Beth opened her mouth to say something, he held up his hand to silence her. He waited to see if he heard the popping noises again, but the sounds weren't repeated. Still, he knew what they'd been. Gunshots. Had he still been human, he couldn't have heard them from four floors below.

If he was to go downstairs, he knew what he'd find—the guard lying dead, most likely with two puncture wounds on the side of his neck. The difference between tonight and the first night the vampires had broken into the Van Horne building was that this time, the guard had managed to squeeze off a few rounds of his gun before he met his end.

There would be another difference, too. They'd know that Dirk was here with Beth, protecting her, and they would have brought plenty of reinforcements.

"Turn off anything that might burn or explode," he ordered Beth, briefly tearing his attention from the door to look at her.

She hesitated only a moment while she studied his face and then hurried about the lab, doing as he'd instructed. When she finished, she came to stand beside him.

"Quietly," he whispered as he led her to the doorway. Peering out, he scanned the hallway. So far, all was quiet. He hesitated only a second and then stepped out, motioning her to follow. They hadn't taken but a couple of steps when Dirk heard the sound of footsteps coming from the stairwell.

Grabbing Beth's arm, he propelled them down the hall in the opposite direction, his mind racing. The last thing he wanted to do was go back to the lab. It would be the first place the vampires would look. He scanned the hallway for options and his gaze fell on the utility closet.

Running for it, he hurried them inside and had just enough time to pull the door closed when the stairwell door opened and five vampires stepped into view. Dirk watched them from the cracked opening, praying that none of the creatures was astute or observant enough to notice the door standing slightly ajar.

The closet was small with barely enough room to accommodate them. Under other circumstances, Dirk might have taken advantage of the cozy confines. Beth's breathing sounded ragged behind him and he longed to turn around, take her in his arms and comfort her, but he dared not take his attention off the hallway.

The vampires came toward them, moving soundlessly. When they reached the first door to Beth's lab, they went inside. It wouldn't take them long to realize it was empty and then they'd start searching the building. If they opened the closet . . . he didn't want to think about that. They had to make a run for it while the vampires were busy.

With no time to second-guess himself, Dirk grabbed Beth's hand and pulled her from the closet and down the hallway toward the elevator. They were almost to it when a "dinging" noise announced its arrival. Dirk, not willing to leave a hapless employee in the wrong place at the wrong time to their fate, waited for the doors to open. As they did, he found himself staring into the faces of two more vampires.

Dirk shoved Bethany toward the stairwell and through the door. With the two vampires right behind them, there was no way to outrun them. Glancing over the side rail and looking to the landing three flights down, Dirk made his decision.

"Hang on." He pulled Beth to him and held her in an ironlike embrace with one arm as he propelled them over the railing with the other.

Chapter
10

B eth's scream reverberated off the walls as they fell to the ground level, the air whooshing past them. Dirk absorbed the impact of their landing with his legs, quickly setting her down and pulling her toward the exit door. The sound of the two vampires landing behind him stopped him in his tracks.

Pushing Bethany to the side, he grabbed the fire extinguisher from the wall and turned just as the first vampire charged. Dirk smashed the canister into the creature's face, denting the canister and causing white foam to spew forth. The vampire's eyes rolled up and as the body started to crumple, Dirk was reaching for his dagger with his free hand. A quick flick of his wrist sent it flying into the chest of the second creature. His aim was true and the second vampire hung suspended in the air for a moment before it, too, fell to the ground.

Tossing the extinguisher aside, Dirk grabbed Bethany

by the arm, pushed open the exit door, and together they dashed outside.

He never saw the fist that hit him. One second they were running, the next he was sailing into the side of the building with such force that when he hit, the bricks cracked.

He fell to the ground, stunned and out of breath. His vision faded to black—except for the bright white light flashing beneath the lids of his closed eyes. Almost as if it came from a great distance away, he heard Beth's scream and though he wasn't sure he could stand, he placed both hands flat on the ground and pushed himself up.

A short distance off, Bethany, carried by two vampires, was struggling and fighting like the very demons of hell were after her—which they were.

He raced after them, catching up to them not far from the parking garage. Grabbing the first vampire by the shoulder, he yanked him around and slammed his fist into the creature's face with enough force that the vampire staggered back, stumbled, and fell. Before the body even hit the ground, Dirk grabbed Beth's arm and pulled her from the other vampire's clutches, at the same time smashing his fist into the creature's face just as hard as he could. The vampire went down like a rock.

"Are you all right?" He could tell she was frightened and wanted to reassure her, but at that moment, he heard the sound of the fire exit opening. "Let's go," he shouted to Beth, pulling her along behind him as he hurried toward the parking garage where his Expedition was parked. If they could get to it before the others caught up to them, they might just survive the night.

Inside the garage, Dirk steered them toward the elevator. With no sign yet of their pursuers, they stepped inside.

As he searched for his keys, he felt Beth shudder beside him.

"My car is just off to the right," he tried to reassure her. "As soon as the doors open, make a run for it."

"They're still out there, aren't they?" Her voice was little more than a whisper.

"Yeah, they are." He wasn't going to lie to her. "But we have a small advantage. They don't know exactly what floor we're on."

She looked up, her eyes wide with fear. "There're so many—you can't fight them all."

He wanted to tell her that everything would be fine, but since he couldn't guarantee it, he made the only promise he could. "If they want you, they'll have to go through me first."

Just then, the elevator slowed to a stop and the doors whooshed open. Dirk stepped out to scan the area. So far, there was no sign of the vampires, but he knew they were close. The hairs on the back of his neck prickled with the anticipation of their arrival. "Run for the car."

He paced her, deactivating the locks just as she reached the passenger side and climbed in. He'd just opened his door when he heard the sound of racing feet in the stairwell.

Climbing into the driver's seat, he slammed his door shut and activated the locks. Then he started the engine, put the SUV in reverse, and backed up. Through the rear-view window, he saw the vampires emerge from the stairwell. They were closing fast and Dirk hurriedly shifted into drive and slammed his foot down on the accelerator. The SUV shot forward.

He made no effort to steer around the charging group.

Several of the creatures lunged to the side to get out of the way. One, however, leaped at the vehicle as it shot past, and Dirk heard the thump as the creature cleared the hood and landed on the roof.

There was no time to worry about their unwanted passenger, so Dirk concentrated on getting out of the garage as expediently as possible.

Reaching the end of the floor, Dirk hit the brake as he spun the wheel, taking the corner practically on two tires. The exit ramp to the next level was straight ahead now, at the opposite end. Scanning the area for errant humans, grateful none were about, Dirk sped up and when they reached the ramp, he took the sharp half-circle curve without slowing down.

When they shot onto the floor below, they were moving so fast that Dirk thought they'd be lucky not to crash. It took his entire focused attention to drive.

They were on the third floor, about to take the next ramp down when he heard the squeal of tires. Then a large black car appeared behind them and quickly began closing the distance between them.

From the corner of his eye, he saw Beth look back over her shoulder. Then she turned and gaped at him. "They're chasing us—in a car." She sounded stunned. "I didn't think they could drive."

"Yeah? Well, guess what?" They hit the ramp, barely slowing enough to make the curve to the bottom.

They entered the second level and still the black car gained on them. When it was close enough, it rammed the rear of the Expedition and Dirk fought to control the wheel. Above him, he heard scraping sounds, reminding him that a vampire still clung to the roof. Dirk knew he was going to have to do some fast thinking and sharp driving to get out of this one.

"Hang on." He stamped on the accelerator and the Expedition shot forward. The small lead Dirk and Beth had was soon lost as the black car also sped up. "That's right, asshole. Be sure to keep up," Dirk muttered.

The Expedition hit the down ramp at a dangerously high speed. Dirk gripped the steering wheel more firmly as he fought to control the SUV as it made the tight curve. Behind them came the squeal of tires followed by the chalkboardlike scraping of metal along concrete as their pursuers' car hugged the wall.

But still they came.

The Expedition barreled onto the street level and Dirk barely managed to straighten the wheel before they smashed into a support column.

The vampires weren't as lucky and as Dirk and Beth raced for the exit, they heard the satisfying crunch of metal as the black car smashed into the same support column Dirk had narrowly avoided.

Dirk didn't slow down. The exit was dead ahead and they had almost reached it when another black car, similar to the first one, suddenly appeared out of nowhere and blocked their escape.

Bethany gasped. They were trapped and yet the Expedition barreled forward, Dirk seemingly unaware of the problem. "Dirk," she screamed, bracing for the inevitable collision. "We're going to cra—"

At the last second, Dirk swerved and the SUV shot out the entrance gate. There were four sharp explosions as the one-way tracks blew out their tires, but Dirk kept going, turning onto the street.

Bethany cast a nervous glance out the rearview window, too afraid to let go of the support handle she was gripping. "I don't see anyone behind us. Maybe we lost them." Her dry throat gave the words a rough-sounding edge.

"Not yet. Brace your feet against the dashboard—and tighten your seat belt."

Wary, she did as instructed. Dirk slammed on the brakes and she lurched forward, but the seat belt and her feet braced against the dash kept her from flying through the windshield. Dirk fought to control the wheel as the SUV started to dovetail, the screeching of the tire rims scraping across the asphalt filling the eerie silence. Then Bethany heard the sound of something large hitting the hood.

She looked up just in time to see a vampire bounce off the hood and disappear under the front of the vehicle, which then heaved like it'd hit a speed bump, but kept on going.

Her mind froze as she remembered the vampire on the roof. She knew her eyes must be as round as saucers as she stared at Dirk in horror. "Is he . . . it . . . dead?"

His expression was solemn as he focused on the road. "Do we care?" He continued to drive for another two blocks, gradually slowing the SUV until he could wrench the wheel enough to turn into the moderately full parking lot of a nightclub.

He didn't so much park the car as let it come to a stop along the side of the building. "Are you all right?"

She nodded. "A little shaken, but for the most part— yeah, I'm fine. You?"

"Yeah. Come on." He undid his seat belt and climbed

out of the SUV. Bethany hesitated a moment and then followed suit. She nervously glanced around, expecting vampires to jump out at them, but except for one or two "humans" heading into the bar, they were alone.

She hurried around the vehicle to stand by Dirk, who was talking on his cell phone.

"They hit the lab again. Yeah, we're fine—for now." He looked up at the name on the nearby sign. "We're at The Dark Velvet nightclub. All right. See you then."

"Mac's on his way," he told her, disconnecting the call. "It'll take him about an hour to get here."

Panic hit Bethany. "What are we supposed to do until then? We can't just wait out here."

Dirk studied her face for a moment and she thought she saw a slight softening of his expression before he turned his head to scan the area. Then he looked back at her.

"Feel like a drink?"

She glanced nervously at the bar, skeptical of its rundown appearance, and imagined the type of patrons it attracted. "I don't know. We might be safer with the vampires," she muttered. "Maybe we should wait here for Mac." She rubbed her hands up and down her arms, trying to fight the chill of the evening—and fear.

"Hey, it'll be all right." His sympathetic tone was a balm to her frayed nerves and when he gathered her close, she let him, wrapping her arms around his waist and laying her head against his chest. He made her feel safe and it wasn't until that moment that she realized just how frightened she'd really been.

"They're never going to give up." She fought against the tears stinging her eyes.

"They will, eventually."

"No." She shook her head. "They'll just keep attacking—and each time they do, someone else will die. Another guard; another innocent victim. And it's all my fault." Her arms tightened around him. "I couldn't bear it if something happened to you." She'd barely whispered the words, but he'd heard her anyway.

"Beth?" When she refused to meet his eyes, he put his finger under her chin and tilted her face up. "Your safety is the most important thing to me. I'll do whatever I have to, to keep you safe. But if something happens to me, it's not your fault, okay? None of this is your fault. Understand?"

She gazed into his eyes, losing herself in their hidden depths, searching for answers to questions she didn't know she had. When they started to glow with their strange inner red light, she knew neither one of them was thinking about vampires anymore.

She longed to feel his lips on hers and tried to use the strength of her own desire to will him to kiss her. Her breasts grew heavy and where their bodies touched, flames seemed to ignite. The light in his eyes grew brighter, like an inferno, evidence of his own heightened emotion, and she felt herself being consumed by their heat.

"Don't look at me like that," he begged in a voice grown husky with need. "We're already walking a thin line here and I'm real close to not giving a damn that you're engaged to someone else."

He dropped his arms and stepped away from her. Bethany struggled for composure. He was right, but that didn't make his actions feel any less like rejection.

"Let's go inside," he suggested after a minute. "I think we could both use that drink."

Inside the bar, Dirk placed their order and then found them a nice quiet table in the back where they could sit and wait. The noise in the place precluded them from talking, so they sat in silence, each lost in their own thoughts. Neither made an effort to rekindle what had started between them outside, which was just as well because Bethany was more confused than ever about her feelings for Dirk and Miles.

When Mac arrived forty-five minutes later, she was glad to leave, and when they finally arrived back at the mansion, she went immediately to her room where she slipped gratefully into bed and fell into an exhausted sleep.

Dirk woke up that evening as the sun started to set. The day's sleep hadn't put him in any better a mood than he'd been when he'd gone to bed earlier that day, and learning that Miles Van Horne had been invited to dinner just made things worse.

Throughout the immeasurably long meal, he sat quietly, answering only the questions directed to him and ignoring the rest of the inane chitchat. Too often, his gaze, like his thoughts, strayed to Beth sitting across from him.

She had no idea how close she'd come to ending up in the back of his Expedition. He'd wanted her with the lust of a hormone-ridden teenager. And he didn't think making love to her once was going to be enough. It was better to have no taste of her at all than to know what Miles could enjoy whenever he wanted.

The thought of Beth's fiancé burned with an impotent rage and he hated having the man there in the admiral's house, sitting next to his wo— *Not* his woman, Dirk forcefully corrected himself.

Taking a deep breath, he brought his attention back to the dinner table and endured the rest of the meal. Finally, it ended and the group retired to the living room for drinks. If Dirk thought he was uncomfortable at dinner, it was nothing compared to the feeling he got sitting in an armchair off by himself while everyone else, either by design or by accident, paired off. Mac sat on the arm of Lanie's chair, the admiral and Julia sat together on the sofa, and Miles and Bethany sat on the adjacent love seat.

"Charles, that was a delightful meal," Miles said.

"Yes, it was, but I had nothing to do with it. Julia made all the arrangements for me," the admiral replied, bestowing a proud smile on the woman sitting beside him.

Julia's smile beamed back at him. "It was nothing, really."

The others voiced their appreciation for the meal, causing the woman to blush daintily, and Dirk wasn't surprised when the admiral reached over and gave her hand an affectionate squeeze. He and Mac exchanged meaningful glances. It was the first time since they'd known the admiral that he'd shown an interest in anyone. Dirk thought it might be a good idea to spend a little extra time getting to know the woman who had captured his mentor's attention.

As the conversation hit another lull, Miles cleared his throat, drawing all eyes to him. "As you may know, tomorrow is the Rod O'Connor Award dinner and ceremony." He draped an arm about Bethany and hugged her close. "You are all invited to be our guests."

"I'm afraid that won't be possible," Dirk said. "None

of us will be going—including Beth." He looked at her, feeling like a heel, hoping she'd understand once he explained. "I know this is a big honor for you, Beth, but it would be extremely dangerous for you to attend that ceremony."

"Why?" Miles sounded indignant.

"Because everyone will be *expecting* her to make an appearance," Dirk explained. "She'll be an easy target and I'm not willing to risk her safety for the sake of an award." He glared at Miles. "Are you?"

Miles had the decency to look abashed. "No, of course not. I would never place her in danger." He turned to Bethany and his face softened. "I'm sorry, my dear. I suppose they're right, it's too dangerous. If you'd like, I will go to the ceremony and accept the award on your behalf."

Dirk saw the disappointment in her eyes when she reluctantly nodded to Miles and he vowed that somehow he'd make it up to her.

With the subject of the ceremony put to rest, the conversation returned to more of the chatter that Dirk hated so much. After listening for what seemed an eternity, he finally stood up.

"If you'll excuse me, I have work to do. Julia, the meal was spectacular." He gave the others a curt nod and then let his gaze travel over to Bethany. "I'm sorry, Beth. I hope you understand why I can't let you go to the ceremony."

She nodded, even though disappointment showed in her eyes. Knowing there was nothing he could do about it right then, he turned and walked from the room.

Bethany watched Dirk leave and wondered where he was going. He hadn't talked much through the meal and she'd gotten the impression that he hadn't wanted to be there at all. Well, she could understand that. Even she was wishing the night were over. She'd been under so much stress lately that she just wanted a chance to relax. Heaving a silent sigh, she wondered when Miles would go home.

Glancing at him, she realized it was going to be a long night. Miles and the admiral had ventured onto the topic of financial investments and both men were in their element. Bethany leaned back against the couch and though she found the topic extremely dry, she politely listened.

After what had to be an hour, Bethany heard a small noise from across the room. Looking over, she saw Lanie stifling a yawn that might not have been totally authentic. "Oh, pardon me," Lanie apologized. "I didn't realize how tired I was."

"Oh, dear." Miles looked at his watch. "It *is* late, I'm sorry to have kept you up." He smiled at them indulgently. "I keep forgetting that not everyone is the night owl that I am."

Bethany had to swallow her smile, grateful when the admiral drew attention away from her when he rose to his feet. "Miles, it was nice visiting with you," he said.

"Thank you, Charles, for inviting me."

Bethany allowed Miles to pull her to her feet and then followed dutifully along as Admiral Winslow walked Miles to the door. There, he made his farewell and left them alone.

"I'll call you tomorrow, all right?" Miles said, his hands on her shoulders.

She nodded.

"And don't worry about the lab," he continued. "I'll

have the maintenance crew clean it up, again. I'm just grateful you weren't hurt last night."

"Thank you, Miles. I appreciate that."

"Good night, my dear." He leaned forward to kiss her, but suddenly Bethany couldn't do it. She turned her head at the last minute and the kiss landed on her cheek. Miles gave her a funny look, but said nothing.

Bethany closed the door after he left and went back into the family room. By now, she was alone. Thinking everyone else must have gone to bed—or was otherwise occupied—she headed for the study in hopes of finding a book to read. She'd taken only a few steps in that direction when she heard the sound of a television.

Following the noise down the main hallway, she stopped in front of a door and knocked.

"It's open," a voice grunted from within.

She opened the door and stepped inside. The minute she saw who it was, though, she quickly stammered her apologies and started to back out.

"Where are you going?" Dirk asked.

"I, uh, didn't mean to intrude."

He gave an impatient sigh. "You're not. What do you want?"

"Nothing. I heard the television, that's all."

He gestured to the set before him. "The only set in this entire mansion. Come on in."

She eyed the small couch, the only available seat in the room, and memories of the night before came rushing back with all the force of a small explosion. "I'd better not."

"Afraid?" he taunted her. "I promise not to bite, unless you want me to."

She felt the heat rush to her cheeks and couldn't bring herself to move from her spot. Apparently seeing her indecision, Dirk sighed, stood up, and walked over to her.

"Beth, what happened last night—at the lab and then later—my fault and it won't happen again. I promise."

She studied his face, trying to decide if he was sincere, and saw his frustration.

"Please, Beth. The last thing in the world I want is for you to be uncomfortable around me. Tell you what. I'll leave. You can stay here and watch TV. I'll go read a book or something."

She smiled at the thought of this always-on-the-go man sitting long enough to read a novel. He caught her smile and gave her a look of mock disdain. "I *can* read, you know."

"Well," she countered sweetly. "I wouldn't want you to strain yourself."

"Ouch." He chuckled and Bethany felt some of the tension between them ease.

"Is there anything good on?" she asked.

He handed her the remote. "See for yourself."

She took it from him, went over to sit on the couch, and brought up the online guide. Then she noticed that Dirk was still standing at the door. She looked up and caught an almost wistful expression on his face that quickly disappeared as soon as he noticed her looking at him.

"Find something worth watching?" he asked.

"What you had on is fine. Aren't you going to finish watching it?"

"If you're sure you don't mind."

She smiled. "I'm sure." Turning her attention back to

the television, Bethany was soon lost in the story unfolding before her. She couldn't remember the last time she'd been able to simply sit and relax. It felt wonderful.

When the show ended, neither made a move to leave. Instead, feeling much at ease, Bethany kicked off her shoes and tucked her legs up under her. As a movie came on, Dirk stood up.

"Don't move," he ordered as he walked to the back of the room. Curious, she turned and saw him cross to a stack of afghans folded on a chair beside the bookshelf stacked full of paperback novels. He grabbed several off the top and brought them back to the love seat where he proceeded to spread one across her lap and drape another around her shoulders. "Better?"

"Mmm. Much better." She hadn't noticed the chill in the air until the blanket enveloped her. "Thank you."

He smiled. "You're welcome."

As the movie played, the release of stress and the blanket's warmth soon had her fighting to stay awake.

When she slumped sideways, Dirk shifted slightly, wrapping his arm around her until her head rested on his chest. He stared down at her and smiled. A thousand vampires could storm the castle at that very moment and he'd let them, as long as he could continue to hold Beth in his arms.

He'd never felt such contentment, which should have bothered him, but he refused to dwell on it. For tonight, he told himself, he would simply enjoy the moment. Which wouldn't be long, he thought. As soon as she woke and realized what she'd done, she'd be mortified. In her mind, she'd equate it to "sleeping" with him. If he was a real gentleman, he'd wake her now, send her to bed, and save her the embarrassment, but he'd already proven he wasn't.

He turned down the TV, not wanting the noise to wake her, and continued to watch. Shortly after dawn, Dirk, unable to fight the fatigue that accompanied the rising sun, drifted off.

Across town, Detective John Boehler stared at the body of another dead drug dealer, his emotions and thoughts conflicted. The body had been found behind a Dumpster, in the same condition as several others that had been recovered over the past several months.

It had the two puncture wounds in the neck, marking it as the work of the Exsanguinators; the "terrorists" hunted by Admiral Winslow and his security team. John and Admiral Winslow had never actually used the word "vampire" when they discussed the perpetrators of these crimes, but John wasn't stupid. He'd been on the force a long time and seen shit that would curl your toes and make you want to crawl home to momma. He knew exactly what atrocities one human could inflict on another; things that couldn't possibly be considered humane. And though these deaths weren't the most violent he'd seen, he was almost positive that no human had committed them. But that's where John left it alone. For now.

When he'd met Mac Knight and Dirk Adams, he'd sensed something dark about them. After getting to know them, he knew two things. They could be as dangerous as the monsters they hunted and he trusted them with his life.

The game being played, as John knew it, was that when the terrorists killed innocent people, the admiral's team hunted down and killed the terrorists. John's role was to keep Mac and Dirk informed any time he came across a new victim. Lately, though, John had noticed a subtle change in the game—and it was this change that left him baffled.

It seemed that, more recently, not-so-innocent people were getting killed. People that John, personally, felt the community was better rid of. These victims were such scum that the entire precinct was hard-pressed to make more than a cursory effort to find their killers—and if they ever did find them . . . well, accidents happened, criminals escaped, and paperwork got lost—especially when it was for the greater good of the community.

That's why John was no longer sure he wanted this particular "terrorist" killed—and why, for the third time that month, he didn't pick up the phone to call Winslow's team. Any clues that might otherwise lead Mac or Dirk to this particular vampire would be lost tonight.

And if John had a hard time sleeping tonight because he was covering up the truth in hopes of serving a greater good, then that made tonight no different from any other night.

Chapter 11

Feeling unusually refreshed, Bethany opened her eyes expecting to greet the golden rays of dawn filtering through the curtains to fill her room with light.

Instead, she met the bright glare of the lit TV screen in an otherwise dark and unfamiliar room. Her confusion as to her whereabouts lasted only a second as her memory of the night came rushing back. In the same instant, she realized that the "bed" she was stretched out on was a living breathing man. From the steady rise and fall of his chest, Bethany guessed that Dirk was fast asleep and she took advantage of the situation to linger a few minutes more. Now that she was awake, she could appreciate the hard strength of his body and the way his arm wrapped around her, anchoring her to him, keeping her safe.

Guilt hit her like a neutron bomb. Nothing had happened, yet she couldn't stop the overwhelming feeling that she'd betrayed Miles—again.

"Dirk, wake up." She shook him gently, trying to rouse

him. He never stirred. She tried again, this time pushing a little harder. "Dirk, it's morning." His arm kept her pinned to him and her first efforts to get up were futile. The strength she'd so admired in him earlier was now proving to be a hindrance.

"Come on," she muttered.

When it was obvious that he wasn't going to wake, she twisted her body this way and that until she was able to slip out from under his arm and onto the floor.

She landed in a graceless heap, but there was no one to notice. Standing up, she smoothed her clothes as best she could and then gazed down at the sleeping man. She was amazed at how soundly he slept, but then remembered him telling her how the daylight affected changelings. It was the influence of their vampire half, she supposed.

He didn't look particularly comfortable and she worried how sore and stiff he would be when he finally did awaken. She tried one last time to rouse him, but when that failed, she spread a blanket over him so he wouldn't get cold and quietly left the room.

From his place at the kitchen table, Charles Winslow watched as Bethany crossed the foyer to the stairs and felt as if another weight had been added to his load.

"You're furrowing your brow," Julia, sitting next to him, pointed out gently.

"I'm worried about Dirk and Bethany," he admitted.

"Worried because they appear to be getting involved and you *don't* approve? Or because you *do* approve?"

He smiled. "I guess that is the question, isn't it?" He took another drink of his tea and set the cup down slowly. "Dirk and Mac are like sons to me."

Julia politely scoffed. "Please, you're not old enough to have sons that age."

He smiled, glad she didn't think him old. "All right, if not sons then younger brothers. I've just met Bethany, but I've grown fond of her as well. I want only what's best for them all and I hate to see any of them get hurt."

Julia placed her hand over his, light and comforting. "Hurt is a part of life, Charles, and you can't keep it from touching those you care about, no matter how hard you try—nor should you, but you can be there for them when they need you."

Charles looked into the warm ginger eyes gazing back at him. There was no censure or bitterness in either her tone or expression, yet something in the depths of her eyes told him that she'd suffered in the past. "You sound as if you speak from experience."

There was a hint of sorrow in the smile she gave him. "Life is what it is."

He liked this woman, more than he should, probably. She had a smooth, elegant manner about her that made him think of long evenings sitting in front of a crackling fire, sipping hot toddies, safe and warm while snowstorms raged outside. It was a combination of her comforting manner and his own loneliness that brought such images to mind.

"I'm very glad you came to work for me," he told her, at that moment realizing the full depth of his feelings. They extended far beyond the employer-employee relationship, but he was old enough and wise enough to know he shouldn't rush things. There was, however, something that needed to be done. "Do you like tea?"

His sudden change in topic caught her off guard but

she was too poised to do more than blink once or twice. "Why, yes, I drink it from time to time."

"Good." He pushed away from the table and set about filling the teakettle with water before placing it on the stove to heat. "I go to England every couple of years to visit my family and they grow a special tea there that I think you might like."

He reached into the pantry and found the plain metal canister sitting near the front of the shelf. He opened it, peering at the contents inside. It was more than half empty. He'd have to write his cousin, Gerard, and have more sent over, especially if things around D.C. continued the way they had.

"Is that what your family does?" Julia asked, turning in her chair so she could face him. "They're tea growers?"

"No, growing tea is something they do for family and friends—sort of a hobby that over the years became a tradition." He poured some of the tea into the palm of his hand and showed it to her. "As you can see, it doesn't look much different from the dried leaves you're used to. What makes this tea unique are the dried blue flower blossoms."

"What kind of flowers are those?"

"They're called *la fleur de vivre,* the flower of life."

He took two steeping balls from a drawer and filled them with the tea before placing them into fresh cups. Then he took the teakettle of now boiling water from the stove and poured it over the balls.

Immediately, a hot, moist sweet scent drifted upward, reminding Charles of the summers he'd spent in England as a child, running through fields of wildflowers, playing with his cousins.

Julia closed her eyes and inhaled. "It smells wonderful," she said, opening her eyes and giving him a smile he couldn't resist returning.

"Wait until you try it," he promised. He added a spoon-ful of honey to both cups and then handed one to her. He felt like a kid, holding his breath, as he watched her take a sip. Let her think him a dotty old fool with eccentric tastes, if she liked—as long as she drank the tea.

"Hmmmm, it *is* good."

He let out his breath, picked up his own cup, and took a sip. "I feel like my day is somehow better if I start it off by enjoying a cup," he commented. "I would consider it a great honor if you would join me each morning in my little ritual."

Her eyes lit up over the rim of her cup and he could tell he'd pleased her with his invitation.

"I'm usually more of a coffee drinker, but thank you," she said. "I'd enjoy that."

He nodded. "Good, then it'll be a standing date."

For several moments, neither spoke as they enjoyed their drinks. After a while, Julia broke the silence. "Charles," she started, using his first name as he'd insisted. "I wanted to talk to you about the gargoyle statue."

He could tell from the hesitant way she brought up the subject that it wasn't something she felt comfortable talk-ing about.

"Is it still showing up on your desk every morning?"

"Yes, and though it's not a big effort to move it, I can't help but wonder why it continues to be necessary. I really don't mean to make so much out of it . . ."

When she paused, he reached out and covered her hand with his. "No, you're right. It shouldn't be so difficult to control the whereabouts of one little statue. I'll take care of it, okay?"

She opened her mouth to say something, then seemed to change her mind and simply nodded in acceptance.

He made a mental note to talk to Lanie and hoped that between the two of them, they could make sure to move Gem off the desk in the mornings before Julia arrived.

"Well," he said with a smile, "now that that's taken care of, shall we take our tea into the study and get started on today's list of appointments?"

Bethany showered and dressed before going down to the kitchen for something to eat. The admiral and Julia were hard at work in the smaller study that served as Julia's office. Not needing to be in the lab until much later, Bethany found herself with several hours of free time.

Having finished the one book she'd started, she remembered the stack of paperbacks in the TV room. She thought about going to get one but then changed her mind. If Dirk was still asleep in there, she didn't want to risk waking him. So instead, she went in search of something to read from the admiral's study.

A few minutes later, she was back in her room, curled up on the bed with a book in front of her. Unfortunately, the admiral's taste in fiction ran to espionage and war stories and by late afternoon, not even the U.S. military blowing up a battalion of Germans was enough to keep her awake.

It was some time later when she was roused from her sleep by a soft knock on her door.

"Come in," she said groggily.

"Hi." Dirk poked his head inside and gave her a smile. "How are you?"

She smiled back. "Good, and you?"

He moved his shoulders about. "A little stiff in places, but otherwise in good shape. I don't remember you leaving."

She considered telling him that she'd awakened in the middle of the night and returned to her room, but chances were that he'd stayed up late and would know she was lying. "I tried to wake you, but the sun was up and you seemed pretty out of it."

"So it wasn't a dream," she thought she heard him say. Then louder, "Did you cover me?"

She felt her face heat up. "Yes, I did."

He seemed pleased. "Thanks."

"You're welcome."

He looked down at his watch then. "Ready to go to the lab?"

Three hours later, Bethany was hard at work on her latest test. The second attack on the lab left her feeling jumpy and it was hard to concentrate on her work. Squeezing several drops of the modified extract into the wells of the gel electrophoresis, she hooked up the electrodes that would run a charge through the instrument, separating this new derivation into its positively and negatively charged components. She went about her tests as if she were on autopilot, lost in brooding thoughts.

She hadn't had a chance to talk to Miles today, so she'd not been able to ask him about the man she'd seen him talking to. Nor had she had a chance to discuss her concerns about the substance. She'd dragged her feet in analyzing it, but lately there'd been no need for artificial delays.

"What's wrong?" Dirk's voice cut into her thoughts as he came up behind her and started rubbing her shoulders. She knew she shouldn't let him, but her muscles ached from bending over the equipment and his fingers felt like magic.

"I guess I'm tired," she offered as an excuse, wishing she could tell him the truth. It would be nice to share her concerns with someone—that there was something about the extract that even she couldn't identify. "Maybe I'm not as smart as everyone thinks I am."

"I doubt that's true," he scoffed. "More like the stress of the last couple of days is getting to you." He stopped rubbing her shoulders, but didn't remove his hands. "I'm sorry about the ceremony tonight."

"That's okay."

At that moment, his cell phone rang. "Excuse me." He stepped out into the hallway to talk and Bethany reluctantly returned to her work.

An hour later, she glanced around the lab and realized that Dirk hadn't come back from his phone call. She was wondering where he'd gone when her stomach growled, reminding her that she hadn't had dinner and it was growing late. Finally at a good breaking point, she was at the sink washing her hands when Dirk walked in.

"Where have you been?"

"Around," he answered vaguely. "Are you hungry?"

"Yes. As a matter of fact, I'm starved."

"Good, let's go eat."

"Oh." Bethany looked around the lab at the various

experiments running. "I really don't have enough time to go out."

"Not a problem," Dirk said. "I had food delivered."

She stared at him amazed. "You did?"

He smiled. "Shall we?" He gestured for her to precede him out of the lab and they walked down the hall together. "It's in here," he said, stopping in front of the lounge and opening the door.

The minute she stepped into the room, she came to an immediate stop. The overhead lights in the lounge had been turned off and the room was lit by the glow of two dozen candles arranged around the room. The table was covered in a white linen tablecloth and set for two, with dinner being kept warm under metal plate covers. Two lit tapers graced the ends of the table and in the center sat a purple *cattleya* orchid in full bloom.

With soft music playing in the background and champagne chilling in an ice bucket, it was the most spectacular thing Bethany had ever seen. She blinked her eyes, trying to fight the tears that threatened to spill, and just made out the words on the banner hanging from the ceiling.

"Congratulations Bethany!"

Chapter 12

"It's beautiful," she whispered past the constriction of her throat.

She felt Dirk's hand at the small of her back and allowed him to guide her to the table.

"I know you'd rather be at the big dinner and celebration, getting your award in person."

She stood before the table, letting her finger trail over the linen cloth, overwhelmed. "I think this is the nicest thing anyone's ever done for me." She turned to him, willing him to see the sincerity in her eyes. "Thank you."

His gaze softened and the corners of his lips lifted slightly. "You're welcome."

"Where'd you get all the candles? And the music?"

"I am not without resources," he said jokingly.

Her eyes fell on the orchid at the center of the table. "Oh! A *cattleya*. My favorite."

He laughed. "Yeah, who would have guessed?" he said sarcastically. At her questioning look, he went on. "Let's see. Your mouse pad has the picture of a cattleya on it; you have a small ceramic one on your desk; your screen saver is a picture of orchids; you have an orchid lapel pin stuck to your lab coat," he paused. "Shall I go on?"

"Well," she said with a laugh, "when you put it like that . . ."

"Yeah. A person would have to be blind *and* stupid not to know." He moved over to one of the chairs and pulled it out for her. "Now let's eat. The food is getting cold."

She moved forward, but then stopped, feeling worried. "What if the vampires attack tonight?"

"That's not very likely. They've tried twice and failed. Besides, Mac is outside patrolling." He pulled out his cell phone and laid it on the table. "If he sees anything, he'll call."

Bethany tried to take comfort from that and this time, when Dirk held out her chair, she sat down. "What's for dinner?" She felt almost like a child, excitement starting to build inside her, and stared at the plate expectantly as he placed his hand on the cover and prepared to pull it off.

"It's a special night and so I wanted to get something equally special to celebrate." His tone was very serious. "And knowing how fond you are of fondue"—he whipped off the cover—"I couldn't do that again, sorry."

She clapped her hands together as she caught a whiff of grilled mesquite. "Burgers and fries!"

"It's not fancy," he started to apologize.

"It's perfect. This is terrific, Dirk. Thank you so much." She waited until he sat down and uncovered his food.

He smiled. "Dig in."

Looking at everything, she saw that he'd even remembered to provide a linen napkin. Draping it across her lap, she picked up her sandwich.

"Oh," she said after swallowing her first bite. "I think I died and went to heaven. This is wonderful." Suddenly she was so hungry, she could hardly stand it. She focused on eating, savoring each and every bite. Dirk must have been hungry, too, because neither spoke for the longest time.

After a while, Dirk reached over and pulled out the bottle sitting in the ice bucket. Running his hand across the surface, he wiped off the excess moisture and then peeled the foil from around the top. Angling the bottle away from them, he popped the cork, preventing any of the contents from spilling.

"Champagne?" He didn't wait for her answer, but poured her a glass and held it out to her. When she'd taken it, he poured a glass for himself and then put the bottle back in the bucket. Turning to her, he held his glass aloft. "A toast—to you, Bethany. You are an amazing woman."

She smiled as they touched glasses and then took a tentative sip. Surprised at how good it tasted, she took another, larger swallow. When she felt Dirk watching her, she looked up but couldn't read the expression on his face. "What?"

"I'm impressed, that's all."

The statement confused her even as it sent a tiny thrill through her. "Thank you."

"Your folks must be proud of you."

"Hmm, this is good," she said around a mouthful of food, trying to change the subject.

Dirk was too sharp for that. "You did tell your folks, didn't you?"

His direct gaze made her squirm in her seat. "No, I sort of—forgot."

"No, you didn't. Why didn't you tell them?"

"My folks are divorced and all they ever do is bitch about one another. I don't talk to them much anymore. Now my grandmother—she would have been thrilled."

"You were close to her?"

"Yeah. She always had time for me and was constantly urging me to pursue my dreams." The image of the well-loved face sprang to mind, followed quickly by the pain of losing the one memento she'd had of her grandmother—the small clown doll. It had still been in her purse when the vampires attacked and in their ransacking of the lab, they'd found her purse and taken it.

She felt Dirk's gaze on her and his sympathetic expression made her wonder if he'd had someone he'd been close to growing up. "What about you?" she asked, setting down her glass. "Are you close to your parents?"

She knew the minute she saw his clouded expression that she'd said something wrong.

"Not exactly," he said, his tone void of emotion. "When I was five, my father shot himself."

"Oh, Dirk. That's horrible. Why?" She immediately felt chagrined. "I'm sorry. That was rude. It's none of my business."

He shrugged. "It was a long time ago. I guess he couldn't handle the responsibilities of a job, marriage, and one small child."

"What about your mother?"

His laugh held no humor. "There's another winner. After my father's death, she started drinking. Six months later, she died of alcohol poisoning."

Bethany couldn't stop herself from reaching out and placing her hand on Dirk's arm. She found his revelation shocking and her heart cried out for the small abandoned boy he had been; for the small lonely boy she sensed still lay deep inside him. "I'm so sorry." She felt ungrateful for belittling her parents. Compared to his life, she'd been blessed.

He raised his glass, effectively breaking her contact with him. "It was a harsh life lesson, but one I learned well." He threw back the contents of his drink as if it were whiskey, not champagne, then lowered his empty glass to the table and stared off into the room, no doubt seeing a past she couldn't. "After my mother died, I lived in a series of foster homes, never staying in one place for any length of time. I was angry with the world and no one seemed to know what to do with me."

"Didn't you have any other family you could stay with?"

"I used to long for a grandparent, or an aunt or uncle, to come for me, but if either of my parents had living relatives, they never stepped forward to claim me. After a few years, I gave up wishing for something that was never going to happen."

"That's so sad."

"By the time I was eighteen, I had been in so much trouble with the law, it was just a matter of time before I ended up in jail." A humorless laugh escaped him. "When the inevitable happened, the judge gave me a choice: jail or enlist. I chose the Navy and it was the best thing that ever happened to me."

At that moment, Bethany heard the distant drone of the

buzzer in the lab, but she made no move to get up from the table.

"Doesn't that mean your tests are done?" Dirk asked.

"Yes, but they can wait." If there was anything else Dirk wanted to share with her, she wanted to be here for him. But he didn't. Instead, he pushed away from the table and stood. "Come on. I'll walk you to the lab, then I'll come back and clean up while you finish."

She stood up as well. "Are you sure?"

"Yeah."

She fought a rush of disappointment. Dirk had finally opened up to her and shared a side of him she doubted many others had seen. She hated to have that interrupted.

They left the candles burning and as they walked, Dirk pulled out his cell phone and placed a call. After a moment, she heard him say, "We're done. Thanks."

Bethany was amazed. He'd gone to so much trouble to make this night special for her. She tried to remember when anyone had done that much for her—without wanting something in return.

When they reached the lab, Dirk did a quick check of the lab. "All clear. I'll be back in a minute."

She nodded and then impulsively put a hand on his arm as she stood on tiptoe and kissed his cheek. "Thank you, Dirk, for making the evening so special."

He nodded his head once. "You're welcome." Then he turned and walked down the hall, leaving her to go back into the lab and finish her work.

It was almost one in the morning when Dirk and Bethany returned to the mansion. She was feeling especially good. Not only had dinner with Dirk been special, but in rerunning an earlier test, she'd discovered an error that Stuart had made in recording the earlier results. Having the correct data shed new light on the project and she felt that, finally, she was close to being done with her analysis. Miles wouldn't like her conclusions, but she'd deal with that later.

Right now, though, she was tired and relaxing in the living room, talking with Dirk and the others, sounded good.

"There you are," Lanie greeted them with a smile when they walked through the door. "How was your evening?"

Bethany smiled. "It was special."

Lanie seemed pleased. "I'm glad." She glanced back to the living room. "You have a visitor."

"I do?"

At that moment Miles walked out. In one hand he carried a bouquet of roses and in the other a plaque that had to be her award. "Bethany, my dear, I wish you could have been there." He came up to her and kissed her cheek before holding out the roses. Then he seemed to notice the orchid she already held. A slight frown creased his brow and he shot an accusing glance at Dirk.

Not wanting any trouble between the two, she balanced the orchid pot in one hand as she took the bouquet of roses from Miles. "Thank you, Miles. They're lovely."

Behind her, she heard Dirk mutter something. She couldn't make out the words, but decided that might be for the best.

"This is a surprise," she said instead. "I didn't expect you to be here."

"I couldn't let the biggest night of your life go by without doing something to celebrate." If his tone sounded artificial and patronizing, Bethany did her best to ignore it.

"That was very thoughtful of you," she replied. "What did you have in mind?"

"Knowing we couldn't go out, I thought we might have a little private celebration." He looked pointedly at Dirk, whose expression Bethany couldn't see.

"Don't leave the mansion," Dirk muttered to her before turning to Lanie. "Where's Mac?"

"He's in the study with Uncle Charles. I'll go with you."

The two walked off, leaving Bethany and Miles standing alone in the foyer.

"Do you want to go into the living room?" she asked him.

He smiled, putting his hand at her elbow, and steered her to the stairs. "No, I had something else in mind. Let's go to your room."

She mustered up a wan smile, wondering why she had a hard time feeling excited about spending time with Miles. After all, spending the rest of her life with him was what she wanted, wasn't it? Confused, she led him upstairs.

Once inside her room, she saw the ice bucket placed on the small corner table with the chilling bottle of champagne. While Bethany had never been a big drinker, tonight was looking like the perfect time to start.

She crossed the room to her dresser and set down the orchids. A crystal vase sat beside the ice bucket, so Bethany busied herself with arranging the roses in the vase while Miles opened the champagne.

Her thoughts were a crazed whirlwind inside her head

as she tried to make sense of her emotions. Distantly, she heard the cork pop and Miles had to call her name twice to get her attention when he handed her a filled glass.

"To Van Horne Technologies' leading biochemist."

As Bethany touched her glass to his, she couldn't help comparing his toast to Dirk's more personal one.

"Here you are, my dear. Here's the plaque you worked so hard to win."

He handed it to her and there was a sense of pride when she finally held it. There weren't many who earned the distinction and she would display it proudly in her office where she could see it every day. "Thank you for accepting this for me, Miles. I wish I could have been there."

"Oh, Bethany. You would have enjoyed it. Everyone who's anyone in the field was there . . . except the guest of honor." He gave her a sad smile. "I'm sorry. I don't mean to make it worse by telling you what you missed."

She shook her head. "That's okay. I want to hear all about it."

Bethany sipped her drink as Miles described the elaborate decorations at the reception hall and all the notable persons who attended, but as his voice droned on, she found her thoughts turning elsewhere.

Dirk had gone to such elaborate measures to make the evening nice for her. Miles, a man of means, had brought her a bottle of champagne and roses.

Her gaze wandered about the room, coming to rest on the orchid sitting on her dresser. Why hadn't Miles bought her orchids? She'd dated him for over a year and known him for five, yet he didn't know that orchids were her favorite flower.

Suddenly that one little detail became significant. Miles didn't know her at all and if she was honest with herself, she didn't know him either. The full weight of that realization hit her.

"I can't do this."

Miles, who'd been rattling on about the award ceremony, stopped and stared at her, clearly confused.

She searched his eyes, beseeching him to understand. "I'm sorry, Miles. I can't marry you."

"Of course you can," he assured her. "Your winning this award doesn't change anything."

She bowed her head. It wasn't going to be easy to explain. She set down her glass and pulled her engagement ring from her finger. "I'm sorry. I thought this would work but over the last several days I've come to realize that I don't really know you. And more important, while I like you a lot, I don't love you. People should marry for love, don't you think?" She held the ring out to him until he took it from her.

"It's just the stress of everything that's happened over the last couple of days," he said patiently. "It's bound to confuse you. If you need more time, we'll postpone the wedding, but please, Bethany, don't call it off."

"Miles, I'm sorry, but it would never work."

"It's him, isn't it?"

She didn't pretend to misunderstand. "In part. I do feel something for him. Something I shouldn't feel if I'm in love with you." She hated the hurt look that came into his eyes when he looked at her.

"I was afraid something like this might happen. It's one of the risks that comes with dating a woman so much younger than myself. I knew you hadn't been with a lot of men when we first started dating, but I'd hoped I would be enough." When she would have interrupted, he took both her hands in his and looked deeply into her eyes. "I understand. You need to explore these feelings you have—you need to see what life can offer you. Afterward, maybe you'll discover that what you're really looking for is me—and I'll be waiting."

She started to shake her head and tell him that he was wrong, but she couldn't. She'd already hurt him enough. There was no reason to make it worse by robbing him of all hope.

Abruptly she stood up and crossed to her dresser. Inside the top drawer, she found the box the engagement ring had come in. She pulled it out and gave it to him, watching as he placed the ring back inside and snapped the lid shut. An uncomfortable silence fell between them and Bethany found herself staring at the roses.

"Are you going to make me take those back, too?" he asked softly.

She couldn't tell from his tone whether he was serious or not, but when she looked at him, he was smiling.

"No, I'd like to keep them, if you don't mind."

"I don't mind, but you might want to give them water before they wilt."

It was something that could wait, but she was afraid he'd think she didn't care about his gift if she didn't do it immediately, so she picked up the vase and carried it into the bathroom. When she walked back into the bedroom, Miles was standing by the dresser, waiting for her.

"I guess I should say good night."

"Thank you for—everything."

He started for the door, but stopped after taking a single step. "This is just personal, right? You're not breaking up with me professionally, too? You will continue your work at the lab?"

He caught her by surprise. She couldn't believe she'd forgotten about what it would be like to work for him now. "It might be uncomfortable for us both if I stayed," she began. "But I don't want to leave my job."

"Good, then don't." He smiled as he leaned over and kissed her cheek. "I'll see myself out."

Bethany stared at the door after he left, replaying their conversation over in her mind, amazed at how well Miles had taken the breakup.

Spying the nearly full bottle of champagne, she went over and refilled her glass. As she drank, she let her thoughts turn to Dirk. For some reason, she felt an inexplicable need to tell him that she was no longer engaged. Before she could talk herself out of it, she set down her glass and left the room.

Dirk's bedroom door wasn't far from hers and she encountered no one along the way. When she got there, she knocked once and waited. From inside came a muffled response. Unsure whether it was an invitation to come in or an order to leave, she tried the knob. It turned easily in her hand.

She poked her head into the room and spotted Dirk sitting on the bed, wearing only his jeans, unbuttoned at the waist, leaning against the headboard, a half-empty bottle of whiskey in his hand. He barely looked up when she walked in.

"What are you doing here?" he half snarled. "I thought you were with Van Horne."

"He just left."

He stared straight ahead, letting the words sink in, then raised the bottle and took a drink. He swallowed, then rested his head back against the headboard and closed his eyes. "Go back to your room, Beth."

"I want to talk to you."

"Now's not a good time."

"Why?"

He gave her a disgusted look. "I'm busy." He raised the bottle and drank deeply.

She tried to ignore the way the muscles in his chest bulged when he lifted the bottle or the sight of his strong hands wrapped around the neck of it. "You're drunk." She heard the censure in her voice.

"God, I hope so." He wiped his mouth with the back of his hand and stared at her with a focused intensity that told her he wasn't as drunk as she'd first thought. "What do you want?"

She hesitated. For a man who'd spent so much time flirting with her in the lab, now he seemed totally uninterested. She'd come here expecting . . . what? That he would seduce her? Carry through on all the suggestive promises he'd made.

The announcement she had planned to make died on her lips. How pathetic of her to have thought it would interest him. She looked for another excuse for her presence. "I wanted to thank you again for the dinner and the flowers."

"You already did that."

"Well, I wanted to make sure you knew I meant it," she said, her frustration making her irritable.

"Go away, Beth."

"Why?"

He made a strangled sound in his voice. "Fine, stick around, but I won't be responsible for what happens." He made it sound like a thinly veiled threat.

"You won't hurt me." She said it softly and moved a little farther into the room, closer to the bed.

"What makes you so sure?" He lifted the bottle and took another swallow.

"I know you." She took another step forward, nervously brushing a strand of hair from her eyes. His eyes followed her motions and, curious, she lowered her hand to the base of her throat.

His eyes tracked her every move, almost scorching her with their intensity, giving her the courage to be daring. "I want to make love to you."

The bottle froze midway to his mouth. "Careful. My control right now is not what it should be. In fact," he growled, "it's not good at all."

"That's okay," she whispered, so nervous her knees began to shake. "You don't have to do a thing." She reached for the top button of her blouse and slowly undid it. His hungry gaze watched as she undid the next. And the next.

Too soon, she ran out of buttons. It was the moment of truth and she wasn't sure if she could continue—if she *should* continue, yet the way his eyes devoured her excited her as nothing else had. *He* excited her as no one else had.

She let the blouse slide off her shoulders until it slipped to the floor. She stood, now, before him in a bra that was more decoration than support. Her nipples hardened beneath his gaze and she wondered if she had the courage to undo the hooks at the back and continue her daring seduction.

"Bethany," he choked out in a harsh voice, "for God's sake, what are you doing?"

She spoke provocatively. "I'm trying to seduce you." She was at the edge of the bed now and was about to crawl onto the mattress when his next words stopped her cold.

"Seduce me?" he growled. "Why? The old man shoot his wad too soon? Did he leave you unsatisfied?"

His crude accusations stabbed her through the heart. "Wh-what?"

"I don't usually do sloppy seconds, but what the hell. Let's go." He set the bottle on the table beside him and reached for the zipper of his jeans, pulling it down.

Mortified, tears filling her eyes, she looked away, blindly backing off the bed.

"What's the matter?" he taunted. "You change your mind? Then go, but you'd better run—before I change my mind about letting you leave."

She picked her blouse up off the floor and, holding it to her, raced for the door.

She never heard him move, but felt the rush of air right before she slammed into his rock-solid body. His hands gripped her arms, holding her helpless before him.

Feeling the heat of his gaze, she dared to look into his face and saw his eyes glowing red.

"Too damn late."

Chapter 13

He ground his mouth against hers and she tensed, expecting it to be as painful as the words he'd hurled at her. Instead, it was sensual and demanding, robbing her of all thought until she was responding with growing desperation. It was as if she couldn't get enough. His kiss was a drug and she the addict.

Her blouse fell to the floor, forgotten, as she wrapped her arms around his waist, pulling him close. His tongue forced its way past her lips and delved inside her mouth to tease hers. Through the sheer fabric of her bra, she pressed against the silky warmth of his chest. Every primal instinct in her reveled in the feel and taste of him, and the tingling that started deep in her stomach built until she rubbed against him shamelessly.

When Dirk tore his mouth from hers, she wanted to cry out in protest. Then he lowered his head and began to tease one of her nipples through the bra, causing her to whimper instead. In a bold, daring move, she ran her hand along his side, down past his hip until she could reach between their bodies. He filled her hand and when she stroked him through his jeans, he groaned with pleasure. Knowing she could elicit that type of response from him encouraged her and she started to slip her hand inside his zipper when he stopped her.

Though it was by far the most difficult thing he'd ever done, Dirk pulled Bethany's hand away until she no longer touched him. When she opened her mouth to protest, he shushed her to silence and, resting his forehead against hers, closed his eyes and prayed for strength.

"Beth, we can't do this." She started to speak, but he cut her off. "You're not thinking clearly right now, but trust me, you'd never forgive yourself or me."

"You don't want me?" she asked softly, sounding hurt. The question was so ludicrous that he groaned aloud.

"Not making love to you will be the hardest thing I've ever done, but I won't make love to a woman engaged to someone else." She opened her mouth again, and knowing he couldn't bear to hear her protests, he captured her lips in a heated kiss. The last one, he told himself. When he felt himself losing his resolve, he broke the kiss and stepped back.

It was a mistake. Her lingerie was more enticing than if she'd been nude and his already throbbing member grew harder at the sight. As if she knew the war he waged with himself, knew how close he was to losing, she smiled. "Miles and I are no longer engaged."

He blinked, staring at her dumbly as his brain struggled to understand. "As of when?"

She stepped closer and trailed her hand down his chest as she gazed up at him through sultry green eyes. "As of about twenty minutes ago, when I called the whole thing off and gave back his ring."

Like a drowning man suddenly thrown a life jacket, he caught her to him and kissed her as he'd wanted to do for so long, taking extra care not to cut her with his fangs. His body reacted to the lush mounds and curves pressed against him. He would no longer be denied.

Scooping her into his arms, he carried her to the bed and lay down beside her. "You are so beautiful. Knowing you were with Van Horne was killing me."

"We didn't do anything," she said softly. He heard the worry in her voice and almost kicked himself for his earlier crude remarks. He'd been hurting and had lashed out.

"Hush, I know," he said tenderly, placing his finger across her lips. She pulled it into her mouth, sucking on it gently, and he felt an immediate reaction below.

He let her continue as his gaze followed the line of her jaw down to the column of her throat, so long and slender. With his acute senses, he heard her pulse pounding below the surface and it was a siren's song, drawing him closer until he pressed his mouth against her neck, stroking the skin with his tongue and then sucking ever so slightly.

Bethany gasped at the erotic feelings stirring deep inside her. When Dirk's hand cupped her breast, she arched into it, needing to feel his touch. For several long seconds, she helplessly clutched at his shoulders while he teased one nipple with the tip of his finger through the silky fabric of her bra. Then he pulled his mouth from her neck and lowered his head until his tongue replaced his finger.

Awash in sensations she had never felt before, Bethany almost came undone when Dirk unclasped her bra so he could suckle her with his mouth. So overwhelmed was she that she hardly noticed when he stopped momentarily to rid them both of their clothes.

Before she could miss him, he was back, his hard body poised between her parted legs, his shaft pressing against her. "It's not too late to say no," he offered, his voice sounding huskier than normal. For a brief moment she wondered if he'd really stop if she asked him to and then, knowing that he would, she caught his head between her hands so she could peer into his face. "Make love to me."

It was all the invitation he needed. He surged into her, stretching her, filling her until she thought her body could take no more, and then he held himself still for a long moment, letting her adjust to his size, before pulling back. Then she felt the entire length of him ease into her again, oh so slowly, and it left her gasping from the sheer pleasure of it.

Wrapping her legs around his waist, she held on tightly as his body moved with powerful smooth strokes. With each thrust, the pressure inside her built, taking her closer and closer to an explosion she'd only heard about, but never before experienced.

When she felt the first scrapings of his fangs against her neck, she wasn't afraid. But when his rhythm faltered, she knew that *he* had reservations. "Don't stop," she breathed.

"I'll hurt you." His arms strained to hold himself above her as he searched her face.

She smiled and wrapped her arms around his neck, pulling him down. "No, you won't. I promise."

Once more, she felt his mouth at her throat and his powerful body resumed its primitive rhythm, driving into her, pushing her to the edge. Just when she thought she could take no more, go no further, his fangs sank into her neck and her entire body felt as if it burst into a thousand sizzling points of light and energy.

Above her, Dirk surged into her one last time and then went rigid as he found his own release.

Moments later, he collapsed beside her and pulled her into his arms. He felt better than he ever had before. With the sun starting to rise, he should have been exhausted and yet he felt as if he could go on forever. He knew why. It was the gift of her blood, freely given, that made him feel so alive.

Humbled that she shared her blood with him, he tipped her face up to his and saw tears in her eyes.

"Beth?" His euphoric mood collapsed into worry. "Did I hurt you?" She laid a hand on his chest, but didn't push him away, so he covered it with his own. "Are you sorry we made love?"

"Sorry?" She gave a nervous, short laugh. "No. Surprised? Amazed? Yes. I didn't know it could be like this. I mean, I've heard other women talk, but I thought they were exaggerating."

Dirk did his best to follow this female logic, but it was beyond him. "I'm sorry, honey. I don't understand."

Her face grew red and after glancing at him, she looked away, unable to meet his eyes. "Dirk, I thought there was something wrong with me because I'd never had . . ." Her words trailed off, but Dirk finally understood.

"You've never had an orgasm."

She nodded.

A very male sense of pride filled him to know that he had been the one to give her that experience. She saw it and laughed. "Go ahead and beat your chest if you want.

You deserve to. You have no idea what this means to me. I thought there was something wrong with me, like maybe I was frigid or something."

This time he laughed out loud, remembering her responses while they'd made love. "Honey, let me assure you. You are most definitely not frigid."

"No?" She began to play with the hairs on his chest.

"Absolutely not." He bent down to kiss her, but one taste of her lips only whetted his appetite. He pulled her to him, kissing her with a hunger that might never go away, and proceeded to show her just how frigid she wasn't.

Julia arrived that morning to a quiet mansion. As expected, Charles was gone, having driven into town for an early breakfast meeting, and none of the others were about.

Going to the study to finish her work, she hesitated when she reached the desk. For a change, the gargoyle statue was not sitting in the middle as expected. Instead, she spotted it in the wastebasket next to the desk. For several seconds, she simply stared at it. It had to be a mistake, she thought, bending over to pluck it out. No matter that the statue wasn't something she would have bought herself—she found its appearance worrisome—it must still have some value. Why would someone just throw it away?

Setting it on the desk, she pulled her hand away and noticed something sticky on her fingers. Looking at them, she found them covered in a light brown substance that smelled of sweet maple. It was the same sticky substance coating the front of the statue. She pulled a Kleenex from a nearby box and tried to wipe the substance off both her hand and the gargoyle. It was nearly impossible to do. Tossing the tissue in the wastebasket, she noticed a broken jar of syrup. That explained the stickiness.

Wondering what she should do about the statue, she noticed the note from Charles lying on the desk.

Julia, I feel bad having to dispose of this, but I think it's for the best. Please see that it goes out in today's trash.—Charles.

It seemed a bit dramatic to throw out the statue, but if this was how Charles wanted to deal with the problem she'd been having, then who was she to argue?

Placing the statue back in the wastebasket, she checked the time. The garbage collectors usually came early and she didn't want to miss them, so she carried the wastebasket outside and dumped the contents, statue and all, into the large trash canister. Feeling slightly better, Julia went back inside and washed her hands.

The sun was up when Dirk rolled over and pressed tiny kisses along Beth's eyes, forehead, and lips. "Time to get up," he whispered.

"Do we have to?" she mumbled.

"Afraid so."

She stretched in bed beside him and it was all he could do to not run his hand along her perfect form, but he knew if he did, they'd both be in trouble. "Come on." He rolled out of bed and pulled on his jeans.

"Where are you going?"

"Where are *we* going—and the answer is—I'm going to walk you to your room before the whole house realizes you spent the night with me. It would be better if you had a chance to tell them you broke off the engagement with

Miles *before* they learned about us." He bent over her and pressed a kiss to her forehead. "So you should get up and get dressed unless you want to walk down the hall naked."

"Okay, okay."

She got out of bed and Dirk almost groaned aloud. "You are so beautiful."

Her eyes lit up and she smiled shyly. "Thank you."

He pulled her into his arms and kissed her because he couldn't resist, then sighed and let her go. "Now let's look for your clothes." He searched around the bottom of the bed until he found them. Picking them up, he held them out to her and watched with unabashed interest as she put them on. He remembered watching her pack and the memory of a particular purple bra and panties still haunted him. He wanted to see her in them.

He smiled at the thought, then opened the door to his room to check the hallway. Finding it empty, he ushered her out and they headed for her room.

"The sun's up, aren't you tired?" she asked him as they walked.

"A little," he admitted. "Maybe there's something to that blood freely given thing after all."

They reached her door and he opened it for her, but didn't follow her in. "You should get some rest," he told her.

She shook her head. "I'm not really that tired. I'll probably take a shower and then go scrounge up a cup of coffee while I go over my lab notes. What are you going to do?"

"I think I'll go catch Mac before he goes to bed. There are a couple of things we need to talk about. After that, I'll probably get some sleep. Do you need to go to the lab tonight?"

"Yes, but not until about eight."

"Okay. That'll give us time to break the news about you and Miles. Then, before the questions become too personal, we can leave." He closed the distance between them and pulled her into his arms. "It's going to be hard not seeing you all day," he said softly, just before he kissed her.

She melted against him, returning his kiss with enthusiasm. It was with great willpower that he stepped away from her and closed the door.

She stood for a moment in a daze, hardly daring to believe everything that had happened. It was enough to make her giddy and she wrapped her arms about herself in a hug, unable to stop the smile that spread across her face. Then she caught a look at her reflection in the mirror and froze.

She was a mess. Running her fingers through her hair, she tried to comb it into place, even though it did no good. She groaned to think that Dirk had seen her looking like this. Embarrassed, she hurried to the bathroom and started the water for her shower.

Shedding her clothes, she stepped inside and let the warm water flow over her body, soothing muscles she hadn't realized were sore. It felt so good that she closed her eyes and fell into a kind of trance.

"Got room for two in there?"

Her eyes flew open as she turned to the door. Dirk stood there, smiling and staring at her with a hunger in his eyes that left her feeling both self-conscious and excited.

"I thought you went to talk to Mac."

"He's already gone to bed, so I thought I'd bring you a cup of coffee." She looked past him and spotted the two cups sitting on the counter, but he made no move to hand one to her. Instead, his hands went to the fly of his jeans and he unzipped his pants. She already knew he wore nothing underneath but still held her breath in anticipation as he peeled the fabric down his hips and legs. He was magnificent.

Tossing his jeans to the side, he stepped into the shower, letting the water hit his body. Little droplets clung to his bronzed skin and she ran her hand across his chest, wiping them away so they could form again. He had the wide shoulders and broad chest of a swimmer and she envisioned him sitting at a lifeguard's station over a pool, his bleached blond hair in sharp contrast to the dark golden glow of his skin.

Feeling his gaze on her, she looked up and realized that he'd been watching her stare at him. When he smiled, she blushed.

He put his hands on her hips and slowly turned her to face the shower. Standing behind her, he rubbed a bar of soap between his hands until he'd worked up a lather, then began massaging the tops of her shoulders, moving his hands in ever-widening circles.

His palms slid smoothly across her flesh, awakening every nerve inside her. When he reached her breasts, he pushed the twin lobes together and lifted them, testing their weight, massaging their fullness.

Bethany's breathing came faster and she leaned her head back against his chest, losing herself in the tactile sensations he stirred to life. He was hard where he pressed against her and it made her squirm. When she heard his breath catch, she smiled. Opening her eyes, she reached out and ran her hand along the bar of soap. Then she leaned forward slightly, filling Dirk's hands with her breasts as she reached back and took him in hers, his length slipping in and out of her grip.

"Sweet Jesus," he moaned and then he was bending her forward at the waist until she was braced against the wall in front of her. Before she had time to understand what he was doing, he grabbed her hips and held her as he buried himself in her with a single thrust. The soap eased his passage and he took her with animalistic fury.

The water hitting her back ran down her sides and along her breasts until a steady stream ran from her nipples to the shower floor. The sounds of their coming together echoed in the stall, and the now familiar tension built low in her belly. She could do nothing more than hang on for the ride.

Then Dirk changed his rhythm and when he buried himself, instead of pulling out, he moved his hips, sinking himself a little deeper into her. At the same time, he slipped one arm across the front of her hips to hold her in place while the other hand moved to her breast where he rolled and lightly squeezed her nipple between his fingers.

The double assault was too much and she hit her climax with the force of a speeding car hitting a brick wall. She was still spiraling from the impact when Dirk tensed, spilling himself into her.

For long moments, they remained joined together, the warm water coursing over them. Then slowly, Dirk eased himself out of her.

"Wow," he said, sounding surprised. "I think I'm still seeing stars. Are you all right?" He turned her toward him and tilted her head up so he could study her face, his concern obvious.

"Never better," she assured him, feeling a small thrill at his reaction.

He took the soap and again lathered his hands. He started to bathe her, then stopped and gave her an apologetic smile. "We're never going to get out of here if I do this. Tell you what. I'll bathe and get out so you can finish."

It didn't take him long and soon she was in the shower by herself, pouring shampoo into her hand to wash her hair as he dried off.

"I'll be out here waiting for you," he told her. "You want your coffee before I go?"

"No, I won't be long." She heard him leave and ducked her head under the water to rinse her hair. She quickly soaped off and rinsed her body, not letting herself think about the way Dirk's hands had felt when he'd washed her. She was flushed by the time she stepped out of the shower.

There was no noise coming from the bedroom as she dried and she wondered if Dirk had gone back to his room after all. Working a comb through her hair, she then wrapped a towel around her, and then stepped into the room.

Dirk was there, standing beside the dresser, his expression dark and closed. Beside him, her new purple bra and panties lay on top of the dresser, next to the orchid and roses.

"Is something wrong?" she asked.

"I thought you ended the engagement." His tone was unusually calm, but no less accusing.

She stared, confused, at her engagement ring, now in his hand. "Where did you get that?"

"I found it in your drawer when I went to get these." He nodded to the lingerie on top. "I saw you pack them and wanted to see you in them. I'm sure it's the last place you expected me to look. Sorry if I ruined your little scheme."

"What scheme?"

He shook his head. "Now it all makes sense. You never really broke up with Miles, did you?"

"Of course I did," she snapped. "Do you really think I'd make love to you while I was engaged to someone else?"

He closed the distance between them, his eyes flashing. "Yes, I do."

It was a slap in the face and she didn't know if she was more stunned or hurt. "Why would I do that?"

"Curiosity."

"About what?"

His heated gaze raked over her and when he ran a finger along the edge of the towel where it wrapped across her breasts, she couldn't stop her body from responding to his touch. Then she understood.

His insinuation immediately ignited her temper and she knocked his hand away. "Get out of my room, now."

He didn't move. Hurt and frustration swelled up inside her and she wanted to scream or cry, but she did neither. Giving him her coldest stare, she kept her voice steady and even. "Get out now or I will scream until everyone in the house comes running."

A full minute went by as they glared at each other. The closeness they'd shared so recently withered and died. Then Dirk snapped shut the lid of the jewelry box and tossed it onto the bed as he walked out of the room.

Chapter 14

Bethany couldn't move. She was still tensed for a fight, her breathing erratically fast as anger and hurt burned deep inside her, making her sick to her stomach. Only when she realized Dirk wasn't coming back did she allow herself to relax slightly.

She went over to the bed and picked up the jewelry box. How had it gotten into her drawer? She distinctly remembered giving it back to Miles. She slipped the box into her purse and crossed to the dresser to put away the purple lingerie that Dirk had pulled out. Her eyes fell on the vase of roses and a memory from the night before surfaced. Miles could have slipped the ring into her drawer while she'd been filling the vase with water, but why?

The only explanation she could think of was that maybe he was having trouble accepting that things really were over between them. If so, she'd have to explain it to him again when she gave back the ring.

Dirk was another problem. Her feelings for him were

complicated and it hurt that he didn't trust her. After listening to the stories of his childhood, she understood why trust was hard for him, but she didn't think she could live under the umbrella of continual suspicion.

Besides, he'd hurt her, humiliated her. Every time she saw him now, it would be there, hanging between them, along with the memory of their lovemaking. The thought of living under the same roof with him for even another day suddenly became intolerable. After she dressed, she pulled her suitcases from the closet and began to pack her clothes.

The vampires were still out there, but if she made good use of her daylight hours, she could be far away from Washington, D.C., by nightfall. She'd pick a destination at random, so there'd be no easy way to follow her.

You're running away. The words echoed in her head. *No, it's a fresh start,* a defiant voice countered. There was nothing holding her here. Not Miles. Certainly not Dirk.

What about the project?

She paused in the act of folding a shirt. Her work was a definite roadblock. After last night, she was close to finishing. Just a few more tests—but there was still the question of what the drug was to be used for. It was a question only Miles could answer. If he was up to something illegal, then she'd walk; leave her work unfinished. If it wasn't illegal, she'd finish it as fast as she could—and then she'd leave.

Unbidden, her thoughts turned to Dirk. If a small part of her had hoped he would come crawling back, asking her for forgiveness, then it was time to face reality. Taking a deep breath, she finished packing.

Minutes later, she went downstairs, helped herself to

another cup of coffee, and then went into the living room where she found Lanie standing in the middle of the room, looking lost.

"Good morning. Is something wrong?"

Lanie jumped at the sound of her voice and then smiled apologetically. "I'm sorry. I'm looking for Gem. Uncle Charles asked me to keep an eye on her, but I sort of got distracted this morning when Mac came home." She blushed, giving Bethany a pretty good idea of how, exactly, she'd been distracted.

"Isn't she on Julia's desk?" Bethany recalled Lanie telling her how the small baby chupacabra had developed a sweet tooth and was constantly nibbling on the mints Julia kept sitting on her desk.

Lanie shook her head. "It's the first place I looked."

"Did you ask Julia if she'd seen her?"

Lanie looked embarrassed. "Not yet. I didn't want to make a big deal out of it. She already thinks one of us is playing a joke on her—I didn't want her thinking it was me."

Bethany understood. Everyone liked Julia and though it was necessary to keep secrets from her, no one liked doing it. "I'll help you look."

Lanie flashed her a smile. "Thanks, I'd appreciate it."

"Where have you looked so far?"

"I've checked the study, the living room, and the kitchen. She's not in my room and there's no way she'd go to Dirk's room."

"Why's that?" Bethany asked out of curiosity.

"She looks too much like the adult who attacked him," Lanie said as they walked down the hall to check some of the other rooms. "He kicks her out whenever she wanders in by mistake."

"But Mac's okay being around her?"

"That's a little different. Even though the adult attacked Mac, when Burton almost killed me, it was Gem who saved my life. Mac swore then to always take care of her."

They'd reached the room where she and Dirk had watched TV, and the conversation came to a halt as they searched it. It took time because they couldn't do just a cursory look around. They had to explore every possible nook and cranny, wherever a playful creature might hide.

After they concluded that she wasn't in the den, they moved to the next room. Four rooms later, they still hadn't found her. By now, Bethany knew Lanie was seriously worried about the little creature.

Going into the kitchen for lunch, they were sitting at the table, picking over their food, when Julia walked in. She took one look at their faces and her own became concerned. "Something's wrong." It was a statement more than a question.

Bethany wasn't sure Lanie would say anything to the woman, so she did. "I'm afraid that the gargoyle statue is missing. It's kind of a long, complicated story that I'm not at liberty to share, but it has great sentimental value and it seems to be missing. Have you seen it?"

For a moment Bethany thought Julia might know something. Her eyes grew wide and though she was too refined to let her jaw hang open, Bethany got the impression she was nevertheless dumbfounded. "I . . . I," she swallowed. "No. Are you sure you looked everywhere?"

"Not yet," Lanie admitted, her voice sounding resigned. "I guess I'll have to go through the rest of the rooms in the west wing." She pushed away from the table, leaving her food untouched. "I think I'll keep looking."

Bethany started to stand when Lanie waved her back. "I know you have better things to do. I'm okay looking by myself, thanks. There's no real urgency until nightfall." She gave Bethany a meaningful look. "Then I'll have to ask Mac and Dirk for help."

"Are you sure, because I don't mind helping," Bethany said.

"Yes, thanks. I'm sure."

Bethany watched her walk out of the room. Julia now seemed preoccupied so Bethany finished eating lunch. She really needed to talk to Miles.

"I have to run into town for a bit," Julia announced suddenly.

Bethany jumped at the opportunity. "Would you mind if I went along? I need to do some work at the lab."

At first she thought Julia might say no, but then the woman smiled. "Of course not. I'll drop you off. Let me make a quick phone call and then we can be on our way."

Julia left the kitchen and hurried to the study where she closed the door. Her heart was racing and she fought to stay calm. What had she done? What had she been thinking? Of course they wouldn't throw away the statue. How idiotic of her to think otherwise.

She knew Lanie wouldn't find the statue in the west wing. In fact, Lanie wouldn't find the statue anywhere on the premises because the trash collectors had come earlier that morning.

Picking up the phone, she called the number for the waste management company. It took the better part of ten minutes, but she finally got the information she needed. Grabbing her purse, she went back into the kitchen to find Bethany waiting for her.

"Ready?"

Bethany nodded, and for a brief second, Julia was tempted to tell her what had happened. Then she thought better of it.

Forty minutes later, Bethany climbed out of Julia's car and watched the woman drive off. She knew there was something troubling her, but Julia hadn't shared and Bethany hadn't pried.

As the car disappeared from sight, Bethany hurried toward the front entrance of the Van Horne building, constantly scanning her surroundings as she went. She remembered what Dirk had told her about vampires hiring humans to help them during the day, but thought if she remained alert, she'd be okay. She was almost to the door when she saw a familiar-looking man walking out. It took her a minute to remember where she'd seen him, but it finally hit her. It was the same man she'd overheard talking to Miles; the one with the orange hair.

Hurrying past him, she went to her lab, picked up the phone, and dialed Miles's office, only to be told by the secretary that he was in a meeting. After getting the secretary's agreement to call her when Miles was free, Bethany put on a pot of coffee and, while it brewed, reviewed her notes up to this point. She couldn't help the sense of urgency pushing her to hurry. The one lesson she'd learned was that she absolutely didn't want to be at the lab after dark.

Going to the refrigerator, she pulled out the last batch

of synthetic extract that she'd made and carried it to the table. About to pick up a tube to examine under the microscope, she hesitated, hand suspended over the rack as she did a quick count. Nine tubes, which meant three were missing. She counted again and came up with the same results.

Going back to the refrigerator, she checked inside, wondering if the missing vials had fallen out or gotten misplaced. She went back to her notes from the night before, in case she'd used more of the synthetic than she could recall. She hadn't.

The ringing phone startled her and she hurried to answer it.

"He can see you now," Miles's secretary informed her.

Promising to be right down, Bethany put the vials back in the fridge and walked out.

"Bethany, this is an unexpected surprise," Miles said a few minutes later as she entered his office. "Are you alone?"

She ignored the question. "I think we should talk."

"Of course. Let's sit down." He led her to the sofa off to one side of his office and sat beside her. Being alone with him now felt awkward. It more or less confirmed her suspicion that it would be difficult to continue working for Van Horne Technologies.

"I wanted to talk to you about the plant extract."

"Okay."

"I created a nearly perfect synthetic replica days ago but there's an element in the original sample that eludes me. I'm afraid that until I can figure out what it is, the synthetics are unstable. The chemical bonds won't hold them together and the resulting elements could be very dangerous."

"I'm not sure I follow," he said.

"It's sort of like table salt," she explained, "only on a more complex scale. When sodium and chlorine are chemically bound together, they make table salt, completely palatable. But if that chemical bond breaks, we end up with sodium, which is a volatile explosive, and chlorine, which is a poisonous gas—neither of which is particularly healthy to ingest."

Miles's brow furrowed but he didn't say anything.

"I want to know what you're planning to do with the extract if I succeed in duplicating it." She kept her gaze level and steady, willing him to take her seriously. "I know about Mr. Santi."

"You do?" She could tell the news caught him off guard.

She nodded. "Yes. I came up here to talk to you the other day and he was in your office. The door was open and I overheard your conversation."

His eyes narrowed as he studied her. "What, exactly, did you hear?"

She was skating on thin ice and debated how much further she could bluff her way through the conversation because she hadn't actually heard that much. "Enough to know that you've got a deal with him to distribute the drug."

Miles nodded solemnly. "Yes, that's true—and you're afraid that I'm doing something illegal?"

She nodded. "I don't want to see anything bad happen to you."

Something flashed across his eyes that she couldn't

interpret, but then he smiled, taking her hand in his. "I'm very fortunate to have someone who cares about me. As a matter of fact, I *am* trying to work out a deal with Mr. Santi, but it's all perfectly legitimate. You see, Mr. Santi is with Burkford Pharmaceuticals."

"He is?"

He nodded. "It's a relatively new company that deals in herbal-based remedies. Because they're still starting up, they have to outsource much of their baseline research on new drugs. All strictly on the up and up, I assure you."

A smile spread across Bethany's face as she digested what he'd told her. "Oh, I'm so relieved to hear that. I can't tell you the things I imagined." She wanted to laugh at her own foolishness. "Mr. Santi doesn't look like your typical drug rep—I'm afraid I assumed the worst." She sobered as she saw Miles's understanding expression. "I'm afraid that I thought the worst of you, too. I'm sorry."

He patted her hand. "I can't have you thinking I'm a saint in all of this," he replied. "The truth is that Burkford Pharmaceuticals is paying Van Horne Technologies a hefty fee to analyze the extract."

"But they're paying it over the table," she said.

"Yes." For several moments, he gazed at her, and then something in his eyes changed. "I know I saw you last night, but I miss you."

In that moment, she knew that she could tell him that she'd changed her mind and he'd take her back. Things could return to the way they'd been before Dirk and the vampires. For the briefest moment, it was tempting, but then she knew she wouldn't do it. "Miles, I—"

"Please, don't say it," he interrupted her. "Hearing it once last night was enough. I don't think I can handle a second rejection in so many days." The smile he gave her was bittersweet. "I'm glad you came to see me. Like I said before, it's nice to know you still care."

"I'll always care," she said, meaning every word. Feeling uncomfortable once again, she knew that she couldn't leave until she took care of one more thing. Reaching into the pocket of her lab coat, she pulled out the small jewelry box and held it up, watching his face. He had the decency to look abashed. "I think you forgot this last night," she said.

He reached out and took it from her. "I was hoping that when you found it, you might have second thoughts."

"I'm sorry, Miles. I won't change my mind."

He nodded, and watching him place the ring into his pocket, she hoped she wouldn't see it again.

"I need to get back to work," she told him. They both stood up and he walked her to the door. They had almost reached it when she thought of something else. "The wedding announcement."

"What about it? Oh, yes. Sorry. I'll take care of it."

She smiled. "Thanks, Miles."

She left, feeling better about one part of her life. She might be fighting with Dirk and vampires might still be after her, but at least now she didn't have to worry about Miles going to jail because he was doing something illegal.

Returning to her lab, Bethany set to work. She was determined to finish before darkness fell and resigned herself to spending at least one more night in the safety of the mansion. Tomorrow, when the sun came up, she would leave.

Julia tried to keep her eyes on the road as she drove. Charles would be so disappointed with her if he knew what she'd done. Not *if,* she amended the thought. When. She had every intention of confessing, but first wanted to see if she could make things right.

Thirty minutes later, Julia stood at the foot of almost an acre of garbage, thinking that she'd seriously underestimated the task at hand. Searching the dumpsite was not only going to take a long time, it promised to be extremely unpleasant. If the rancid odor was anything to judge by, there could very well be a dozen rotting bodies in there, along with other things she didn't want to consider.

Resigning herself to the inevitable, she heaved a sigh and then immediately regretted it as she gasped for clean, odor-free air.

"Well, Julia, putting it off won't make it easier," she told herself. "Best get to it."

After dropping off Bethany earlier, she'd stopped at the first hardware store she came to and purchased a set of coveralls, rubber boots, and a box of gloves. Then she'd driven to the address she'd been given by the city clerk. Now, decked out in her new purchases, she set to work.

Initially, she found sifting through the trash educational—both in terms of what people threw out and in discovering her gag threshold. As with so many things, success was dependent on how disciplined one's mind was. It also helped that Julia was looking for something big, allowing her to skip over the many small, less pleasant items.

The first section she searched proved to be disappointing, so she moved to another section where her efforts were no more fruitful. Still, she persevered, moving to another part of the massive dumpsite. By the end of the day, Julia was tired, depressed, and had nothing to show for her efforts except a stench she hoped wasn't permanent. A small part of her worried that somewhere along the route, either the garbage collectors or someone else had spotted the statue among the rest of the trash, liked it, and now had it in their possession. If that was the case, then she would never see it again.

Now, with the hour getting late, Julia worked her way systematically around a relatively fresh mountain of trash, concerned that the sun might not stay up long enough for her to finish. She also worried about what was happening at the mansion. By now, they had to be wondering where she was.

As the smell of the garbage grew stronger, she pulled her small perfume atomizer from her pocket and sprayed herself, hoping it was strong enough to mask some of the more offensive odors clinging to her.

The sun's dying rays cast an orange glow across the landscape, throwing one side of the large pile into shadow. She walked to the far side and stood with her back to the sun, so she could see, and began to pick through the debris.

Soon lost in thought, a flicker of movement off to the side startled her. She froze in place and waited. She had just decided that it had been a figment of her imagination when it came again.

Apprehension shot through her. Though she had yet to see any, it wasn't inconceivable for there to be dogs or even rats digging through the pile, she told herself. The problem was that, in all likelihood, the animal was a stray and potentially dangerous.

Hoping to avoid it, she inched her way around the pile. Unfortunately, the animal moved with her, almost as if it were tracking her. She froze once more and it moved into view, sniffing through the pile. In the dim light, it was hard to see exactly what type of animal it was.

The hair was cut so short that the creature appeared furless, although there seemed to be tufts of hair running down its back. As she strained to get a better look at it, the animal raised its head and saw her.

Its eyes glowed red and Julia was positive that she saw long, sharp teeth protruding from its mouth. Suddenly she was very afraid. No one knew she was out here and she'd left her cell phone in the car.

Moving slowly, she backed down the heap of garbage and had just reached the bottom when she heard the growl. In a desperate attempt to save herself, she raced toward her car. She'd taken only a couple of steps when her luck ran out.

Chapter
15

Dirk woke up in a foul mood. He'd been played with and he didn't like it. The old Dirk wouldn't have minded so much. He might even have taken advantage of the situation by enjoying the woman until he got tired of her and then sending her back to her fiancé when he was done. For some reason, he found that hard to do with Bethany. From the first moment he'd seen her, she'd affected him strangely.

He now realized that what had been between them was purely physical, nothing more. And now, even that was gone. He steeled himself against an overwhelming sense of loss, refusing to let it affect him. He still had a job to do and he'd be damned if he'd let this get in the way. He would guard Bethany with his life. Still, as long as she was at the mansion, she was safe. In the six months they'd been hunting Harris and Patterson, the two Primes had never dared attack the mansion. To do so would be suicidal and the former SEALs knew better.

Dirk sighed. Despite his reluctance to get out of bed, a sense of urgency plagued him until he could no longer ignore it. Getting out of bed, he dressed quickly and headed downstairs.

Mac was in the living room, his arms wrapped around Lanie who was clearly upset. Admiral Winslow was also there, pacing back and forth, looking grim. One look at Mac's face and Dirk knew the sense of urgency he'd felt had come through the psychic link the two men shared.

"We have to find Gem," Lanie pleaded with Mac.

"I know, baby, we will. I promise." He looked around and saw Dirk and, for a moment, his expression relaxed. "Dirk and I will go out and find her, but you have to promise me you'll stay here."

Dirk looked from Mac to the admiral, and then back again. "What's going on?"

"Gem's disappeared," the admiral said.

Dirk couldn't help glancing around the room and noticed for the first time that the small chupacabra wasn't lurking nearby as it usually was. "Well, she can't have gone far. The sun only set about an hour ago," he reasoned. "Maybe she's outside."

Lanie was shaking her head before he finished. "I spent the entire day looking for her—I've combed every inch of this place, inside and out. She's not here."

"Why didn't you come wake me," Mac quietly chided his wife.

"You needed your sleep. Besides, I thought I'd find her. I mean, she's so small, where could she go?" Her voice broke over this last part and she fell silent.

"Maybe Julia found her and put her someplace," Dirk suggested.

"That's the other problem," Mac said, his tone accusing. "Julia left earlier today and never came back. She hasn't called either."

The admiral stopped pacing in order to face Mac. Dirk saw the lines of worry etched in his face and the rigid way in which he held himself. "Young man, I hope you're not suggesting that Julia had something to do with Gem's disappearance."

"That is exactly what I'm suggesting," Mac countered, moving Lanie behind him so he could square off with the admiral.

Dirk thought it was an indication of just how upset the two men were that they were so close to blows. He was about to step between them when the sound of the front door opening caught his attention.

Dirk spun around as the newcomer appeared, catching a whiff of something foul. Julia stood there, wearing a one-piece jumpsuit that was so filthy, Dirk had no idea what color it had once been. Her hair was a wild mass on top of her head and her face was streaked with mud.

Admiral Winslow took a step toward her, but then stopped, no doubt driven back by the odor. "Julia, what in God's name . . ."

"I'm sorry," she said. "I made a mistake today. I don't expect you to forgive me, but I didn't want you to fire me before I had a chance to make things right."

The admiral looked as confused as Dirk felt. "What are you talking about?"

"The statue."

The mere mention of the word caused the tension in the room to escalate.

"What do you know about the statue?" Mac's tone was deadly serious.

Julia looked as if she wanted to run away, but Dirk gave her credit for having the courage to remain where she was. "I know what happened to it." She turned to look at Lanie. "I'm so sorry. When you asked me earlier where it was, I lied."

Lanie gasped but Julia hurried on before anyone could interrupt. "You see, I came in this morning and found the statue in the wastebasket." She turned to the admiral. "After our talk yesterday, you said you'd take care of it. I thought that had been your solution—to throw it away. Especially after I read your note."

"My note?"

All eyes turned to the admiral and for a second he looked confused, then he sighed and nodded his head. "I was late for my breakfast meeting downtown. I was going through my mail to make sure there was nothing there I needed when I noticed a package from an old friend. I opened it and found several small bottles of syrup, one of which had broken. I threw it in the trash and left Julia a note to dispose of it."

Lanie turned then to Mac, her expression hopeful. "She's probably out in the trash canister. Would you go check?"

"Of course." He squeezed her hand and started for the door when the admiral cleared his throat.

"She won't be there," the admiral said tightly. "Today is collection day."

Julia peered at Lanie with a resigned expression on her face. "When you asked about the statue, I realized I had made a mistake, but by then, it was too late to correct it. The trash had already been collected."

"We need to find out where they dumped the trash," Lanie said, clearly distressed. "Maybe she'll still be there."

"I'll take care of it." Mac looked at Dirk, who nodded that he was ready to help search for the small creature.

"I wanted to help—" Julia began, but Mac cut her off, his tone cold, bordering on cruel.

"I think you've done enough already."

He turned to go, but with almost changeling speed, the admiral crossed the room and gripped Mac's arm in a viselike grip, spinning him around.

Mac's eyes flared a bright red and Dirk saw him fight to control his reaction, out of respect for the older man. For several seconds, they glared at each other. Dirk edged closer, wondering if he was going to have to break up a fight, then Mac heaved a sigh, releasing his anger. He turned to face Julia, who still hadn't moved from where she stood half inside the living room. "I'm sorry. I was out of line."

"No," she replied. "You have every right to be upset. All I wanted to say is that you don't have to go anywhere." She ducked out of view for a moment and when she came back, she was holding the baby chupacabra in her arms.

Lanie squealed with delight and ran to the creature. Gem emitted a noise somewhere between a bark and a growl, which Dirk assumed meant she was excited. She leaped into Lanie's arms and almost knocked her over.

Dirk watched the happy reunion, wondering when

everyone would realize that there was now one more person who knew their secret—or at least part of their secret.

It didn't take long. With Gem cradled against her side
like a baby, Lanie stared at Julia in amazement. "How?" It
seemed all she was capable of asking.

Julia smiled. "It wasn't that hard. I called the city to
find out where the trash is dumped. That's where I've
been all afternoon."

"But you were looking for a statue," Lanie pointed out.
"When did you realize that Gem really isn't a statue?"

"Right after the sun went down and I thought she was
going to rip out my throat."

The admiral went to her. "Are you all right? You're not
hurt, are you?"

"No, I'm fine," she replied, looking at the admiral with
a mixture of hope and longing that made Dirk wonder if
the admiral realized just how much she cared for him. "I
admit, I thought I was dead when she knocked me over
and went for my throat."

Everyone in the room gasped in alarm, but Julia remained calm. She reached into the upper pocket of her
coveralls and pulled out a mint, like the ones she kept on
her desk, and held it out to the baby chupacabra, who
snatched it from her hand and began licking it. "It turned
out that she wasn't going for my throat after all. Once I realized I wasn't about to die, I had a chance to study her.
That's when I noticed the similarity to the statue."

"I'm impressed," Dirk admitted, speaking for the first
time. "There aren't many people who would have remained calm under those circumstances."

Julia gave a small laugh. "Then I won't tell you about
the small breakdown I had."

The admiral's smile was warm and gentle. "I suspect you have a few questions."

"Actually," she admitted, "I only have one."

They all turned to her expectantly and waited.

"Are you going to kill me?"

Everyone stared at her and Dirk wondered if they, like he, were trying to figure out if she was joking or serious. He suspected the latter and it bothered him.

The admiral, however, looked to be the most upset. "Julia, why would you even ask that?"

Her gaze was level when she answered him. "You say you're running a security agency, but you only have one client, as far as I can tell, and she's not paying you to watch her. All the money you get for the philanthropic activities is coming from somewhere, but I have no clue where. You're former military and you work with the local police. Dirk and Mac work mostly at night and except for an occasional meal, you go to great lengths to see that I'm not here after dark. I know you were trying to keep whatever it is you do confidential and this creature, whatever it is, is part of that. So, I just wondered if you were going to kill me in order to keep your secret."

"Of course we're not going to kill you." The admiral sounded outraged. "I'm highly offended that you would even suggest such a thing. I'll admit that we have kept certain things from you, but only for your own protection."

Julia laid her hand on his arm. "You don't owe me any explanations. I'm not going to tell anyone what I've seen. I'll just clean out my desk and be out of your way as soon as I can."

"You're quitting?" Lanie asked, her face showing concern as she set the baby chupacabra on the floor to play so she could approach Julia.

It was Julia's turn to look surprised as she looked at Lanie and then the admiral. "No, I'm not quitting. I mean, I don't want to quit, but I thought, after what happened, that you wouldn't . . . that is to say, I thought I was fired."

The admiral smiled. "No, you're not fired. I can't stop you if you want to leave, but I hope you'll stay."

Julia smiled up at him, the dirt on her face giving her a particularly waiflike appearance. "Well, I do like it here."

"Good," the admiral said, as if things had been decided. "But this does change things a little." He exchanged meaningful looks with Dirk and the others and they all silently nodded. Turning back to Julia, the admiral continued. "I'm afraid that there is much more to what we do than what little you've figured out. I think it's time we told you all of it, but first, perhaps you'd like to freshen up a bit?"

Julia's eyes widened in horror as she raised a hand to her hair. "Oh, my, I must look, and smell, a mess."

"I think you look stunning," the admiral replied gallantly. "Lanie, would you show Julia to a guest room so she can shower and perhaps either you or Bethany has a change of clothes she can borrow."

"Bethany's about your size," Lanie said, leading Julia upstairs. They were gone for a few minutes before Lanie called down. "Has anyone seen Bethany? She's not in her room."

Dirk tensed. "What do you mean, she's not there?" he growled, racing up to Bethany's room. He immediately spotted the suitcases sitting on the bed, lids opened to reveal the packed clothes inside. She was leaving?

The discovery came as a shock, followed closely by anger, frustration, and the trickling of fear. "Where the hell is she?"

"Maybe she's still at the lab," Julia offered, drawing everyone's attention. "I dropped her off earlier today." She looked around. "Oh, dear," she sighed. "Was that wrong?"

Dirk didn't say a word. He simply raced outside, jumped into his SUV, and headed into town.

Harris approached the farm, his senses alert to every sound and movement. He knew the adult chupacabra was near because he'd felt her presence through the psychic link.

He'd driven himself out into the country, but had left the car down the road, not wanting to frighten her off. He wasn't expecting miracles tonight. He knew that her trust would be hard to win, thanks to Burton's cruelty. Once again, Harris felt the familiar hate and anger well up inside until it almost choked him. It took great discipline to tamp it down, but Harris still had that discipline, which was a miracle in itself.

Every day, it got a little harder to control the monster within, but every day, Harris found the strength to do it.

Climbing through the rails of a wood fence, he walked across the pasture, heading for the barn. He had only gone a few feet when he found the first animal carcass. Though it was night, he had no trouble making out the two puncture wounds in the neck. He walked a bit farther before spotting two more dead cows. These bodies hadn't been dead that long. He climbed the upward slope of the pasture until he stood at the very top and then, looking down into the small valley below, he saw the darker forms.

The adult was feeding, but she must have sensed him there because she stopped and looked up. He froze, not wanting to scare her away. It was enough that he was this close and she wasn't running from him.

He remained where he was until she finished eating and then he used the shared psychic link to send her an image of her own departure. He didn't want her remaining at the farm long enough to be spotted. That wouldn't be good.

She stood watching him for several seconds and then finally turned and lumbered off. Once she was out of his sight, Harris turned around and headed back to his car. He was feeling good. He'd gotten this close and she hadn't run from him. Tonight's encounter could be considered a success.

Bethany placed a drop of her latest batch of synthetic extract on a slide and placed it under the microscope next to the first one. She'd run every test she could think of and in all cases the synthetic had reacted just as the original— for about ten minutes. Staring at both the original and synthetic for the thousandth time as if the answer were in front of her if she could only see it, she tried to accept her own failure.

She tried to be objective, but couldn't. She didn't like failing. Taking a deep breath, she set up another round of experiments, refusing to give up.

"What the hell do you think you're doing?"

Dirk's sudden appearance startled her and the sound of

his voice set her pulse to racing, though she tried not to show it. "I'm working."

Coming up behind her, he grabbed her arm and spun her around on the stool until she was staring up into angry blue eyes tinged with a red glowing light. "I told you specifically not to go out by yourself."

She glared back. "News flash," she said heatedly, "I don't take orders from you." She started to turn her back on him, but he grabbed her arm again and refused to let her go.

"What you did was dangerous." His eyes practically shot sparks of light and his lips curled, revealing his fangs. She didn't know if he was trying to frighten her on purpose or whether he was even aware of how he looked. Either way, he was crowding her, making it hard for her to focus on anything but him. It wasn't fear, though, that she felt. Despite everything, she still wanted him and that, to her, was the cruelest blow of all.

She managed to push off the stool and stood toe to toe, looking up at him. He didn't move. "You're in my way," she said between clenched teeth, staring up at him defiantly.

"We're not through talking."

"Oh, yes, we are." She placed her hand against his chest and shoved. He didn't budge, making her feel small and ineffectual. Anger, frustration, and hurt bubbled up, almost choking her as she shoved at him again, this time harder. "Get away from me."

"You should have told me where you were going," he growled.

"Told you where I was going?" she yelled, incredulous. "Why?" She fisted her hands and rode the wave of anger coursing through her. "Would you have believed me? After all, in your twisted little reality, I'm a liar and a cheat. You don't give a damn what happens to me."

"I don't want anything to hurt you," he said—and she lost it.

Pounding him with her fists, she started yelling. "You don't want anything to hurt me? Well, guess what, you jerk? In the last two weeks, the only *thing* that's hurt me is you. You. You." Each word was punctuated with a blow to his chest.

Dirk stood there and let her vent, guilt hitting him with a force far stronger than anything she could dole out. After finding the ring in her drawer, it had never occurred to him that she had been honest with him—that she would give up the wealth and affluence Miles could give her for a chance to be with him.

He stood there patiently waiting as her blows grew weaker and then finally stopped. He looked down and saw that she wasn't trying to fight him now, wasn't glaring at him. She was merely standing there, her head bowed, crying.

He pulled her to him, not allowing her to resist, and wrapped his arms around her. "I'm sorry," he whispered into her hair. "I'm sorry I hurt you. I'm sorry . . . for everything."

He stroked her back, relishing the feel of her in his arms for as long as she'd let him hold her. She hated him—how could she not? And it was his own fault.

Looking down at her, he put a finger under her chin and tipped her tear-streaked face up toward him. Her eyes were swollen, her mascara had run, and her nose was red, yet he'd never thought she looked more beautiful. He wanted one last kiss—to last a lifetime.

He moved slowly, giving her time to pull away or turn her head, then his mouth was on hers and his tongue teased the seam of her closed lips until she opened for him. He heard her sigh and realized he was wrong when he'd thought that all there was between them was a physical attraction.

Somewhere along the way, Beth had become the most important thing in his life.

"I finished."

Patterson looked up as Stuart walked into the chamber where he kept the prisoners. "Really? And this is different from the others how?"

"The problem was the enzyme—"

Patterson held up his hand, silencing the young man. "Spare me the technical explanation. Just tell me—how sure are you that this is a perfect match to the real venom?"

He saw Stuart's confident, cocky expression. "Positive."

Patterson smiled, not bothering to hide his fangs. "Positive?" he echoed. "Then let's test it, shall we?" He looked at the wall where the bodies of the previous test subjects lay withered and dead on the floor. All but one cowering man.

"Do you have a syringe?"

Stuart nodded, holding it up. "I've already filled it."

"Excellent." He reached for the syringe and was stunned when the other man pulled his hand back out of reach.

"Remember our agreement," Stuart said. "I know you're planning to sell this and I expect you'll make a ton of money. All I'm asking for is a piece of the action. I think that's only fair."

The two stared at each other while Patterson fought to control his temper. Then he smiled. "Of course." He held out his hand again and this time Stuart gave him the syringe. Patterson took it and held it up to the light. "I trust you've made extensive notes on the formula?"

"Of course," Stuart mimicked Patterson's condescending tone.

"Good." Patterson never gave Stuart a chance to anticipate his demise. The first rush of warm blood filling his mouth was like ambrosia and he drank deeply. Whether the venom worked this time or not, he was glad to be rid of this young man.

When Stuart sagged in his arms, Patterson lowered him to the ground. Pulling the syringe from his lifeless fingers, Patterson injected the contents into Stuart's heart. "A piece of the action—as promised."

Chapter
16

Bethany woke late the next day still feeling tired and emotionally drained. She and Dirk were no longer fighting, but their relationship was still at an awkward phase.

After the kiss, he'd let her get back to work. It had been hard to focus with him so close, but she had run a battery of experiments and finally concluded that the latest batch of synthetic plant extract was as close to the real thing as anyone was likely to get—but it wasn't close enough. In her professional opinion, if the pharmaceutical company wanted to use the plant extract in a new drug, they were going to have to get it from the plants themselves.

By the time Dirk had driven them home, the sun was already coming up over the horizon and as soon as they'd arrived at the mansion, they'd gone straight to bed—Dirk to his and she to hers.

Tired and depressed, she slept fitfully throughout the

day. Every time she woke up, she merely rolled over and forced herself to go back to sleep. There wasn't much point in getting up, as far as she was concerned. She didn't have to go into the lab, and having tentatively made up with Dirk, she'd put her plans to leave town on hold.

Thinking of Dirk made her groan and she pulled the covers higher. The truth was that she didn't know where she stood with him, which meant their next encounter was bound to be uncomfortable. In anticipation of it, she rolled over and closed her eyes, determined to stay in bed as long as possible.

Finally, by late afternoon, she was starving and tired of hiding. She took a leisurely shower, dressed casually in jeans and a sweater, and went downstairs.

She hoped she might be able to enjoy a cup of coffee by herself, but those hopes vanished when she walked into the kitchen and found Dirk sitting at the table, a cup of coffee in front of him and a dour expression on his face.

"You're up early," she said, surprised to see him before nightfall. "Didn't you sleep well?"

"Well enough," he answered vaguely.

Bethany couldn't judge his mood and it worried her. Trying to act as if nothing was wrong, she poured herself a cup of coffee and joined him at the table.

"You had a phone call earlier," he informed her.

"Really? Who?"

"Miles." He made it sound like an accusation.

She couldn't help it if Miles called her and she refused to let Dirk make her feel guilty. "What did he want?"

"He didn't say, but I'm guessing it had something to do with this." He pushed the folded newspaper across the table to her. It was opened to the society section and when she looked, she saw her own face staring back at her.

"Oh, no." She set down her cup and picked up the paper, needing to take a closer look.

"It's a good photo of you both, don't you think?" His tone was snide and Bethany wanted to scream.

Instead, she took a deep breath and let it out slowly. "I don't know how many times I have to tell you that I broke up with him, but this is the last time I'm going to do it. So listen up. I. Broke. Up. With. Him." She tossed the paper back at him. "Despite all evidence to the contrary."

"Yeah? Maybe he didn't get the message."

She stared at Dirk in disbelief. "You're being absurd." She pushed away from the table, going for the phone. She punched in Miles's phone number and waited. After a few rings, he answered.

"Hello?"

"Miles, it's Bethany."

"Oh, I'm so glad you called. Listen, I wanted to warn you that our engagement announcement is in today's paper."

She heaved a sigh. "I saw it."

"I'm sorry, Bethany," he said, sounding sincere. "I tried to cancel it, but it was too late. I can ask them to print a retraction. I'm sure they won't mind. That kind of scandal is sure to boost their sales."

He was right. As a member of the prominent Van Horne family, the papers would have a heyday with this latest twist over his engagement. The media wouldn't be satisfied until they discovered why Bethany and Miles had called off their plans. In pursuit of an explanation, there was a good chance that Dirk and the rest of the admiral's security team would be dragged into it. She didn't think they'd appreciate the exposure.

"No, don't do anything. The less publicity, the better."

"Really, Bethany. It's no problem."

Bethany glanced at Dirk's sour expression. "Just leave it."

"Okay, if you're sure. Listen, I'm glad you called," he continued. "I wanted to go over your lab notes."

"All right. I'll come in so we can go over them."

"That won't be necessary. I have your notebook here in front of me."

Bethany frowned. "You have *my* notebook?" She'd been tired and distracted last night, but was almost positive that she'd locked the notebook in her desk before leaving. She never left it lying about in the open.

"Yes, it was on the counter when I went into your lab hoping to find you." Now he sounded a little confused. "Is there a problem?"

She guessed she'd been more tired than she remembered. "No, no problem. Okay, if you'll turn to the last couple of pages, you'll see . . ."

For the next ten minutes, while Dirk sat at the table and drank his coffee, she rattled off her findings and answered his questions. She could tell that Miles didn't like her conclusion.

"Are you positive?" he asked when she was finished.

"I'm sorry, Miles. I know you were counting on selling the formula for a good price."

She heard his sigh. "I have to go. I'll talk to you later."

She hung up the phone and turned to find Dirk watching her. His expression hadn't changed much and she was getting tired of his constant distrust. "He tried to cancel," she told him, glancing again at the article, "but it was too late."

"Bullshit."

She jerked her head up in surprise. "Excuse me?"

"You heard me." He shoved a slip of paper across the table toward her. She made no move to take it, but saw it had a phone number scrawled across it. "That's the phone number to the paper. When you decide you're ready to face the truth about Miles, call the paper and ask when their deadline for canceling an announcement is and if anyone called to cancel that particular one."

With that parting statement, he stood and walked out of the room, leaving her alone at the table, silently fuming. She counted to ten, then got up from the table, fixed herself a snack, and poured another cup of coffee. As she passed the kitchen table, her gaze fell on the slip of paper. With a disgusted sigh, she snatched it up and went back to her room.

That night, Julia, who had now learned all about the vampires, stayed for dinner. With a few hours to kill before they drove into town to patrol the streets, Mac and Dirk joined the others in the great room.

As they took their seats, Gem appeared. She'd just finished consuming a meal of pig's blood, which Lanie purchased from the local butcher shop. Now, she walked to Julia, sitting beside the admiral on the couch.

"I just can't believe that vampires and creatures such as this exist," she said, stroking Gem's head. "Where did she come from?"

"Gem was found in the Amazon jungle," the admiral replied. "At least, that's where we found her and the adult, but if you mean where the species originates, I don't really know."

"There are various theories on the chupacabras' true origin," Lanie piped up. "One is that they are aliens stranded on Earth from some earlier visit. Along those same lines is a related theory that the chupacabra is the result of a NASA alien/animal experiment gone awry—although I think we can now discount that one since the admiral's family has been hunting vampires long before NASA existed. Of a less scientific nature is the theory that chupacabras are transdimensional spirits or dark angels, children of Lucifer, which manifest into physical form while in our dimension, turning to stone during the day to avoid detection."

Julia looked as confused as Bethany felt. "Which one is correct?"

"Maybe none of them," Lanie said. She pinned the admiral with a look. "You knew chupacabras existed before you sent my father to study them last year, didn't you?"

"I knew there were creatures that had the ability to convert humans into vampires, but I didn't know, specifically, that it was the chupacabra, although your father and I discussed the possibility at great length over the years. It's one of the reasons I asked him to be the one to study them. However, I never expected we'd lose him like that." His expression grew sad. "Sending him was a mistake that I'll regret the rest of my life."

"No, you mustn't," Lanie hurried to reassure him. "You gave him the opportunity of a lifetime. It's what he always wanted and I know that even with the way things turned out, he doesn't regret it. You mustn't either."

He nodded, but the troubled look remained on his face.

"Your family has known about vampires for generations," Mac said to the admiral. "They had to have learned something in all that time about vampires and where they come from. I mean, the person who forged the Death Rider sword wasn't an average blacksmith. How did your family get involved?"

The admiral smiled. "No, Ewan Winslow was no ordinary blacksmith and I don't know what went into making that blade—how much magic and how much science. That line of the family is charged with making the blade and they've passed down their secrets from father to son, just as my side has handed down the charge of finding the changelings.

"Much of the legend has been lost over time," he went on, "but the story goes like this. Centuries ago, four brothers were out doing some night hunting when they came across a creature in the woods. Not recognizing the beast, the eldest brother, Angus, advised his brothers that they should leave the creature alone and return home. Ewan and Sean, the middle twins, agreed, but the youngest and most foolhardy, Erik, thought it would be great sport to hunt the creature and he took up his sword and tried to slay it. The creature attacked and killed Erik before his brothers could react. By the time they'd drawn their weapons, the creature had run off.

"The three brothers bore Erik's body home and for two days the townspeople paid homage to it. On the second night, the eve of his burial, Erik came back to life as a vampire. He was crazed and hungry, yearning for blood. He'd killed several people before he realized what he was doing and then was horrified both at what he'd become and what he'd done.

"The townspeople wanted him slain, but Angus, Ewan, and Sean, who loved their youngest brother, couldn't do it. Instead, they took him home and allowed him to live in the basement of their castle where they fed him the blood of animals and kept him safe. Sean, who dabbled in the black arts, began looking for a spell that would reverse what had happened to his brother. He needed the blood of the creature, so Angus and Ewan armed themselves with weapons and went to find it.

"Many nights they went out and returned empty-handed. Then, one foggy night, they found it. Together, the brothers attacked. They fought fiercely, but the creature was stronger. In the ensuing battle, Ewan was knocked unconscious. Left alone, Angus continued the battle, but in the end, fell to the creature. He was near death when the sun rose and the creature turned to stone.

"Ewan awoke and took Angus home where the brothers prepared for another death in the family. It never came. Instead of dying, Angus healed almost overnight from his wounds."

"He became a changeling," Lanie whispered.

The admiral smiled. "The first changeling, though at the time, the brothers didn't see much difference between Angus and Erik. They had the same eyes and teeth, superior strength, speed, and hearing—they thought they were the same, except for two differences. Angus had no interest in blood and he could go out during the day.

"By this time, Erik's victims had begun to rise, but instead of learning to control their bloodlust, as Erik seemed able to do, they killed indiscriminately. There were soon as many vampires as there were humans and at night it was difficult to tell the difference between them until it was too late.

"The brothers decided it was their responsibility to rid the town of the vampires, but they knew they needed to be smart about how they did it. Angus, now as strong as Erik and the other vampires, was the logical choice to hunt them, but he needed a special blade—one that would strike true each time. Ewan undertook the task of forging it. Meanwhile, Sean used Erik's blood to make an amulet that would glow in the presence of a vampire so that Angus would not be fooled into thinking a vampire was human. There were so many vampires, however, that not even Angus could hunt them all. So a second sword was forged and Erik joined the fight."

"Did they ever find the chupacabra?" Julia asked.

"They found what they believed to be a chupacabra lair in the woods near the border of Scotland, but they never found the creature," the admiral said. "Over the years, however, there have been sightings and even a couple of run-ins with the creatures."

"You never learned where they came from?" Lanie asked.

"Remember, this was a long time ago and the brothers were afraid to commit what they knew to paper. So what I know today is what has been passed down through the generations, subject to embellishment."

Everyone watched the admiral attentively, waiting for him to continue. "Whether the creatures were aliens stranded here eons ago or prehistoric creatures that managed to survive undetected or the actual children of the gods, the chupacabra has its roots in Egyptian mythology. We know this because about a hundred years ago, a small piece of the Egyptian Book of the Dead was found. In it was a reference to the guardian of one of the twelve realms of the underworld and a picture of the chupacabra."

Lanie frowned. "I don't remember seeing that in any of my research."

"No, you wouldn't have. Erik sneaked into the dig site one night and stole it before anyone else had a chance to study it."

Dirk, who'd been quiet up until now, suddenly piped up. "Erik? Of the Original Four?"

"One and the same."

Dirk frowned. "How is that possible?"

"Because Erik, as far as I know, is still alive."

A hush fell over the room. It was Lanie who finally asked the question that Bethany was dying to ask. "Have you met him?"

The admiral shook his head. "No, but my cousin, Gerard, has. He lives in the family castle where Erik still resides." He smiled. "Gerard is a character. I hope you get a chance to meet him."

"What about Angus?" Lanie continued. "Is he still alive? Do changelings live as long as vampires?"

"No, Angus is dead. He died a long time ago. As for how long changelings live, I'm afraid I don't know the answer to that," the admiral said solemnly. "Hunting vampires has always been a dangerous occupation and over the centuries there have only been a few changelings— and I'm afraid they all died fighting vampires. It's impossible to know how long they might have lived otherwise."

Bethany saw Mac reach over and take his wife's hand, giving it a reassuring squeeze. She couldn't help but glance at Dirk, sitting there, staring at the fire, wondering what he was thinking or feeling. On the other side of the room, Julia stood up, mumbling something about making a pot of coffee. Bethany watched her leave, envying her the escape.

"If the chupacabra originated in Egypt, how did they wind up being in England and the Amazon jungle?" Bethany asked.

"I'm not exactly sure," the admiral replied. "But the family theory is that they were mistaken for statuary by the Romans when they were in Egypt. For some reason, the gargoyle figures appealed to them and as the Romans slowly conquered Europe, they took the statues with them.

"I'm sure that over the years, several of the creatures were left at various points along the way, but some clearly made it as far as England and Spain. We think the Spanish conquistadors brought the chupacabras with them to South America."

"Where the chupacabras went, they had to have left behind vampires and changelings. How come the world isn't crawling with the undead?" Mac asked.

"The story of the Original Four is just how my family got involved with slaying vampires. I assume there have been others with similar stories throughout history."

"Speaking of family," Mac said, "were you able to get in touch with your cousin about making another sword?"

"Yes. In fact, he's been working on it. He's supposed to let me know when he's finished."

The talk turned to weapons and Bethany, already feeling overwhelmed with everything she'd heard, excused herself and went to join Julia in the kitchen.

She found the other woman leaning against the counter,

staring out the back window into the night while the sound of coffee brewing filled the kitchen. "It's almost unbeliev-able, isn't it?" she commented softly, going to stand be-side the woman.

Julia glanced at her and smiled. "Yes, it is. If I hadn't seen the chupacabra for myself, I would have thought the whole thing was an elaborate hoax at my expense."

"Ignorance is bliss?"

She gave a soft laugh. "Something like that."

"I felt the same way," Bethany admitted. "Even after I saw the vampires with my own eyes. And believe me, they're not as romantic and debonair as the movies make them out to be. At least, not the ones I saw."

"Is Mac a changeling?"

Bethany turned to her, studying her face. "Dirk, too. You didn't know?"

Julia shook her head. "Charles tried to explain every-thing to me earlier today, but it was so much to take in all at once." She fell silent for a long time until Bethany thought she might have lost interest in talking. Then she asked, "Is Charles a changeling?"

"I don't think so," Bethany said honestly. "I've never heard anyone say he was, but like you, a lot of this is still new to me."

Bethany felt a chill air brush across her and folded her arms, shivering. "Do you mind if I close this?" she asked, spotting the open sliding glass door.

Julia's eyes grew round. "Oh, dear." She looked around the kitchen. "Where is she?"

"Who?"

"Gem. She followed me in here and went straight for the door. She started scratching and pawing at it, making such a terrible racket, I thought she'd break the glass. I opened the door a crack and that seemed to calm her down. She stood there, enjoying the breeze, so I left her while I made the coffee. Then I'm afraid I got lost in my thoughts, and well, I simply forgot about her." She rolled her eyes. "I'd better go after her before the others notice she's missing. They'll have my head if they find out I lost her—again." She looked worried. "I hope she hasn't wandered too far."

"Come on," Bethany said. "I'll help you look for her."

Grabbing a couple of jackets hanging inside the utility room, they put them on as they went out the back door.

She and Julia took turns calling the young chupacabra's name. When she didn't come, they widened the pattern of their search. They had wandered several hundred yards from the mansion when a whooshing sound caught Bethany's attention.

The hairs on the back of her neck rose as she pulled Julia to a stop. She glanced around and even though she didn't see anything, she knew they were there. *Vampires.*

"We have to get inside—now." Grabbing Julia's arm, she pushed her toward the house.

They hadn't gone but a few steps when a figure suddenly appeared on the lawn in front of them, blocking their path. Bethany felt her heart lurch. From this distance, she couldn't see him clearly enough to know if it was Mac or Dirk—or something far more dangerous.

She pulled Julia to a stop. "Dirk? Is that you?" she shouted.

At the figure's continued silence, she quickly looked around. He seemed to be alone. She spotted an old shed, fifty yards away. It was closer to them than the house and Bethany thought that if they could just get there . . .

A flash of movement caught her eye as the figure closed the distance between them. Bethany didn't recognize him, but she knew what he was. His eyes glowed a bright red and when he smiled, his fangs shone a pearly white. Terrified, Bethany couldn't think, couldn't move.

Then the vampire grabbed Julia and sank his teeth into her throat.

Chapter
17

As Julia went limp in the vampire's grip, Bethany snapped into action. Screaming for help, she beat at him with both fists.

Suddenly Julia was free. As she fell to the ground, the vampire's face contorted into a mask of pain. He stood as if frozen, making no attempt to seize Bethany as she bent to grab Julia and drag her off.

Then, to Bethany's shocked amazement, he collapsed to the ground and lay there unmoving.

Bethany waited for him to get up, but after several seconds, realized that he was dead—permanently dead.

With no time to figure out what had happened, she bent over Julia and saw blood covering her neck. She was in shock, but conscious.

"We can't stay here," Bethany said, casting a nervous look around. "Can you stand?"

Julia nodded and, with Bethany's help, got unsteadily to her feet. Bethany wondered if there were other vampires nearby, waiting to attack them. Suddenly the mansion seemed very far away.

"I think we need to run for the shed. It's closer. Maybe we can hide there until we know it's safe." She nodded to the structure off to the side. "Can you make it?"

"Try and keep up," Julia said bravely, though Bethany thought she looked shaken.

Grabbing her by the arm, Bethany ran. All the while, her pounding heart kept beat to the litany of prayers she sent heavenward that the shed doors were unlocked. Luck was with them.

Hurrying inside, Bethany looked around. Faint moonlight filtered through the windows provided barely enough light to see. The shed was older than she had first assumed, and larger. It might have, at one time, been used as the garage, at least until the one closer to the mansion had been built. Now, it stood empty, except for a single car, covered by a large tarp.

Jerking her attention back to the door, Bethany felt her heart sink. "There's no lock. What're we going to do?"

"What about the crowbar?"

Bethany looked to where Julia pointed and spotted the collection of tools on the counter. She grabbed the crowbar and slid it through the metal door handles, hooking it so it would stay and praying it would hold against a vampire's strength.

Turning to take stock of their surroundings, Bethany felt a sense of hopelessness. Other than a small collection of dusty mechanic's tools, there was nothing. She longed for Dirk's presence and, barring that, wished she at least had his sword.

The first impact of a body against the door tore a scream

from them both. Next they heard the sound of someone on the roof. Bethany refused to stand there helplessly while the vampires searched for a way inside. Letting go of Julia's hand, she started looking for something she could use as a weapon.

"I never expected them to be like that."

Bethany spared a quick glance at Julia, who stood with a hand pressed to her neck. "How are you?" she asked, nodding to the woman's neck.

Julia pulled her hand away. It was covered with blood. "Do you suppose they carry diseases? Like a rat?"

Bethany didn't know. "You're lucky you're still alive."

Julia grimaced. "If we get out of this alive, remind me to speak to Charles about hazard pay."

The comment struck Bethany as funny but another commotion on the roof caused her smile to fade. "I can't tell how many there are."

Julia's eyes darted to the ceiling. "It sounds like they're all around us."

"We need weapons." Bethany resumed her search.

"Do you think the others heard our shouts?"

"I'm sure they did," Bethany said with a confidence she didn't feel, not wanting to upset the woman further; needing to believe for herself that it might be true.

An incessant pounding started on the shed doors, jerking both women's attention in that direction.

"They won't hold much longer," Bethany said. "Maybe instead of looking for a weapon, we should find someplace to hide." She studied the covered car, but quickly dismissed the idea of hiding inside it. They'd be like rabbits trapped in a burrow.

She looked around. "Maybe we can hide in the back."

She pointed and together the women moved in that direction.

Bethany didn't see the spot lamp on the ground until her foot hit it. Picking it up, she wondered if it still worked. There was a fine coating of dust on it, but it wasn't as thick as the coating on some of the other items lying around.

Pulling the trigger, she quickly put a hand to her eyes. The lamp worked. The burst of light that shot out was far more powerful than any she'd come across before. It had so much candlepower, it would have turned the darkest night into the brightest day.

Wanting to save the battery, she let up on the trigger and the inside of the garage was instantly plunged into pitch-black.

For long minutes, only the sound of their breathing could be heard. Then came the sound of splintering wood as something crashed through the shed doors. Her eyes now adjusted again to the dark, Bethany stared, horrified, at the vampire standing there, silhouetted by the moonlight behind him, red glowing eyes staring out from an eerily pale face.

She shrank back, wishing she could disappear into the woodwork. A cold chill of fear raced down her spine as he looked around the garage. Then his gaze locked with hers just before he launched himself across the room, little more than a blur.

Bethany and Julia scrambled back, trying to get away as he dived across the car, his arms outstretched to grab them. Instinctively, Bethany lifted the lamp to knock him away. Her finger, still on the trigger, involuntarily tightened and the blinding light filled the room.

She waited to feel the impact of the vampire's body hitting hers; waited for the pain that would come when he ripped out her throat. Nothing happened.

The vampire seemed frozen in midflight, his arm outstretched, still reaching for her. He didn't blink. In fact, he no longer looked alive.

Taking a closer look, she noticed something odd about his appearance. His face, still very pale, now had the gritty appearance of stone. She moved the lamp's beam and noticed that wherever it touched, the vampire's skin hardened.

"I think he's turned to stone," she whispered, leaning to one side, letting her gaze travel down the length of him and saw his foot twitch. "At least, most of him has."

"It's the lamp," Julia said in an equally awed tone. Bethany cringed, wondering what would have happened had she spotlighted the lower half of his body first? Would the upper half of his body still be alive?

Just then, the lamp's light flickered. "I need to turn it off," she said. "In case we need it again." Not wanting to be near the vampire when the light went out, she and Julia moved along the space between the workbench and the car.

As they moved, so did the lamp's beam, turning more of the vampire's body into stone. As the now heavier weight of the upper torso pulled the body downward, it started to slide.

"Hurry," Bethany shouted. They had barely enough time to scramble out of the way before the vampire toppled forward. The moment his head hit the workbench, it exploded in a cloud of dust, along with part of his upper torso. Only the lower part of his body remained intact.

Bethany doused the light and the two women stood huddled together.

"Did you know that would happen?" Julia whispered.

"No," Bethany admitted.

"I thought vampires were supposed to burst into flames if the sun touched them."

Bethany shook her head. "The chupacabras turn to stone during the day. Maybe it has something to do with the candlepower of the spotlight being so high. Regular fluorescent lights don't seem to affect the vampires this way."

Julia turned suddenly and went to the workbench.

"What are you doing?" Bethany whispered to her.

"I'm looking for a weapon. If there are more of those creatures out there, I want to be prepared."

Bethany nodded. "We need a stake or knife or something like that. That's how Dirk kills them. He stabs them through the heart with his dagger."

The sound of more splintering wood caused them to look up as the roof came crashing down. Then a vampire jumped through the opening.

Boldly taking a step forward, Bethany pointed the lamp and pulled the trigger. Brilliant light flared out, momentarily stopping the creature as he threw up his arms to protect his eyes.

Bethany watched in fascination as the creature's skin thickened, taking on the rough, gritty texture, but it was happening more slowly this time, and she found herself straining to see. With a shock, she realized that the lamp was dying.

Trapped in a slow-moving nightmare, Bethany stared as the lamplight grew dimmer. Then Julia was there, swinging a crowbar like a baseball bat. When she finished her swing, the tip of the crowbar was embedded in the chest of the vampire, sinking deep into the spot where his heart was.

A look of surprise crossed the creature's face right before he crumpled to the ground, dead.

Bethany stared at Julia with something akin to shock. "You just impaled a vampire with a crowbar."

"Why, yes. I believe I did." She stopped in the process of pulling down the cuffs of her blouse and smoothing the wrinkles from her slacks to look at Bethany as if she was shocked that Bethany should be so surprised. "You did say they could be killed by stabbing them through the heart, did you not?"

A slow smile crept over Bethany's face. "Yes, I did." Her admiration for Julia went up another notch.

Still inordinately preoccupied with straightening her clothes, Julia gave her an exasperated look. "Oh, please, do stop gawking. It isn't ladylike. Now, I don't hear anything at the moment. Do you suppose it might be safe for us to make a run for the house?"

Reminded of their situation, Bethany grew serious once more. She cocked her head to listen, but like Julia didn't hear anything. "I don't know. I could have sworn I heard more than one up there. I'm afraid that if we try to leave, then they'll jump us or—" She paused to listen. "What was that?"

The faint sound of shouting could be heard outside. Bethany's heart gave a lurch of joy, quickly replaced by fear for Dirk's safety. "Dirk! Vampires!" There wasn't time for lengthy explanations and she prayed he understood.

"The old garage," she heard Mac's distant shout. Through the shattered garage doors, she caught sight of movement, then a whooshing noise. Minutes later, the sound of fighting drifted to them and waiting to learn if Dirk was safe proved too much for Bethany to patiently endure.

With parts of the garage door lying in pieces, she set the spotlight aside and searched through the debris until she found a board that wasn't too heavy to carry. The splintered end was sharp enough to be used as a stake.

She started for the door when Julia stopped her. For a second she was afraid the woman would try to talk her out of going, but instead Julia only wanted time to select a piece of wood for herself. Hers was smaller and she held it like a dagger. "Shall we?" she asked when she was ready.

The two crept slowly to the garage door, half expecting a vampire to leap out at them. When none did, they stepped outside.

The sounds of fighting grew louder as they ran up the small incline leading to the back of the mansion. As they crested the hill, both women drew to a halt. The sight before them was beyond anything Bethany could have imagined. Someone had turned on the mansion's back-yard lights and three pairs of men could be seen fighting.

Mac and Dirk were engaged in hand-to-hand combat with two vampires, moving with a swiftness and apparent strength equal to the vampires they fought. The admiral stood off a short distance, using a sword to fend off another vampire. Bethany would have thought the admiral, a mere human, would be an easy target, but she saw from the flashes of steel in the yard lights that he was holding his own.

Two vampires lay on the ground, near Mac and Dirk. Bethany couldn't help moving closer, drawn by the scene. Eyes glowing, fangs bared, they *all* looked like vampires. It seemed to Bethany that the fight would go on forever, but at that moment the admiral made a sweep of his sword. As his opponent dropped to the ground, the admiral flung out his arm and sent the sword sailing. Neither Mac nor Dirk seemed aware of it arcing toward them, but then Mac's hand shot out. In one smooth motion, he plucked the sword from the air and made a sweeping cutting motion. The vampire he'd been fighting suddenly stilled and even before the body collapsed, Mac threw the sword.

As Mac's had earlier, Dirk's hand shot out, grabbed the sword in midflight, and in a single swift lunge he buried the sword in the vampire's heart and eased the creature to the ground.

The three men stood unmoving. Bethany got the sense that they were listening, preparing for the next attack. Then she heard the admiral's voice. "Anything?"

Mac's face was tense. "I'm picking up something, but I don't know what."

Bethany's eyes met Dirk's across the distance and unable to stop herself, she ran to him. She hadn't taken four steps before he was there, pulling her to him, holding her close, his head bent forward to whisper soothing words of reassurance.

"Are you okay?" He stroked the back of her head. "I was so worried when I realized you were gone." He sighed. "Why did you go outside?"

"We were looking for Gem."

"Julia, you're hurt." Admiral Winslow hurried to the woman's side and lightly touched her neck.

"I'm fine," she assured him, although Bethany thought she looked pale.

"Where's Lanie?" Mac asked, clearly worried, looking around the yard. "She disappeared right after the two of you did—I thought she was with you."

Bethany shook her head, getting a bad feeling. "No, we haven't seen her."

Mac swore and raised his hand at the same time that Dirk tossed him the sword. He caught it and sped toward the house.

Lanie stood near the edge of the woods on the far side of the house. Every fiber of her being tingled with alarm, but she didn't move. When she'd gone into the kitchen earlier and found it empty with the door open, she'd feared the worst. About to call out to Mac, she'd seen Gem race past the back door.

Afraid she'd lose her in the night, Lanie had gone after the small chupacabra. The chase had taken them to the front of the mansion, ending at the line of trees where the appearance of the adult chupacabra brought Lanie to an abrupt halt.

Despite the tremor of fear that shot through her, she was touched. Her father had never determined the exact relationship between the adult chupacabra and Gem, however, both he and, later, Lanie, assumed the adult was Gem's mother. Even now, she nuzzled Gem as a mother would her young.

As Lanie looked on, some of her fear abated. She

knew now that the creature's attacks on Mac, Dirk, and the others had not been malicious.

How long she stood watching, she had no idea, but her awareness of the vampire when he emerged from the woods, not far from the chupacabras, was instantaneous. She knew she couldn't outrun him if he attacked, so she held very still, waiting to see what would happen.

Very slowly, perhaps not wanting to alarm her, the vampire stepped forward until Lanie saw his face.

"Harris," she gasped, staring at the tall, dark-haired vampire.

He smiled, but not enough to show his fangs. "Ms. Weber, I see you remember me."

"I'm not likely to forget the man . . . the creature . . . that almost killed me and my husband," Lanie retorted heatedly.

"Husband? Congratulations." A pained expression crossed his handsome face and then was gone. "I don't expect you to believe me, but I'm glad you're all right."

"I don't believe you. What do you want?"

He nodded to the adult chupacabra. "I came for her."

Fear for the creature lanced through her. "Please, you can't." Harris held up his hand, stanching her protests.

"I'm not going to hurt her. My interests in her are not the same as Patterson's or Burton's."

In the distance, Lanie heard Mac call her name. Her mind raced for some way to warn him of Harris's presence. The shouting grew louder and Lanie knew it was just a matter of seconds before he rounded the corner of the house and saw them.

"I'm not here to harm anyone," Harris said, as if reading her mind.

"Again, I don't believe you."

"I'm not the abomination you think I am." His gaze met hers and the look of sincerity there almost had her believing him. Then she heard Mac's approach and turned to shout a warning.

"Mac, be careful."

A rustle of leaves had her spinning back to face Harris, but he wasn't there. And neither was the adult chupacabra.

Chapter
18

"Are you sure you're not hurt?" the admiral asked, hovering over Julia like a mother hen. Despite everything they'd been through, watching the older man's clear affection for Julia made Bethany want to smile.

Julia shoved his hand aside when he brought a wet cloth up and tried to place it over the wounds in her neck, getting more water on her clothes than anything else. "Please, Charles. I assure you. I'm quite all right."

"But there's blood all over you."

"Yes, but as I've already told you, it's just a scratch really. The vampire bit me and then suddenly keeled over, dead. I mean, really dead."

"It's true," Bethany added. "I saw it."

She looked at Dirk who sat next to her at that table.

"There *was* a body out there that hadn't been staked, decapitated, or"—he cocked an eye at Bethany—"partially turned to stone. I can't explain it." Then he pinned the admiral with a look. "But I bet you can, can't you?"

Everyone turned to look at Admiral Winslow and, surprisingly, he looked embarrassed. Finally, giving up trying to help Julia, he raised his hands in defeat, placed the wet cloth on the kitchen counter, and took an empty seat at the table. "Back in the day of the Original Four, my family experimented with herbs until they created a hybrid that proved to be fatal should a vampire ingest it while drinking the blood of a human who had recently consumed this herb. It's one of the few defenses humans have against vampires, although it's not perfect. It's only effective for about twenty-four hours and, depending on the strength of the vampire, doesn't always work."

"But I've never taken anything," Julia pointed out, confused.

"I've been giving it to you." He had the decency to look embarrassed.

"How? I would have known." Then Julia narrowed her eyes at him. "The tea we've been drinking every morning?"

He nodded. "I couldn't bear the thought of anything happening to you and I couldn't think of any other way to protect you without telling you the truth, which, at the time, I couldn't do."

Julia smiled at him with such tenderness, Bethany knew the woman had already forgiven the admiral. "If that tea can kill vampires, perhaps everyone should be drinking it," she ventured.

Bethany saw the admiral sneak a sideways look at Lanie.

"Actually," Lanie said, "everyone has already been taking the herb. I've been grinding it up and mixing it in with the coffee. It's not as strong that way, but we thought it might help."

"What?" Mac sounded alarmed. "Do you think that's a good idea?" He pinned Lanie with a look. "I remember the first time the admiral tested Dirk and me, to see if we were changelings. We drank some of his blood after he'd taken the herb, but that was only a drop of blood."

Lanie blushed, but it was the admiral who responded to Mac's concern. "As long as you and Dirk are changelings and take only blood that is freely given, then the herb won't hurt you."

That answer seemed to satisfy the others, but left Bethany with a question. "If I've been protected against vampire bites this whole time—"

Dirk didn't let her finish. "The vampires after you aren't interested in biting you, Beth. They want to take you hostage and make you work for them."

"We may have another problem, now," Lanie announced, glancing at Mac, who quietly nodded, encouraging her to proceed. "When I caught up to Gem, she was with the adult chupacabra. And she wasn't alone. Harris was with her."

"Great. Now he and Patterson can rebuild their mercenary army of vampires," Dirk said with disgust.

"We'll just have to find a way to stop them," Mac replied.

"But not tonight," Lanie said, stifling a yawn. "I'm so tired, I can barely think straight." She and Mac stood and, picking up Gem, walked out of the room. Bethany watched them go, envious of the closeness the two shared.

"I think you should stay here," the admiral said to Julia.

"Thank you. I don't want to be an imposition but I would feel safer."

"No imposition at all," the admiral assured her. "I'll show you to a room."

They also walked out, leaving Bethany alone with Dirk. An uncomfortable silence fell.

"How did they find us?" Bethany asked after a while.

Dirk frowned. "It wouldn't have been that hard. Admiral Winslow used to be their C.O., just as he was Mac's and mine. I'm sure they knew Mac and I were living here and they know I'm protecting you, so . . ." He paused. "Don't worry, Beth. They won't come back tonight. We killed most of the team that showed up and now they've lost the element of surprise." He gave her a comforting smile. "You should get some sleep."

"What about you?"

He nodded. "Yeah, I'll probably try to get some rest."

Together, they rose and went upstairs. At her door, she turned to Dirk, wondering—hoping—he'd kiss her, disappointed when he didn't.

"Good night, Beth."

"Good night." It came out little more than a whisper. She hurried into her room, closed the door behind her, and fell back against it, feeling more alone than she ever had before.

Images of vampires filled her head and she hurriedly flipped on the light switch, afraid of the dark for the first time in her life. It was going to be a long night.

Heaving a sigh, she pushed away from the door, pulled off her clothes, and took the fastest shower of her life. While the rational part of her mind accepted that she was safe, her imagination ran rampant. Leaving the lights on, she climbed into bed, but didn't stretch out. Instead, she leaned against the headboard, clutching her legs to her chest, waiting for sleep to claim her.

Every little noise haunted her and it wasn't long before her nerves were strung tight. After an hour, Bethany was so tired, she wanted to cry. There was only one way she was going to get any sleep at all.

Throwing back the covers, she crept to the door of her room, pressed her ear to it, and listened. No sounds came from the other side so she opened it and looked into the hallway. It was empty of vampires, ghosts, and things that go bump in the night.

She moved quickly to Dirk's door and softly tapped on it, not wanting to wake the entire household. When there was no answer, she considered going back to her room. Instead, she tried his doorknob and found it unlocked. Slowly, she opened it and slipped inside.

His room was dark but she could hear the sound of his steady breathing. He was asleep and the thought of waking him almost made her go back.

"What are you doing here?" His voice rumbled across the darkness.

"I . . . I couldn't sleep." He didn't say anything and her courage fled. "I'm sorry. I shouldn't have bothered you." She backed toward the door, fumbling for the knob.

"Beth, come here." His voice was gentle, but firm as he held up the bedcovers and waited for her.

Ignoring the small voice of common sense that told her to return to her room, she hurried to the bed and climbed in beside him. Maybe this had been a mistake, she thought, lying so close to him that she felt his body heat reach out to envelop her.

"Relax," he whispered. "Close your eyes and go to sleep."

She wasn't sure she could, but even as she thought it, she grew drowsy.

Dirk listened to her breathing and knew the moment she fell asleep. He longed to touch her, though he hadn't, yet. He waited until he was sure she wouldn't wake up and then slipped from the bed.

He crossed the room and closed the window, still open from his late-night prowl. He locked it, now that there was no longer a need to sneak out and lurk on her balcony. Never before had the vampires come so close to the mansion. They were either daring or stupid. Either way, despite what he'd told Beth, Dirk didn't trust them not to try again.

Keeping watch on her balcony, it had been hard not to let his attention stray to the woman inside. He'd seen the fear in her eyes and regretted that he hadn't done a better job of protecting her. It had caught him off guard when she slipped out into the hallway. He'd had to move extra fast to make it back to his window, intending to slip into the hallway to follow her, never imagining that her destination was *his* room. He'd barely had time to slip under the covers and pretend to be asleep before she'd knocked and walked in.

He studied her now as she slept, feeling confused. Perhaps he'd been too hasty in judging her when he found the engagement ring. It was more likely something Miles had done—like the announcement. He knew, for a fact, that Miles had made no attempt to cancel it because he had called the paper himself. What he didn't know was why Miles refused to acknowledge it was over between him and

Beth. That bothered Dirk the most. Maybe Miles wasn't ready to give up on Bethany, hoping that she'd change her mind after spending more time with Dirk. After all, Dirk couldn't possibly offer her what Miles could.

Such thoughts were destructive and they were taking their toll. Dirk was a man of action and he didn't like not knowing where he stood with Beth. One thing he knew for sure, though, was that he was tired of doing nothing. He'd never given up without a fight and he sure as hell wasn't going to do it now. Bethany wasn't indifferent to him and she'd turned to him when she was frightened. If he and Miles were fighting to win her heart, it had been a real setback for him not to believe her. He needed to have more faith in her. Starting tomorrow, things would be different. He may have lost a battle, but he was still in the war—and he was determined to win.

Feeling better, he peeled off the clothes he still wore and climbed into bed. Bethany stirred, but he whispered soothing words to quiet her as his body spooned with hers. The feel of her pressed against him almost caused him to moan aloud, but he held himself in check. Tonight, he wanted to hold her, nothing more. Tomorrow, when they woke, he'd begin the battle to win her over.

Across town, Miles pressed a hand against the pocket of his jacket. The vial of synthetic extract was a reassuring presence and though the solution was imperfect, he intended to keep that critical piece of information to himself.

It was early morning, hours before the sun would rise. He hurried down the park path toward the rendezvous site, fear and exhilaration filling him. What he was about to do was the most dangerous thing he'd ever done and while it was not without risks, he felt the payoff would be worth it.

He reached the curve in the paved walk and stopped to let a lone jogger pass. He shook his head, musing at the effort so many people put into trying to stay young. When the jogger disappeared, Miles left the path and continued his trek across the grass, past the trees, and down a small ravine to a little used area. Here he stopped and looked around. There was no one about.

He remained there almost twenty minutes before he heard a noise come from out of the darkness.

He whirled around and saw several figures approach. "There you are. I've been waiting."

"I had other things to attend to," Kent Patterson said, not bothering to hurry his pace. His fangs were visible when he smiled and his eyes glowed eerily in the moonlight. Miles swallowed forcefully. He mustn't show fear, he told himself.

He reached into his pocket and pulled out the vial, holding it out to the vampire. "Here it is—as promised."

Patterson stepped forward, cocking an eyebrow. "Really? It's done—a perfect duplicate?"

Miles didn't even blink. "Yes."

Patterson took it and held it up. "This is different from the others you brought me?"

Again, Miles nodded.

Patterson turned to the vampires with him. "Bring me someone. I want to test it."

This was an unexpected twist that Miles wasn't prepared for, but there was nothing he could do about it. He waited, not saying a word. One thing he'd learned in business was not to fill the silence with nervous chatter—that's when mistakes were made.

They didn't have to wait long before the vampires returned, blood dripping from their mouths and carrying a middle-aged man between them. He wore blue running shorts and a white Nike T-shirt and Miles recognized the jogger he'd seen earlier. Miles couldn't tell if he was unconscious or dead until they dropped his lifeless body at Patterson's feet.

Patterson reached into his pocket and pulled out an empty syringe, which he filled with the synthetic mixture. Then he leaned over and injected it into the dead man's heart. "We won't know for a few nights if this works or not." Patterson looked at Miles. "Do you have the formula?"

It was now or never, Miles realized. "Yes, and I'll give it to you after I collect my payment."

Patterson gave him a skeptical look. "You expect me to pay you now? Before we know if the formula works?"

"The way I see it," Miles explained, "I delivered the best possible synthetic. Whether it works or not isn't my fault."

Patterson studied him for several minutes and then shrugged. "Makes no difference to me whether I pay you now or later."

A rush of exhilaration went through Miles in anticipation. This was the moment he'd been waiting for. He stared at Patterson expectantly until a blur of movement distracted him. By the time he realized that Patterson had moved, white-hot pain shot through his neck. A single coherent thought wormed its way past his shocked senses—he was dying.

Chapter 19

Bethany came awake slowly. She was warm, comfortable, and the last thing she wanted to do was get out of bed. She felt too good where she was. Like a cat, she stretched, and then froze when she felt a warm, muscled body behind her.

Opening her eyes, she recognized the inside of Dirk's room and the events of the night before came rushing back. Heat suffused her face at the memory of how she had practically come crawling to him with her nightmares and fears.

She should slip out of the bed before he woke, she realized. It was the right thing to do and yet she hesitated. It felt too wonderful to be in his arms again, for however long it might last. She closed her eyes and fell back asleep.

She awoke some time later to the feel of a hand lightly stroking the underside of her breast while lips teased the back of her neck.

"Good morning," Dirk whispered. "Or rather, good evening."

She smiled and squirmed when he hit a particularly sensitive spot. "Good evening." She let herself enjoy his touch as it both teased and aroused her. It made her think of the last time they had been together and she immediately sobered. "Dirk, thank you for letting me stay with you last night." His hand stopped moving and she hurried on, needing to get everything out before it was too late. "I was really afraid and couldn't sleep and you always make me feel safe, and . . . thank you."

"It's okay, Bethany. I'm glad you came to me."

She nodded and took a deep breath. This was the hard part, she thought. "It's just that I didn't want you to think I came down here to seduce you. I didn't want you to think I was using you again." He'd grown still and she felt mortified, humiliated. "I should go," she muttered, trying to move away from him.

He was forceful, but gentle, when he rolled her onto her back. His expression was serious when he looked down at her. His hand brushed the hair from her forehead and then the back of his fingers caressed her cheek. "How did things get so messed up?"

She traced the line of his furrowed brows with her fingertip, wanting to wipe away his worries. He captured her hand with his and brought it to his mouth where he kissed her fingertips.

"I'm sorry I doubted you. If there was some way I could make it up to you, I would—I just don't know how." His voice was gruff with emotion.

"Then let me show you." Gently, she pulled his head down and kissed him, tenderly, not wanting to assume too much. His response, however, was filled with hunger and passion, releasing her own pent-up desires until they raged out of control.

He held her to him with one arm beneath her while his other hand grazed a path from her hip to her waist and then up farther, moving beneath the fabric of her shirt. His hand molded her breast and she nearly came unglued. When he broke away long enough to pull her shirt over her head, she lifted her arms to accommodate him, gasping aloud when he wrapped the material around her arms so they were bound together.

Then his mouth was at the fleshy mound of her breast, the tips of his fangs teasing the skin. The tempo of his breathing grew faster and she knew he was fighting the temptation to bite her. The thought of his doing so should have frightened her, but it had the opposite effect and she arched into him.

"Yes," she whispered.

His fangs pierced her skin and she rode the thin line that separates pleasure and pain until the sucking motion of his mouth as he drank from her sent her crashing over the edge, into waves of ecstasy.

When he finally raised his head, his eyes shone like brilliant neon lights. She felt a small burn as he ripped her panties from her body and positioned himself between her legs. Already wet with desire, her body welcomed him eagerly and she wrapped her legs tightly around his hips as he made love to her.

Fighting against the shirt binding her arms until she rid herself of it, she clutched at his shoulders, holding on for the wild and furious ride. When her climax came again, she let the explosion take her. Moments later, Dirk went rigid above her and his primitive cry of release was music to her ears.

Much later, Bethany went downstairs alone. The truth of her situation—engaged to Miles one day and sleeping with Dirk the next—was too strange. Even she had a hard time believing it. To expect everyone else to accept it was perhaps asking too much, so she and Dirk decided to wait before revealing to the others the exact nature of their relationship.

Walking into the kitchen, she was greeted by the aromatic smells of dinner cooking.

"Hello," Julia said as she closed the oven door and placed the mitt on the counter. "Did you sleep well?"

"Yes, I did. How about you?" Bethany thought she looked tired. "I hope you didn't stay awake too long."

Julia smiled sympathetically. "No more so than you, I would imagine." She waved to the table. "Sit down. I'll bring you a cup of coffee."

"It smells wonderful in here," a smiling Admiral Winslow said as he walked in to join them. "Bethany. Julia." Bethany thought the admiral's face lit up when he turned to the older woman.

"Good evening, Charles," Julia greeted him, her own smile seeming a little brighter now. "Sit down with Bethany. I'll bring you a cup of coffee." She brought the filled cups over to the table, handing one to Bethany and the other to the admiral, then sat down with her own.

Lanie and Mac wandered into the kitchen then, smiling at each other at a shared joke. "Hello, everyone," Lanie said as she motioned Julia to remain seated while she got their coffee. Taking their cups to the table, she sat beside Mac.

"That was some adventure we had last night, wasn't it?" Mac asked. Bethany studied his face, thinking he looked particularly vibrant and alive. She was at a loss to explain it.

Then Dirk walked into the kitchen, greeting everyone with a smile, though his gaze lingered on Bethany.

"Coffee?" Julia asked him.

"No, thanks. I'm good." He smiled and took the last seat.

"Fighting vampires must agree with you and Mac," Julia observed. "I don't think I've ever seen either of you look so healthy and alive."

Mac and Lanie exchanged a quick look and then their surprised gazes flew to Dirk and Bethany, who couldn't understand why until she remembered what Dirk had told her about the effect on changelings of blood freely given—and the circumstances under which Mac usually took blood from Lanie. Then her cheeks burned with embarrassment and she couldn't bring herself to look at any of them.

Julia continued on, oblivious to the quick looks being exchanged around her. "Do you have to go into the lab tonight, Bethany? I've cooked a big meal for us. After sleeping through most of the day, I thought we needed it."

"No, not tonight. In fact, not for a while. I actually finished the project last night."

"That's great," Julia said.

The timer on the oven went off and Julia jumped up from the table. She opened the oven door and the aroma of roast beef and vegetables filled the room, making Bethany's mouth water.

"Can I help with anything," she offered, wanting to do

something that would provide some small escape from everyone's knowing look.

Julia smiled. "Why don't you set the table while I finish. Then we can eat."

Bethany stood and went to the far cabinet to get the plates. They were heavy and she moved carefully, not wanting to drop one. She'd only taken one down when two familiar arms reached around her into the cabinet. Turning her head, she looked up into Dirk's face.

"Let me help." His warm, reassuring smile as he took down the remaining plates left her feeling that everything would be okay.

Soon enough, the table was set and the food was ready. Bethany, who was dreading the meal, was pleasantly surprised when it turned out to be very enjoyable. The admiral told them more tales about the Original Four and their early exploits in vampire hunting. Then Mac, Dirk, and the admiral shared stories about some of their adventures in the SEALs. Dinner passed quickly and soon she, Dirk, Mac, and Lanie were being dismissed so Julia could do the dishes. She insisted on doing them herself, only allowing the admiral to stay and help her.

The others walked into the living room.

"Are you going out to patrol?" Lanie asked Mac.

He smiled down at her. "Not tonight. I think it would be better if we stayed closer to home. We only need to run out and check the bodies from last night, to make sure they all turned to stone."

"Great, then Bethany and I will find something on TV to watch."

"Come on, Dirk. We've been given our orders."

Dirk, who'd been standing next to Bethany as they listened to the exchange between Mac and Lanie, reached out and gave her arm a reassuring squeeze. "I'll be right back."

"Be careful," she said, a little breathless as she watched them go.

"Don't worry," Lanie said beside her. "They'll be all right. Let's go see what's on."

They went into the small television room where Lanie turned on the TV. She slowly scrolled through the on-screen guide while Bethany sat beside her.

"There's only one way a changeling gets the look that Mac and Dirk had tonight," Lanie said casually, never taking her eyes from the TV.

Bethany knew where she was headed. "I'm not cheating on Miles." She was glad to be able to tell someone. "I broke up with him the night of the awards ceremony."

Lanie looked embarrassed. "I'm sorry to pry. It's just that Dirk means a lot to me. He's like a brother and I'd hate to see him get hurt, and anyone can tell from the way he is around you that he cares about you a great deal." Then, maybe because she realized how serious and threatening she sounded, she hurried to add, "I couldn't be happier to see the two of you together."

"Thanks," Bethany said. "Do you think the others know?"

"Well, Mac knows how Dirk feels, but I don't think he knows about you and Miles. Let's hope Dirk has a chance to explain before they get into a fight."

That got Bethany's attention. "Do you really think they'd hurt one another?"

Lanie smiled. "Don't worry."

Fifteen minutes later, the door opened and Mac and

Dirk walked in. Bethany could tell from the looks on their faces that Dirk had broken the news to Mac. Both men had dirt spots on their clothes and she noticed a sprig of grass in Dirk's hair, leaving her to wonder if Dirk hadn't talked quite fast enough.

The couch was small, but the four of them fit nicely. Mirroring Mac and Lanie, Dirk sat with Bethany pulled close to his side, his arm wrapped securely about her. That was how the admiral found them an hour later.

"Excuse me." He gave them a disapproving look. "Bethany, you have a phone call in the kitchen. Dirk, perhaps I could have a word?"

Dirk helped Bethany to her feet and held her hand as they left the study. He gave her hand a reassuring squeeze before letting her go. She felt like she should stick around and help explain things to the admiral, but one glance at Dirk's face and she knew he didn't want, or need, her there.

Hurrying to the kitchen, she found where the admiral had set the cordless phone on the table and picked it up.

"Hello?"

"Hello, Bethany?"

The voice on the other end sounded familiar but it took her a second to recognize Miles's secretary. "Suzanne? Is that you? Is something wrong?"

"I'm sorry to bother you. I tried your cell phone, but it wasn't on. Mr. Van Horne said you were staying with friends. I found this number in his personal file."

"No, it's fine that you called. Is something wrong?"

"Well," she hesitated, sounding unsure. "Is he with you by any chance?"

"Who? Miles? No, I haven't seen him since yesterday."

"Oh, dear. I hope nothing has happened to him. He never came in today and I haven't heard from him."

The news was surprising. "Maybe he left a message on my cell phone—let me check." She was already rushing through the house and was breathless by the time she ran up the stairs to her room. She turned on her cell phone, but there were no messages. "I'm sorry, Suzanne. He hasn't called me."

"It's not like him to not check in," the secretary continued, clearly upset.

"I guess you've already tried his apartment?"

"Yes. I talked to the building manager and he assured me that Mr. Van Horne was not at home."

Bethany didn't know what to tell her. It wasn't like Miles to simply disappear without leaving word with someone, but usually that someone had been Bethany. Now that they were no longer engaged, there was certainly no reason for him to inform her of his plans.

"Did you call his family?"

"I tried, but they're still in Europe."

"Maybe we should call the police," Bethany finally suggested.

"I already tried, but there's no reason to suspect foul play. Until there is, there's nothing they can, or will, do."

"I guess we don't have much of a choice. We'll just have to wait and hope he shows up."

"I don't like it," Suzanne complained. "It's not like him."

"I know. I'm not happy about it either, but I don't know what to tell you."

Suzanne promised to stay in touch and then hung up. Bethany returned to the TV room. Dirk had obviously finished his conversation with the admiral and was waiting for her.

"Problems?" he asked as she sat next to him.

Deciding that Miles was already a tender subject with him, she thought it best not to say anything. "No, just someone at the lab double-checking something. Everything's fine." She gave him what she hoped was a reassuring smile. "How about here? Everything okay?"

His expression darkened very slightly. "Nothing you need to worry about."

She didn't like the sound of that, but decided not to press. Instead, she turned her attention to the show on TV.

It was nearly dawn when the four of them finally called it a night and retired. Dirk and Bethany went back to his room where he spent a good part of the early dawn making love to her.

They finally fell asleep and woke up much later to the sound of someone pounding on the door. Bethany groaned, wanting to hide beneath the covers. She felt like a teenager caught in her boyfriend's bed by her dad.

"Dirk, wake up," the admiral barked through the door.

"I'm awake," Dirk growled back. "Hell, the whole house is awake. What's the matter?"

"Phone call."

Bethany saw Dirk rub his face. "Take a message. I'm sleeping."

"It's not for you."

Bethany did groan then.

"Stay here," Dirk said, throwing back the covers. He pulled on his jeans and walked to the door, bare-chested, hair rumpled from sleeping. Bethany thought he'd never looked sexier.

He opened the door a crack, reached through, and took the phone. Then, closing the door behind him, he brought it to her.

"Hello?"

"Bethany, this is Suzanne again. It's almost four and I still haven't seen or heard from Mr. Van Horne. He missed all his appointments. I'm really worried now."

Bethany cast a worried glance at Dirk. He wouldn't like it, but she knew he'd help her. "All right, Suzanne. I'll go by his place and see what I can find out. If we haven't heard from him by morning, then you should call the police again."

"Thank you, Bethany. I've felt so lost these last two days."

Bethany disconnected the call and looked up to find Dirk watching her carefully. "Miles hasn't been seen for two days. His secretary is worried and frankly now, so am I. This isn't like him. I think he might be in real trouble."

"Why, because he took some time off for a couple of days without telling anyone?"

"Yes, as a matter of fact. Someone like Miles, who owns a large business and has social obligations, doesn't just disappear."

"Maybe he needed a vacation."

"But going off without telling someone?"

Dirk shrugged. "The man has a right to disappear if he wants to."

"But it's not like him."

Dirk's gaze burned. "Yeah, and you know him so well, right?"

The retort cut deep and she clenched her teeth together so she wouldn't react to the hurt. "No, you're right. Lately, I seem to be a terrible judge of character, but you know what? If you disappeared for two days, I'd worry about you, too."

She struggled to get out of bed, pulling the sheets off to cover herself. She'd barely taken a step before Dirk was there in front of her.

"I'm sorry, Beth. It's just—" He paused and Bethany filled in the blanks herself.

"Miles made you doubt me? No, I don't think so. It was easier to think I was using you than risk letting me get too close."

She held her breath and waited for his denial, but it didn't come. Instead he nodded. "You may be right. I'll help you look for him."

She couldn't believe it. "Really?"

"Beth, you know I don't like the guy and if there was any way in the world I thought I could convince you to stay here, I'd do it. But I know you'll just sit here and worry. And God help me, I don't want you being with me, but thinking about him."

She let the sheet fall to the floor as she wrapped her arms around his neck. "Thank you. I'll let you in on a little secret." She pulled him closer so she could whisper in his ear. "It doesn't matter who I'm with or what I'm doing, you're the only one I ever think about."

Chapter
20

I t was after dark when Bethany and Dirk finally left the mansion and they had just reached the city limits when Bethany's cell phone rang. Looking at the caller ID, she frowned.

"Miles, are you all right? Where have you been? Suzanne and I have been worried sick about you."

"I'm sorry, my dear," he said, sounding fine. "Some unexpected business came up and I was temporarily away. I'm sorry if I worried you, although to be honest, I'm touched that you were."

"Of course, I was worried about you. We're friends— at least I hope we are." She sighed. "Well, if you're okay, then I guess we can go back."

"Go back? Where are you?"

"On our way to your place, to check on you."

"I'm touched. Let me make it up to you—how about dinner?"

Bethany looked at Dirk, certain he'd heard Miles's

offer through the phone. She knew she was right when he shook his head.

"I don't think so," she began.

"Drinks, then—or is Mr. Adams so insecure that you can't even share a drink with an old friend?"

Bethany saw Dirk grip the steering wheel tighter, but he didn't say anything. She wasn't that interested in meeting Miles for drinks, but she was curious to know what had happened to him, because it really wasn't like him to disappear like that with no word to anyone. She made up her mind.

"A drink sounds good, Miles. Where should we meet you?"

Dirk found a place to park outside the bar and grill. He wasn't thrilled to be there and didn't trust Miles at all. To make matters worse, the minute they'd pulled into the lot, Dirk had started to pick up what he privately referred to as "a disturbance in the force"—something bleeding through to him on the psychic link. It was difficult to know what it was, but his senses were on full alert for another vampire attack.

With his hand at the small of her back, Dirk guided Beth to the door, feeling only marginally safer once they were inside. Miles was already seated, waiting for them, and rose when they approached.

"Did you have any problems getting here?" he asked politely as they all sat.

"No," Dirk replied tersely.

"Good." Miles raised his hand to summon the waiter to take their drink orders. "Isn't this nice?" he asked after the waiter left. Dirk wanted to physically wipe the smile from the man's face, but refrained.

"Bethany, I'm glad I got hold of you. Santi was disappointed with the results, but he did pay for the work you did." He looked at Bethany expectantly.

"That's great, Miles," she congratulated, glancing at Dirk, who kept his expression carefully neutral. Half his attention was still focused on the uncomfortable feeling slipping through the link. Instead of it going away as he'd hoped, it had gotten worse, making Dirk wonder if he'd made a mistake in bringing Beth here.

"There are a couple of pieces of new equipment that would be nice to have," Bethany was saying, unaware of Dirk's inner turmoil.

Miles smiled at her. "Excellent suggestion. Maybe you could put together a list and send it to me to review?"

She nodded. "I'd be happy to."

Their drinks arrived then and they opted not to order dinner, much to Dirk's relief. When the waiter left, Miles pulled a paper roll from a briefcase on the floor beside his chair.

"What's that?" Bethany asked.

"It's the blueprint for the new offices I'm thinking of having built."

"Really? Miles, that's so exciting."

"Isn't it?" He smiled as he unrolled the paper in front of her, then scooted his chair closer to hers, so they could both study the pages. He pointed out various aspects of the drawing, but his arm kept bumping into Bethany.

"I'm sorry," he mumbled, finally putting his arm on the back of her chair under the pretense of getting it out of her way.

Dirk didn't like it, but Bethany shot him a look, more or less begging him not to make an issue of it, so instead he downed the contents of his drink and ordered another, praying she'd hurry so they could get out of there.

After what seemed an eternity to Dirk, Miles raised his glass and said, "A toast." He waited until Bethany and Dirk raised their glasses before continuing. "To a bright future and the woman who made it all possible."

Bethany blushed and Dirk wanted to throw up. Surely she saw how transparent Miles was in his attentions? He set his glass down without taking a sip, noticing that even though Miles had raised his glass to his lips, he hadn't actually taken a drink, which Dirk found odd.

Dirk's psychic senses were fairly screaming in alarm now and he scanned the room, looking for the source of it. He felt certain the dark, evil prickling was coming from a vampire, but he didn't know where the creature lurked.

"Thank you, Bethany," Miles said, setting down his glass and reaching for her hand. "I knew you could do it. I've always said we make a great team."

He gave her hand an affectionate squeeze, not bothering to let go. Dirk stared pointedly at their joined hands, feeling his temper skyrocket. Bethany took one look at his face and then excused herself, using the pretense of needing to go to the ladies' room.

Dirk watched her disappear through the crowd, tempted to follow her, to make sure she was safe.

"She's not much in bed, is she?"

The question, as well as the cold, calculating tone coming from Miles, caught Dirk by surprise. "Excuse me?"

Miles gave him a tolerant smile. "Oh, don't get me

wrong. She's a beautiful woman and a brilliant scientist. With her on my arm, I'll be the envy of my peers—and as my wife, her research will keep Van Horne Technologies a financially viable institution for a long time. That's why I don't mind postponing the wedding."

Dirk wondered what game Miles was playing now. "Beth isn't going to marry you."

"Is that what she told you? I'll admit that I was a little put off when she said she wanted to have her fun before getting serious, but like I said, she's worth the wait." He shrugged. "Besides, anything you teach her in bed only benefits me, doesn't it?" He paused, giving Dirk an apologetic half smile. "I hope you weren't getting too attached. You two never really did have a future together. To her, you're nothing more than a phase—a playful interlude, so to speak."

Dirk sat there, wanting nothing more than to beat the shit out of the man, yet there was that small voice in his head that wondered how much of what Miles said might be true. Bethany returned at that moment and Miles stood up to hold her chair. After she sat, he placed his hands on her shoulders and began to massage them.

Dirk fought to control the raging inferno inside as he carefully folded his napkin and stood up. "Time to go."

He could tell the announcement surprised Beth. She glanced anxiously at Miles and he braced for her refusal, but then she grabbed her purse and deftly slid out from under Miles's touch.

"Good night, Miles. I'm glad you're all right," she said, standing. "Be sure to call Suzanne, okay?" she added, walking around the table to stand next to Dirk, who reached into his pocket and pulled out enough cash to pay for his and Beth's drinks. Then, putting his arm around Bethany's waist, he escorted her from the restaurant.

"What was that all about?" she asked the moment they were outside.

Dirk had to give her credit for waiting. The question he wrestled with was how much to tell her. If he told her the truth, she might not believe him. Worse than that, if she did, Miles's comments would crush her and Dirk didn't want to hurt her, not that the old man didn't deserve to lose her friendship.

He used the time it took to climb into the SUV, start the engine, and pull out of the parking lot to think about what he'd say. Finally, he made his decision.

"Do you remember me telling you about the psychic link that Mac and I share through the adult chupacabra?" he asked her.

"The link shared by all those attacked by the same chupacabra? Sure, but I thought you said it was more or less defunct."

"It has been, but every now and then, I pick up something through it. It's like watching TV with really bad reception. Mostly you get snow and white noise, but once in a while, it clears up enough that you can get a signal."

"And tonight, during drinks, you got a signal, so to speak?"

"Yes, and the longer we were there, the worse it got. I was afraid that we were about to face another attack and I wanted to get you out of there before it happened."

She seemed to weigh his words and then Dirk thought he saw her relax as she leaned back and stared out the front windshield. "I was afraid that you and Miles had gotten into it; that maybe he'd said something. I'm glad that's not the case."

They drove along in silence, each lost in their own thoughts.

"Are you hungry?" she asked. "We could stop someplace and grab a bite?"

"Not tonight. I think we'd better eat at the mansion."

"Still picking up a signal on the link?"

He smiled. "Yeah. If there's another attack coming, I'd just as soon be at home where I have a better chance of beating them."

Julia, who was turning out to be an accomplished chef, had once again cooked dinner. Bethany and Dirk arrived back at the mansion in time to join Julia and the admiral for dinner. Mac and Lanie had gone out, wanting to spend time alone.

They were almost through with their meal when Dirk's cell phone rang. He frowned when he saw Detective Boehler's number on the caller ID.

"Dirk here."

"Dirk, it's John. I've got a body you might want to take a look at."

"Now's not a good time," Dirk said, not wanting to leave Beth at the mansion unprotected.

"This one you'll want to see," John replied. "We found it outside of Miles Van Horne's apartment."

Dirk glanced at Beth, then stood up and walked out of the kitchen, going into the living room where he could talk without being overheard.

"Dirk?" John asked when he'd been silent for too long.

"Yeah, I'm here. Who's the victim? It's not Van Horne, is it?"

"No, some John Doe. We're checking missing persons now. I thought that you might want to see it, since you're already watching his fiancée. The two might be related."

Dirk didn't bother telling John that Bethany and Miles were no longer engaged. It didn't have any bearing on the situation. "What about Van Horne? Was he home at the time?"

"No. In fact, we haven't located him yet. The manager said he'd been gone for the last two days but the man couldn't say where. Hell, I don't even know if he's in town."

"He is. I just saw him an hour ago."

"Where?"

Dirk gave him the address.

"Okay. I'll send a car over there now. What about you?"

"On my way." He hung up and went back into the kitchen. "I've got to go out for a while," he told the others.

"Problems?" the admiral asked. "Maybe I should come with you?"

"No, just a John Doe. I can handle it. I need you to stay here." He gave the admiral a meaningful look.

The older man glanced at Bethany and nodded.

Dirk then turned to Bethany. "Walk me to the door?"

She rose and followed him out of the kitchen. He stopped in the foyer to double-check the dagger in its sheath at his waist. When he was ready, he placed his hands on her shoulders, needing to see the emotions reflected in her eyes when he talked to her.

"I'm sorry—I have to go. Hopefully, it won't take

long. While I'm gone, don't, under any circumstances, go outside, okay?"

She stared at him with her impossibly green eyes, worry marring the delicate features of her face. "Be careful. I . . ." It seemed like she wanted to say more, but settled instead for, "Be careful, okay?"

He smiled and kissed her good-bye. Before he could get distracted, he turned and left.

It took twenty minutes to reach Van Horne's apartment building and Dirk spent the entire trip wondering why, all of a sudden, the vampires should have an interest in Miles.

Once there, he took the elevator to the top, flashed his ID to the uniformed officers on guard, and walked down the hall. He knew right away which door was Van Horne's; the body still lay slumped against it. Dirk went to take a closer look.

The deceased appeared to be a man in his mid-thirties. He wore blue jogging shorts and a white Nike T-shirt. Aside from the two puncture wounds in his neck, there wasn't anything overtly different about this body compared to the other vampire victims Dirk had seen. A typical vampire kill. And yet . . .

"What do you think?" John asked, coming up to stand behind Dirk. "Just a coincidence that this man, who's not a tenant of the building, should be found here at this particular door? Or is someone trying to send Van Horne a message?"

Dirk peeled off the gloves he'd used to examine the body and stood up. "I think we both know the answer to that. The question is—what's the message?"

"Maybe they gave up trying to kidnap the fiancée and are going for Van Horne himself."

"But why? That doesn't make sense. Van Horne may own and run a research firm, but he's no biochemist."

"Maybe they were never after a biochemist. Which reminds me, we found Stuart Meyers's body."

"You did?"

"Yeah, earlier today. Same M.O., more or less. Looked like he'd been dead longer, though. Some of his extremities had withered and dried—I've never seen anything like it. The body's at the morgue if you want to swing by and look at it."

Dirk nodded. "I will." He glanced up at the detective. "You mind if I have a few more minutes alone here?"

"Suit yourself." John shrugged. "We're done."

Dirk waited until he walked off before pulling out the small wood stake he'd put in his pocket. He kept a supply of them in his SUV for just such emergencies. He lifted the victim's shirt so he had a clear view of the man's chest and drove the wood deep into the dead man's heart. It would have been difficult to do if he'd been only human, but he wasn't. He would have preferred to haul the body back to the mansion and decapitate it, but too many people had seen this one for it to just disappear. He'd have to be satisfied with staking it. He took some small solace from knowing that the creatures he'd staked the other night at Nicolette's hadn't risen after being stabbed through the heart.

Finished with that chore, he turned his thoughts to Miles. It made no sense that the vampires were now targeting the man and Dirk couldn't help but wonder if there was something he was overlooking. Still troubled, he walked into Miles's apartment to find the detective.

"Still no sign of Van Horne," John informed him, closing his cell phone.

Dirk thought about it. "I'll stay here and wait for him, in case someone shows up to deliver another message."

John thought about it, then nodded. "Okay. I guess we're done. I'll give the master key back to the manager. Be sure to lock up after we leave—and call if Van Horne—or anyone else—shows up."

Bethany sat at the kitchen table, absently playing with her cup of coffee as she worried about what Dirk was doing.

"He'll be okay."

Bethany stared at the admiral blankly, so focused on her thoughts that his words didn't, at first, register. Then she nodded. "I know."

Just then, Mac and Lanie came walking in.

"Where have you two been?" Julia asked.

"We went to dinner and then for a walk," Lanie answered as they joined the others at the table.

"Really? Where'd you go?" the admiral asked, politely interested.

"The zoo."

Julia looked confused. "It's after hours, isn't it closed?"

"Yes, that's why we went." Lanie dug in her purse and pulled out a folded newspaper. "I found this story in today's paper, see?" She held the paper out so Julia and the admiral could read the article she indicated. "Several goats at the petting zoo were found dead this morning.

You can see from the picture here that it looks like they were bitten on the neck. I wondered . . .''

As Lanie went on, Bethany's thoughts returned to Dirk. She stared absently at the back of the newspaper until something about a photo there caught her attention. The orange color of the man's hair stood out, making it easy to identify Mr. Santi.

Curious what the story was about, she stared at the upside-down caption until she made out the words. Trepidation filled her. "May I see that?" she asked Lanie, already reaching out for the paper.

"Uh, sure," Lanie said, handing it to her. "Is everything all right?"

"I'm not sure." Bethany read the article. Juan Santi, second in command of one of the largest East Coast drug rings, was dead of a gunshot wound sustained during a drug deal gone bad, the police believed.

"Bethany, what's the matter?"

Feeling dazed, Bethany showed the article and photo to the others. "This is the drug rep Miles has been doing business with. He must have lied to Miles about who he worked for."

She pushed away from the table and hurried to the phone. "Miles has no idea what he's involved in." Quickly dialing Miles' cell phone number, she waited for him to answer, which he did on the third ring.

"Miles, it's Bethany."

"What's the matter, you sound upset?" He paused. "Does this have anything to do with earlier, because I don't know what Adams may have told you, but—"

"No, no. It doesn't have anything to do with Dirk. Where are you? Are you safe?"

"Yes, I'm fine."

"Where are you?"

"I'm just walking into my apartment building, why?" He sounded confused.

"Have you seen today's paper?"

"No, not yet. I thought I might look at it tonight."

"Well, there's a story in there about Mr. Santi."

"Really?" He didn't sound particularly upset.

"Miles, he's dead. Mr. Santi is dead—and that's not the worst of it. He was a major drug dealer."

There was silence on the other end, then she heard Miles swear softly. "How was he killed?"

"He was shot. The police think it was a drug deal gone bad." She thought she heard Miles's sigh of relief and worried that he wasn't taking this seriously. "If the murderers know you were helping him develop a new drug, even if you did it unknowingly, you could be in trouble, too."

"Calm down, Bethany, everything will be fine. Look, I'm at my apartment. Hang on while I unlock my door. Then we can finish discussing this."

She heard the sound of his key in the door and then—

"What the hell . . . ?"

The phone went dead and Bethany stared at it, trying to figure out what had happened. She hit auto redial, but instead of ringing through, it rolled over into Miles's voice mailbox. Her mind conjured hundreds of scenarios to explain the abruptness with which the call ended—all of them tragic.

Dumbfounded, she hung up.

"Bethany, what's wrong?" Lanie asked.

She turned to look at the others. "The phone went

dead. He was in the middle of talking and then . . . it just went dead." She started wringing her hands together, unable to stop. "Can I borrow someone's car—please."

No one moved and Bethany grew desperate. "Please, I'm afraid someone might be trying to kill him."

"I'll go." Mac pushed away from the table. "I can't let you go if there really is trouble."

As he started walking to the door, Bethany snatched her purse from the counter and hurried after him. "If you think you're leaving me behind, you've got another think coming."

Mac stopped in the hall and turned to face her. "I don't think so."

"I'm going, too," Lanie said, joining Bethany.

"Now wait just a damn minute," Mac protested as the admiral appeared.

"You kids can argue in the car, let's go. I'm driving. You coming, Julia? There's safety in numbers."

"What the hell are you doing here?"

"I've been waiting for you," Dirk said coldly, sitting in the shadows of Miles's apartment.

"Have you now?" Miles tossed his phone onto a nearby counter and sauntered into the room, clearly unperturbed to have found an unwanted visitor waiting for him. "And why would that be? Did you want to continue our earlier conversation?"

"I don't think that will be necessary. I'm here for another reason."

"Really?"

Dirk stood so he could face Miles as the older man

walked about the room. "I know what you're up to and I can't let you get away with it."

"And I suppose you plan to stop me?"

"Yes, I do."

"I'd like to see you try," Miles snarled. In the dim lighting of the room, his eyes glowed a vibrant red and when his lips curled upward, Dirk saw the two newly formed fangs.

Chapter
21

M iles hissed and then frowned. "You don't look surprised."

"I'm not," Dirk admitted. "I've been hunting vampires for a while now; you might say I have a sixth sense for them. I'll admit that you had me fooled at the restaurant. I kept sensing a vampire, but I didn't expect it to be you."

Miles shrugged. "Your reaction is a bit disappointing but I suppose it makes sense. On the night of the attack at the lab, I saw Frank's body. I knew the police called you in because you knew something about vampires."

Another piece of the puzzle fell into place for Dirk. "You've been working with Patterson and Harris all along, haven't you?" He mentally kicked himself for not having seen it earlier.

"Of course," Miles readily admitted.

"And the plant extract Beth's been trying to duplicate?"

"Chupacabra venom."

Dirk was relieved it wasn't biotoxin, but still, he was

confused. "If Beth was already working on duplicating the venom, then why did Patterson and Harris try to kidnap her?"

Miles's face clouded over. "I never meant for that to happen," he admitted. "Patterson felt her research was going too slow; that she was purposely dragging her feet. He thought if he had her at his lair, he might persuade her to work more quickly."

"And you did nothing to try and stop them?" Dirk felt his anger grow. "We won't pretend that what you felt for her was love, but don't you at least care a little about her?"

Miles had the decency to look insulted. "Of course I cared about her. I was going to marry her, wasn't I?"

"You used her. I should kill you for that alone," Dirk spit out.

Miles circled the room, taking slow casual steps, and Dirk continued to move with him. Eventually, Dirk knew he'd have to fight the older man, but not yet. He didn't have all his answers yet. "What are you getting in return for helping the Primes?"

"I get immortality," Miles said proudly, gesturing to himself. "And a percent of the profits when we sell Immortality on the street."

"Not a lot of repeat business in that, is there?"

"At the price Patterson plans to sell it, we don't need repeat business."

"Only one problem," Dirk said, confused. "I thought Beth wasn't able to duplicate the venom."

"True, but I was never in it for the money."

"I suspect Patterson and Harris are, so I can't help but wonder why they agreed to convert you before you delivered the goods?" Then the light went on. "You gave them the stuff Beth was working on and told them it worked."

Miles cocked an eyebrow and smiled.

"And they didn't test the drug for themselves?"

"Of course they did, but as I'm sure you know, it takes a couple of nights."

Dirk shook his head. "You have no idea whom you're dealing with, do you?"

"I don't really care. I got what I wanted. By the time they figure it out, I'll be long gone." There was arrogance in his tone that wouldn't have been there if he really understood what was going on.

"That's your first mistake." Miles raised a curious brow, so Dirk went on. "The police found a body against your door earlier this evening. Middle-aged man, blue jogging shorts, white T-shirt. Sound familiar? From the looks of him, he'd been killed a couple of days ago. He'd converted, but then something went wrong. That body will never rise again. I'd say Patterson already knows your drug doesn't work."

Miles was silent for a moment, seeming lost in thought. Then, as if remembering that he wasn't alone, he turned to Dirk. "Well, I appreciate the information. I guess I'll have to leave town a little sooner than expected."

"I don't think so."

Miles's eyes blazed brighter and he gave a bark of laughter. "What? You think you're going to stop me? You are nothing compared to what I am."

"That's your second mistake," Dirk replied. He gave his anger and hatred for the man free rein. His vision bled to red and his lips instinctively curled back to reveal his fangs. He saw Miles's eyes widen in surprise. "If it's a fight you want, let's do it."

The ride to Miles's apartment was a silent one, except for Bethany giving the admiral directions as he drove. Even though he pushed the upper bounds of the speed limit, it still took twenty minutes to reach the building. The doorman tried to stop them, but the admiral held up some sort of badge Bethany had never seen before and they were allowed to continue.

They stepped on the elevator and Bethany wanted to scream as it slowly carried them to Miles's floor. As soon as the doors opened, she rushed down the hall, heedless of Mac's order to let him go first. They reached the door to Miles' apartment and found it slightly ajar. From inside came the sound of a man's cry followed by the dull thump a body makes when it falls to the floor.

With no thought other than to save Miles, Bethany burst into the room.

The sight that met her was so horrifying that she stopped short and stared, openmouthed. Before her, on the ground, lay Miles' body with Dirk poised over it; eyes glowing red, breathing hard, rivulets of blood running down his arms from myriad scratches—and his hand still gripping the dagger buried to the hilt in Miles' chest.

Dirk slowly became aware that he was no longer alone in the apartment. Looking up, he saw Mac, the admiral, Lanie, Julia, and Bethany standing just inside the door. Their shocked expressions of horror were understandable. The condemnation he saw was not.

"You killed him?" Bethany's voice was barely more than a whisper of sound.

"Bethany . . ." he started to explain, taking a step toward her only to stop when she shied away.

He looked at Mac and the admiral. Both men wore grim expressions of confusion and something worse, disappointment. He knew what they were thinking. In a jealous rage, he'd lost control and killed an innocent old man. They weren't interested in knowing what happened and suddenly Dirk was a teenager again, found guilty without consideration for the truth.

It had been the story of his life for so long, he should have been used to it. Their censure should come as no surprise and certainly shouldn't cause the pain and hurt it did. Seeing Bethany's confusion and horror, her fear of him, was the cruelest blow of all.

He had to get away. Giving them a defiant glare, he brushed past them, unfettered.

Bethany watched him go as grief and horror warred with confusion, leaving her in a type of shock. Miles was dead. Dirk had killed him. Those were the only thoughts she seemed capable of and her mind replayed them over and over. She knew Miles and Dirk had hated each other, but would hate have been enough reason for Dirk to kill Miles?

Finally, a single new thought pierced through her mental fog. No. Irrefutably, no. Dirk might be many things, but he was not a cold-blooded murderer.

In her mind's eye came the image of Dirk's expression when he'd seen them standing there. The hurt that flashed across his eyes tore at her heart and she knew he thought they blamed him.

Pushing past the others, she raced for the elevators, stabbing the button for the lobby repeatedly until the doors closed.

"A man just came this way," she said breathlessly to the doorman when she reached the front of the building. "Tall, blond hair, wearing a black duster. Which way did he go?"

The doorman pointed.

"Thanks." She rushed out the door, heading in the direction the doorman indicated. The night air was cool, but she didn't notice. A few cars were on the streets and the pedestrian traffic at this time of night was light. She scanned the sidewalk ahead of her, but saw no sign of Dirk.

Hoping the doorman had steered her in the right direction, she picked up her pace. After going several blocks, she spotted him in the distance. She ran, hollering for him to stop, afraid that even if he heard her, he wouldn't listen.

Desperate, she ran faster, closing the distance, and almost slammed into him when he suddenly whirled around to confront her. "What the hell do you think you're doing? You shouldn't be out here." He looked beyond her. "Where's Mac?"

"Back at the apartment," she panted.

"You came out here by yourself?" He was yelling now, but she knew his anger stemmed from his concern for her safety.

"I'm not by myself, I'm with you."

He gave a derisive snort. "Yeah, and we both know how safe that is, right?"

"I'm willing to take my chances." She searched his

face for some sign of what he was feeling. "You're not a cold-blooded murderer."

"Don't kid yourself, Beth. I didn't find him dead; I sank my dagger into his chest. The man you were going to marry, I just stabbed through the heart. Don't tell me that doesn't bother you."

She flinched at the hurt and anger in his tone as much as from his words. "I'd like to know what happened," she admitted softly. "But you're wrong about one thing. I wasn't going to marry Miles. I didn't love him." She hesitated, gazing into his eyes, willing him to believe her. "I do, however, love you."

Dirk stood there, shell-shocked. No one had told him that before; no one who'd meant it. "Beth." He breathed out her name as if it were a prayer, grabbed her to him and kissed her. She was his life's blood, his reason for living. He savored the feel of her body and in her arms he found sanctuary and peace. He wanted to tell her how much he loved her, but having never spoken the words before, they stuck in his throat.

"Isn't this romantic?" a snide voice spoke from the darkness.

Dirk froze. "Patterson," he spat out, lifting his head to look around. In doing so, he saw they were surrounded by vampires and knew he had failed to do the one thing he'd vowed to do—keep Beth safe.

Dirk felt at his belt, belatedly remembering where he'd left his dagger. It made him think of the others. Mac wouldn't have allowed Bethany to race out unprotected; he had to be close. All Dirk had to do was stall for time. "What do you want?" he asked the Prime.

"I would think that would be obvious by now, Adams," Patterson said with a smile.

"You're not getting Bethany without going through me." Dirk pushed her behind him, hoping to protect her.

Patterson laughed. "How very noble of you, and yet, totally naive. I have twenty fresh recruits. Do you suppose you can beat them all? Do you think you can beat *me*?"

Dirk knew he couldn't take them all, so he changed tactics. "You don't need her. The venom can't be duplicated."

Patterson shook his head. "No, I don't believe that. Van Horne simply didn't know how to properly motivate his employees."

"What does Miles have to do with this?" Bethany asked quietly from behind Dirk. "What venom?"

Patterson looked at Dirk in surprise. "You didn't tell her how her fiancé was using us all?"

"What?" Dirk heard the disbelief in her voice.

"That's right," the vampire continued. "The night we took Stuart wasn't our first attempt to kidnap a biochemist. The night we kidnapped Van Horne was." He gave a half laugh. "You can imagine our disappointment when we learned he wasn't a scientist at all, merely a wealthy businessman—but one, it seems, with high ambition."

Bethany gasped and Dirk wished he could have spared her the truth, but if it bought them more time, he hoped Patterson continued to talk.

"From the beginning, Van Horne was only interested in what he could gain for himself," Patterson continued. "He convinced us that his research facility could duplicate the venom; that his fiancée was a brilliant scientist and unquestionably devoted to him. I assume he meant you." He gave her a mocking smile.

"The plant extract?" she asked.

Patterson shook his head. "It wasn't plant extract. It was chupacabra venom."

"But why would Miles offer to help?" she asked.

"Not for money. A man like that—wealthy, powerful, in the autumn of his life—only wants one thing, but what the hell. Who am I to deny him? If he kept his word, I intended to keep mine. I told him my plans to sell the venom on the black market and he offered to work with the distributor I'd already lined up."

"Mr. Santi."

"Yes. Fortunately for me, drug dealers don't care much about the nature of their clients, as long as they get paid. Mr. Santi overlooked my vampire status when I presented him with the opportunity to distribute my drug. He acted as an intermediary, delivering my messages to Van Horne and bringing the samples that Van Horne took from the lab so we could check the progress of your work. Two nights ago, Van Horne brought me the finished product himself."

"But I never—"

Patterson held up his hand to stop her. "I am not that gullible, Ms. Stavinoski. When Van Horne demanded payment for the duplicated venom, I paid him."

"By killing him," Dirk said.

"By giving him the immortality he sought," Patterson corrected.

"Immortality with a catch," Dirk clarified.

Patterson didn't bother to hide his fangs when he smiled.

"What do you mean?" Beth asked.

It was Dirk who answered her. "Miles wanted to be a Prime, but only a chupacabra can do that. Patterson didn't have the adult, did you, Patterson? You killed him yourself."

Patterson merely smiled.

"Miles rose tonight as a vampire, but he probably only had about two to four weeks before he lost all traces of his human self and became nothing more than a bloodthirsty brainless creature, living from one victim to the next."

"That's why you killed him," she mumbled to herself, though Dirk heard her.

"It's time to go," Patterson announced. "I'll come back later to deal with Van Horne, personally."

"Don't bother," Dirk replied. "I just killed him."

Patterson seemed surprised, but then he shrugged. "Whatever. It saves me the trouble. Now, let's go."

Dirk glanced at the vampires surrounding him. It was now or never. Mac wasn't going to reach them in time.

He waited until the first vampire came for them, staying close to Beth, afraid one of them might grab her while he was busy fighting the others.

The battle was over almost before it began as Patterson and his team jumped Dirk and bore him to the ground, fighting all the way.

Chapter 22

After what seemed an interminably long trek through the city, Dirk and Bethany were taken to a grated covering that blocked the entrance to the underground sewage system.

"Interesting location you have here," Dirk muttered as they were hauled along the sewer pipelines where the essence of raw sewage assaulted their senses. He was sure the rancid smell might just finish the job the vampires had started on him.

"Are you still alive, Adams?" Patterson joked. "Do you like this? It may not look or smell like much, but it has the advantage of being the last place anyone would think to search."

"What do you plan to do with us?" Dirk asked.

Patterson laughed. "Ms. Stavinoski, of course, will be put to work in the lab. I think you'll be impressed with the setup we have. Much of the equipment was collected while

Dr. Weber was with us, but we've made a few additions, thanks to the suggestions of Mr. Meyers."

"Stuart's here?" Bethany asked.

Patterson looked at her. "Not any longer. It seems that the venom he synthesized wasn't as perfect as he believed when he volunteered to test it."

"More like he was volunteered," Dirk clarified.

"What's the difference? The venom didn't work and now he's dead—permanently."

"I won't do it," Bethany told Patterson. "I won't analyze the venom."

The Prime seemed unconcerned. "My dear, you will hardly have a choice," he said too calmly, extending a finger so his sharp talonlike nail was visible. He moved close to Dirk and pressed the tip against Dirk's throat. Slowly, he drew the nail across the surface, just deep enough that Bethany saw a line of blood well to the surface and trickle down his neck.

"Stop!" she cried in horror. She would have gone to Dirk's side, but two of the vampires held her back.

"Don't agree to anything," Dirk told her, straining futilely against his own guards. "Nothing, do you hear me?"

Patterson leaned forward and, despite Dirk's efforts to get away, licked the blood from Dirk's skin before turning to Bethany. "I want the formula and be assured that I will test each vial you make. If it doesn't work exactly as I expect, then Adams will pay the consequences."

Dirk's stare was fixed on her. "I don't care what he threatens you with, don't do it. You know what he's going to do with that venom—innocent people are going to die."

Bethany was mesmerized by the small ruby-red necklace of blood seeping from Dirk's neck. She knew that he could endure a lot of pain, but she didn't know how much more she could watch. She gathered her determination around her like a thin shield and, blocking Dirk from her mind, shook her head. "No, I won't do it. I won't help you."

Patterson studied her face and then shrugged. "Fine. Then I see no reason to keep Adams alive."

He lunged, grabbing Dirk by the head as the other vampires held him captive, and jerked him forward bodily, sinking his fangs into Dirk's neck in a violent attack. Dirk bucked and fought, but already weak from the earlier fight, he was easily restrained. Bethany could just make out his face in the dim lighting. The pain and agony she saw chipped at her resolve. Patterson was killing the man she loved and it was within her power to stop it.

Patterson continued to drink and Bethany thought there was no way that Dirk could have that much blood in him. When she saw his eyes roll back in his head, the horror of nameless, faceless individuals dying as a result of her efforts to duplicate the venom paled in the face of the current horror. Dirk was dying now.

"Stop," she screamed. "I'll help you."

Patterson ignored her and she grew desperate. "Stop, stop. I said I'd help, but I swear I won't if you kill him. If he dies, then you might as well kill me, too." Still he continued to drink and she finally screamed. "I'm your only chance."

Bethany barely heard the sound of running feet before a form shot past her. Shocked by the sudden appearance of this new vampire, she watched him pry Patterson off Dirk and shove the Prime back several yards. "That's enough," he growled.

The newcomer placed his fingers against Dirk's throat and held them there.

"Is he . . . ?" Bethany couldn't get the words out.

The newcomer shook his head. "He'll live—for now. Take him to the lab," he addressed the two vampires holding Dirk up. Then he turned to Bethany.

"I'm Sheldon Harris. And you are Bethany Stavinoski, I presume?"

She nodded.

He held out his hand, gesturing for her to walk with him as they followed the vampires carrying Dirk.

"Harris!" Patterson's hoarse shout reverberated against the walls. When Bethany turned around, she saw that his eyes shone brightly and there was a crazed look about him. "Don't ever do that again."

"Don't threaten me, Patterson. You know as well as I do that if you kill Adams, you'll never get the woman's cooperation."

He turned then, much more confident that Patterson would not attack them from behind than Bethany was, and continued walking, leading her to the small door through which the other vampires had carried Dirk.

Stepping into the room, Bethany saw it was an almost fully equipped lab. She had to wonder how the vampires had gotten all this equipment down here, and the electricity to run the lights and equipment, but then she remembered that Patterson and Harris used to be SEALs and probably knew how to obtain many things the average person wouldn't be able to.

Off to the side, against the wall, Dirk lay on a cot. Bethany rushed to his side, checking his pulse for herself to make sure that he was all right.

"I can barely feel a pulse," she said worriedly. "We have to get him medical help." She looked up at Harris, standing not far away.

He shook his head. "He'll be fine. Adams is different. I've seen him sustain worse injuries and survive."

"But—"

He held up his hand. "Don't push your luck." He turned to the other vampires. "Leave us."

They nodded obediently and left the room. Suddenly alone with Harris, Bethany wondered what was coming next.

"There's a bathroom over there," he said, pointing to the far corner. "He needs food to help rebuild his blood supply. I'll bring some, as well as a cloth to clean his wounds."

She stared up at him. "What's the point of bringing us food if you're just going to kill us?"

"No one's going to kill you if I can help it," he assured her.

She stood up to face him. "Why are you being so nice?"

A shadow passed over his face. He raised his hand, as if to touch her cheek but then thought better of it and let his hand fall back to his side. "You remind me of someone I used to know."

Something about the way he said it caused Bethany to wonder if he meant a wife or girlfriend. She hadn't considered that a vampire might still have feelings for those he'd left behind. For the first time, she considered this vampire as something other than a hideous monster, briefly glimpsing the man he once was.

He walked to the door, stopping when he reached it. "Don't try to leave. Aside from the fact that the place is crawling with vampires, the pipes are interconnected and confusing. You could easily get lost and spend the rest of your life trying to find your way out." He waited for her to nod that she understood before he continued. "I'll be back shortly."

She waited until the door closed before returning to Dirk's side, whispering his name. "Dirk? Can you hear me?" When he didn't respond, she grew fearful that he might already be dead.

She bent over him, hugging him close as she whispered in his ear. "Please don't die, please don't die. Dirk, can you hear me?"

"Bethany?" His voice was weak and she strained to hear it.

"Yes, love. I'm here."

"Are you . . . okay?"

"Yes, I'm fine." For now, she thought.

"Where . . . ?"

"I think we must be in some abandoned underground maintenance section of the sewer system. The door's locked and Harris went to get food."

Dirk struggled to sit up but was too weak. "We've got to get out of here."

"You're not going anywhere." She forced him to lie down. "You lost a lot of blood and we need to give your body a chance to recover."

He was shaking his head before she finished. "No. Don't trust him. Don't trust Harris."

"Right now, Adams, you don't have anyone else," Harris said from the doorway, startling Bethany who hadn't heard the door open. "I suggest you eat something. In a short while, Patterson will send two of his converts for you. He's decided it will be best to separate you during the day as added protection against either of you leaving while we sleep." Harris gave her a reassuring smile. "No one will bother you."

"I don't care what happens to me. What are you going to do to Dirk?"

She again saw the shadow pass across Harris's eyes. "My apologies." Then he turned to look at Dirk. "Adams, you're a lucky man, to have found someone who cares about you as much as she does." He handed her the food and left.

With effort, she was able to get Dirk to eat several bites, but he was too weak to do more than that. She didn't know how much of his fatigue was due to his weakened condition and how much was because they were so close to dawn, which would normally have made him tired.

As predicted, it wasn't long before several of Patterson's vampire flunkies came and carried Dirk off, locking the door behind them, leaving Bethany alone in a lab filled with equipment and no means of escape.

How long she paced, she had no idea, but it felt like an eternity. She was starting to think that maybe the sun had come up and she would have several hours to herself when she heard the lock turn in the door. Seconds later, Patterson walked in.

Immediately she backed away from him, moving to stand behind a lab table, hoping it might provide some protection.

Patterson, noticing what she'd done, lifted his lips in an evil smile and began to walk around the lab, forcing her to keep moving if she wanted to keep the table between them.

"Well, Ms. Stavinoski—Bethany. May I call you Bethany? I think you'll find the lab is equipped with everything you need. I suggest you make good use of your time. If you try to refuse, well, I don't think Adams can afford to lose much more of his blood."

Their situation was hopeless. "I can't duplicate that formula."

"Can't or won't?"

"Can't," she said emphatically. "There's an element to the venom that is completely unfamiliar to me. I won't go into the scientific explanation, but it's like the chupacabra isn't really from our planet. This element is completely foreign and the way it reacts and combines with the enzymes in our body—well, it's unpredictable. I can't duplicate that. I don't know that anyone can," she added softly.

Patterson's polite facade vanished and his tone grew sharp. In a blur of movement, he was beside her, his hand to her throat, clutching it just tight enough to be uncomfortable, his eyes glowing as they stared at her. "You'd better hope that's not true, because when I come back this evening and check on you, there'd better be venom. If there's not, I'll finish what I started with Adams and then come for you."

"Let her go," Harris said from the doorway.

"Go away, Harris. This is a private conversation."

Harris moved into the room, coming to stand on the other side of her. He didn't try to touch Patterson. "Nothing that involves this woman or Adams is private. I'm in this as much as you are and I won't let you fuck it up because you can't control your temper. Now, back off. It's almost dawn."

Trapped between them, Bethany watched the silent

battle of wills, feeling helpless. Finally, Patterson's grip lessened. She held her breath and only started to breathe again when his hand fell to his side. His attention was no longer on her but riveted on Harris. So much so that Bethany was half afraid the two vampires would battle to the death right there.

Then the moment passed and Patterson strode to the door. "I'm getting tired of your interference, Harris. I'm warning you, I won't tolerate much more." At the door he stopped to look back. "I want that adult chupacabra. Where is she?"

"As I've told you repeatedly, it's not that easy. You don't call her like a dog. I'll let you know as soon as I've made contact with her. Until then, you'll have to wait."

Patterson gave Harris a hard stare and then simply turned and walked out.

Alone with Harris, Bethany stood there confused, not understanding why this vampire would repeatedly protect her from Patterson. "Thank you, again," she said.

"Save your gratitude. If it comes to a fight, I don't know that I can take Patterson. He may still kill you."

"Then you have to help us escape."

Harris gave her an incredulous look. "Why would I do that?"

Bethany wondered if she'd misjudged the man. "I thought . . ." She fumbled for the words. "You're not like him. You're better than that. I know you don't want to see us get hurt."

Harris shook his head. "Don't give me too much credit. I'm as interested in that venom as Patterson."

The announcement shocked her. "I don't believe it."

His gaze was cold and hard as he stared at her. "Well,

you'd better. Oh, don't get me wrong, I have no desire to create a special ops vampire team. My interests lie elsewhere."

"Where, exactly?" She was almost afraid to hear the answer.

"You may find this hard to believe," he began sarcastically, "but I once had a real life, before Burton stole it all from me. I want that life back. I want to be human again. And I expect you to help me."

Bethany froze as the full weight of his words hit her. There was no way to give him what he wanted. That much she knew. Even if she could duplicate the venom perfectly, even if she could find a way to reverse the effects, Harris wouldn't be human again—he'd be dead.

"If you want my help to escape," he continued, "then you have to help me in return. Your choice, but make it now."

Guilt stabbed through her. This man, this vampire, had done nothing but help her and she hated to lead him on, but she had to do what she could to save Dirk and herself.

"All right. I'll help you."

Harris nodded and walked to the door. "Patterson gave you the day to finish the synthetic. Spend that time learning how to reverse the effects of the venom instead, because we leave when the sun goes down."

Chapter 23

Hours after Harris left her, Bethany paced the lab, looking for a way to escape. So far, the only way out appeared to be the door and it was locked. She smashed two stools against it trying to break it down before realizing it was made of steel.

She'd half expected Dirk to show up to save them both, but as more time passed and he didn't appear, her concern for him grew. He would have come for her if he could have, but he'd been in bad shape when they'd taken him. If Patterson had fed off him again . . .

She forced her mind away from the thought. Dirk was alive. She had to believe that. And if he wasn't in a position to help her escape then she'd have to find a way to help him.

With that goal uppermost in her mind, she studied the chemicals available in the lab. With the right ingredients, she might be able to make a bomb or two. She dug through the equipment, pulling out what she needed when she came across a journal.

She didn't recognize the handwriting, but after reading only a couple of pages, she knew it was the work of a highly intelligent scientist. The notes on each experiment were meticulously recorded and supplemented with the writer's private theorems and hypotheses. She wondered if this might be the work of Dr. Weber, Lanie's father. She was about to close it when a notation caught her attention. Eagerly, she read on.

Dr. Weber had developed an antiserum that destroyed the venom in the host's system. Though he didn't come right out and say it, his goal, she could tell, was to find some way to destroy the vampires. More amazing to Bethany was that his concoction had worked. Suddenly the idea of reversing the venom and restoring life wasn't as far-fetched as she'd originally thought.

Unfortunately, figuring out how to do it was going to take a lot longer than a single day. It could take a lifetime.

She sat on the cot and continued to read, fighting to keep her eyes open as she pored over Dr. Weber's notes. Just maybe . . .

Exhaustion stole over her and it wasn't long before she fell asleep.

Something jerked her awake and she felt herself hauled roughly off the cot. Patterson stared at her, his eyes blazing with anger. "What the hell are you doing asleep?" he yelled, slapping her across the face as he held her upright. "Where's my venom?"

Bethany tasted blood at the corner of her mouth where her lip had split. Her heart raced from the combination of adrenaline and terror coursing through her. She opened her mouth to say something, but never got the chance.

"If you're not going to do what I tell you, then I have no use for you," he spat out.

She barely had time to anticipate the pain before he'd yanked her to him and sank his teeth into her neck. Agony ripped through her, spreading along her veins as Patterson drank. She fought against him, hitting and clawing, but her efforts didn't faze him. She thought of the admiral's herb in her bloodstream and hope filled her—until she remembered its twenty-four hour limitation. Her last cup of coffee still sat, untouched, on the kitchen table. As hope died, her strength failed and only Patterson's hold on her kept her from falling. She was dying, but too weak to care.

"What the hell—?"

Suddenly released, she fell to the floor, landing in a crumpled heap. Harris stood over her, confronting Patterson, and though she tried to focus on their words as they argued, she only caught bits and pieces.

". . . crazy? We need her," Harris was saying.

"She's no better than Meyers," Patterson shot back. "We're better off killing her and finding someone new."

"No, it's too late for that." Harris clenched his hands into fists. "Let me take care of this—you go deal with Adams. I'm sure he's awake by now."

Bethany saw the way Patterson stared at the other Prime. There was a decided lack of trust between the two. As if sensing Patterson's hesitation, Harris said, "Leave her to me. I can be very persuasive—or have you already forgotten that time in Iraq?"

Patterson still seemed hesitant, but he finally nodded.

"See that she's cooperating when I get back. Her only value lies in her ability to duplicate the venom. If she's not going to do that, then we might as well enjoy her."

Bethany felt cold fear lance through her at his words and she watched him walk out of the lab. Then she looked up to see Harris standing over her, his expression unreadable, and she didn't know whether to be relieved or afraid.

Dirk woke to find he was alone in an empty room except for the decaying corpse of some unfortunate soul chained to the wall next to him. When his captors had carried him in hours ago, he'd been too weak to put up much of a fight. They'd secured him in the iron cuffs that were chained to the wall and left him. He'd thought if he could find the strength and energy, he could use the time while his captors slept to escape and find Bethany, but as the sun rose, he'd been overwhelmed with fatigue. Unable to fight against it, he'd slept.

While he did, his body had used its special abilities to recuperate. Now, looking at the wall behind him, he saw where the chains were bolted and felt a spurt of hope. The mortar and brick looked old. Cocking his head to listen for the sounds of someone approaching, he heard nothing.

There was enough slack in the chains that if he took a step closer to the wall, he could grab them with his hands. With his feet spread for balance, he strained, pulling with all his might until the muscles in his arms and chest shook with the effort. Sweat broke out over his body and his groans filled the room.

Then one of the bolts moved. Encouraged by this small victory, he renewed his effort. Little by little, the bolts ripped from the wall, sending cracked mortar flying.

Suddenly free, Dirk fell to the ground and stayed there, exhausted. His muscles ached beyond belief and he wasn't sure he could move, but he needed to. He had to find Bethany, if she was still alive.

He refused to consider any other possibility and forced himself to his feet, his chains dangling from the iron bracelets at his wrists, weighing him down. There was no way to get them off, so he didn't waste time trying. He swung his arms around in circles, winding the chains about his forearms to act as a cumbersome type of chain mail.

He'd taken only a step toward the door when it burst open and Patterson appeared. His face was clouded with anger, but at seeing Dirk, he smiled.

"I'm going to enjoy this, Adams," he taunted as they squared off. "I've just enjoyed a taste of your girlfriend— she put up quite a fight. If Harris hadn't come in, there's no telling what I might have done."

Dirk fought to keep his emotions under control. If he lost it now, Patterson would have the advantage. He had to remain calm and look for an opportunity to attack.

"Yes, indeed," Patterson went on. "She was quite a treat. I definitely want another taste—provided there's anything left. You know how Harris gets when he's . . . negotiating. You remember what he did to that Iraqi terrorist responsible for bombing the mission a couple of years ago? Do you think anyone ever found enough of the body to figure out who it was?"

"I guess some things never change, do they?" Dirk scoffed. "I thought you were in charge of this little underground operation, but I see now that it's been Harris all along."

The barb hit its mark and Patterson roared as he attacked. Dirk threw out his arm, pain ripping through the already stressed muscles. The weight of the chain added to the power of his punch and Patterson flew across the room. He recovered quickly and with another yell, charged. This time, he was ready for the impact of the chain and Dirk wasn't able to throw him off.

Patterson jumped on Dirk, bearing him to the ground. For the second time, Dirk felt the vampire's fangs sink into his neck and the warm trickle of blood ran down his skin. Already weak, Dirk struggled to knock him off. Unsuccessful, he pushed himself off the ground, carrying Patterson on his back. Finally, getting his feet under him, he stumbled to the wall and slammed Patterson against it. He had to repeat the move several times before Patterson loosened his hold.

Reaching up, Dirk grabbed the vampire and hauled him over his shoulder. As soon as Patterson landed on the floor, Dirk hit him, breaking the vampire's nose. Patterson rolled to the side, freeing himself from Dirk's grip, and they both staggered to their feet.

Dirk knew that if he didn't beat Patterson soon, he never would. Letting a length of chain unravel off his arm, he waited for Patterson to lunge at him. As he did, Dirk swung a loop around Patterson's neck and caught the other end. Before the Prime knew what Dirk was up to, Dirk pulled the chain tight.

Dirk's original intent was to decapitate the vampire, but between his weakened muscles and the bulk of the chain links, it proved impossible to do, so he pulled the chain as tight as he could and prayed that the vampire needed air to breathe.

Patterson fought to get free, doing everything he could to cause Dirk to loosen his grip, even slamming him bodily into the wall repeatedly. Through it all, Dirk held on, pulling the chains tighter and tighter. Slowly, Patterson's efforts weakened until, finally, he crumpled to the ground. Dirk didn't let go of the chain, worried that Patterson might be faking.

After what seemed like an eternity, Dirk unwound the chains. He moved cautiously, poised to react should Patterson suddenly spring into action. However, even with the chain no longer around his neck, Patterson lay still. Dirk slowly backed out of the room. Closing the door behind him, he turned and raced down the hall, praying he reached Beth before it was too late.

"Can you stand?"

Bethany blinked her eyes, trying to clear the dizziness. She found herself staring up into Harris's eyes and realized she was lying on the floor. She stared at him blankly as her brain did a rewind.

"I don't know," she answered honestly. She struggled to push herself into a sitting position and then paused while the world righted itself. Then she put her hands on the floor and tried to leverage herself up.

"Give me your hand."

Bethany paused in her efforts and stared at Harris's outstretched hand. Did she dare trust him? He stood there patiently while she made up her mind. "What did you do in Iraq?" she asked, finally placing her hand in his and letting him pull her to her feet.

The sudden movement made her light-headed and everything turned black. She felt herself falling, but could do nothing to prevent it. Then strong arms wrapped around her, arresting her fall, holding her while the darkness passed.

"Thank you." Her voice sounded weak, even to her own ears, but she didn't care. She needed to pull herself together if she was to have any chance at all of escaping.

From far off, she heard the sound of a door crashing open and then she was falling again as Harris was tackled to the floor.

She heard grunts of pain and the clanking of metal against concrete. Struggling to her knees, her hands braced against the floor, she looked over and saw someone on top of Harris, arms flailing. With a quickening of her pulse, she realized who it was.

"Dirk?" Her whisper couldn't be heard above the fighting, so she tried again, this time louder. "Dirk?"

Still he didn't respond and as adrenaline shot through her body, she got to her feet. "Stop it," she ordered, going over to grab his arm. He shook her off as if she were nothing more than a fly. A glimpse of Harris's bloodied face gave her the strength to try again.

She pulled at Dirk's arm pinning Harris to the floor by the throat. It was like trying to move a stone column. Giving up, she grabbed Dirk's face and turned it so he stared at her. It was a frightening sight. Never had he looked so much like a vampire. She was almost afraid he wouldn't recognize her.

Keeping her voice smooth and easy, she tried talking to him. "Dirk, look at me. Please. You have to let Harris up."

"Why?" Dirk's voice came out a snarl.

"He saved my life."

Dirk shook his head. "I saw him. He was attacking you."

"No. I was too weak to stand. He was helping me up."

Dirk looked unconvinced, so she hurried on. "Patterson came in here and attacked me. Harris stopped him. Please. I'm begging you. Don't kill him. Please. For me?"

Dirk loosened his grip and she heard Harris draw in a breath. Running her hand down Dirk's arm, she pried his fingers from around the vampire's throat and pulled him away.

Harris lay there, unmoving, his gaze focused on Dirk. Bethany didn't know if he was hurt or just being cautious. Once Dirk and Bethany stepped back to give him room, though, he got to his feet.

He stood there, rubbing his throat. "What now?"

Dirk gestured to Bethany and himself, "We're getting out of here and you're going to let us."

Harris shook his head. "It's not that simple. These pipes run under the entire city; some of them caved in years ago and are impassable—and there are other surprises out there. Unless you know the way, you could be down here a long time before you get out." He nodded to Bethany. "She's not in any shape to be down here that long and from the looks of it, neither are you."

Dirk took a step forward. "How about I just beat the directions out of you?"

Harris shrugged, though his eyes blazed angrily. "I'm already dead. What more do you think you can do to me?"

Dirk started forward again, but Bethany pulled him back. "This isn't helping," she said, looking from changeling to vampire. "We—"

"What did you do to Patterson?" Harris interrupted, his brow furrowed.

"What? I killed him."

Harris gave an impatient jerk of his head. "No, I don't think so. Royally pissed him off, maybe, but you didn't kill him." He looked back at Dirk. "Can't you feel him?"

Bethany watched Dirk cock his head to one side, as if he was listening to a sound she couldn't hear. Then he grabbed her hand. "Time to go—can you make it?"

His blue eyes shone with an intense light. "Yes." She was exhausted beyond belief, and frightened, but she would do whatever he asked of her.

"Get out of our way," Dirk growled when Harris blocked the door.

"Not so fast. Ms. Stavinoski?" Harris stared at her expectantly.

She knew what he wanted and it reminded her of the journal. Releasing Dirk's hand, she crossed the room, picked it up, and hurried back to Dirk's side. Instead of taking his hand, though, she stepped in front of him, facing Harris.

"I'm sorry. I don't know how to make you human again. I lied to you earlier because I wanted to escape and I'm sorry for that." She looked down at Dr. Weber's journal and then held it out to him.

"I think that Dr. Weber might have been on to something. I don't know if there's a cure for you or not, but if there is, the notes in here might help."

"What the hell am I supposed to do with this?" Harris growled, taking it from her. "Kidnap another biochemist?" He threw the book across the room where it smashed several glass flasks sitting on top of the lab table.

"Maybe I could help," she offered hesitantly. "If I can get out of here—to a real lab. Maybe in time—"

She was interrupted by a roar as something powerful hit the door from the other side. Only Harris, leaning against it, held it closed.

"Open the door, Harris," Patterson yelled, his manic tone more frightening than anything Bethany had heard before. She watched as Harris and Dirk stared at each other, volumes of unspoken words passing between them.

Patterson rammed the door again, startling her and apparently breaking the deadlock between vampire and changeling.

Clenching his jaw, his expression world-weary, Harris spoke. "When you leave, stay right. Where it dead-ends, you'll find a set of rungs in the wall leading to the surface. It comes out in the park. From there, you're on your own." He waited until Dirk nodded and then, moving at lightning speed, tore open the door and rushed at Patterson. The sound of the two vampires fighting was more like that of two wild boars.

Dirk grabbed her hand and they took off running through the pipe. The farther they moved away from the vampires' lair, the fainter the sounds of the fight became. They turned right at the first intersection and kept running. The light faded until it finally became too dark for Bethany to see. With his night vision, she knew Dirk would have no trouble, but several times she stumbled and he had to catch her before she fell.

When they neared an intersection where another pipe T-boned into the one they were in, Dirk slowed their pace, bringing them to a stop. Beth moved close and automatically Dirk wrapped his arms around her, holding her. She curled her arms around his neck and froze.

"Is that blood?" She lightly touched his skin and then

pulled her hand away, pressing thumb and index fingers together to check the stickiness.

"I'm okay," he assured her.

"No, you're not. Patterson bled you again, didn't he?"

He captured her hand in his and brought it to his mouth where he kissed it. "I'm okay. Let's keep moving."

They continued down the pipe, stopping occasionally to listen for sounds of pursuit. Bethany wasn't sure how far they'd gone when she heard a noise that chilled her to the bone. Up ahead in the tunnel, blocking their path to freedom, were several of Patterson's abandoned vampires and from the sound of their piercing howls, they were crazed and hungry.

She instinctively clutched Dirk's hand a little harder as she slowed her steps. "How many? Can you see them?"

"Four. Maybe five."

She fought to keep the panic at bay. "Maybe we can find another route?"

"The only other way is back the way we came—that's not much of an option."

"What'll we do?"

"I can fight them," he said grimly.

She thought about that as the sounds of the approaching vampires got louder. "No. You've lost too much blood and besides, you have no weapon. How much of a chance do you have?"

She heard him sigh. "I can't kill them, but if they're busy fighting me, you might be able to sneak past them and escape."

She grabbed his hand and pulled him back a step. "No. I'm not leaving without you. Let's go back. We can hide in a side tunnel until they move past us."

She realized that Dirk must be hurt worse than she originally thought because he didn't argue with her. They retraced their steps, the howls of the vampires trailing after them. At the first side tunnel, they turned, taking it far enough that the approaching vampires wouldn't see them when they passed.

Pressed against the wall, they waited, hardly daring to breathe. When the vampires came to the opening, however, instead of walking past it, they turned in.

Bethany heard Dirk swear softly under his breath as he led her farther down the pipe. The sound of the vampires continued to grow louder, as if they were coming faster. Bethany and Dirk had no choice but to keep moving. It soon became apparent that the vampires knew they were there and were hunting them.

Going down yet another intersecting tunnel, Bethany and Dirk came to a sudden stop.

"What's the matter?" Bethany asked, all too aware of the vampires closing in on them.

"Dead end."

"Really? Do you see rungs leading up?"

There was a moment of silence as Bethany waited, trying not to let herself get too excited. She hated it down in the tunnels. The oppressive dark was suffocating her.

"There's nothing here." He sounded tense. "We'll have to go back."

"But the vampires—"

"I know, but if we stay here, we're trapped."

He tugged her arm and she stumbled after him. It was hard for her to tell how far they'd backtracked before Dirk suddenly pulled her to a stop and pressed her to the wall.

As she opened her mouth to ask what was going on, he covered it with his hand to silence her.

"Vampires," he whispered in her ear, barely loud enough for her to hear.

He pushed her back the way they'd come, hugging the wall as they went. Then suddenly Dirk dropped to the ground.

Panic ripped through her as the image of Dirk lying unconscious flashed through her mind. When a hand grabbed her arm, she nearly cried out.

"It's okay. It's me. I found a shaft. We can hide there, but we need to hurry."

She let Dirk guide her as the sound of the approaching vampires got louder.

"Here," Dirk whispered, bringing her to a stop. "There, at the base of the wall, is a small shaft. It'll be tight but I think we can both fit. Get down on your hands and knees and back into it. I'll guide you."

With Dirk's help, she did as he instructed and backed into the small opening. Just as he'd warned her, it was a tight fit, especially when he squeezed in beside her.

They had no sooner wedged themselves in than the vampires entered their tunnel. Their guttural snarls and heavy breathing reminded her of a pack of wolves on the hunt and if she hadn't already been lying down, she felt certain her legs would have buckled from sheer terror.

She prayed they weren't smart enough to look down and wondered how visible the shaft was to someone with night vision. As the sounds of them grew closer still, Bethany felt something brush her foot. At first, she thought it was Dirk's foot, but then it came again.

"There's something in here with us." There was virtually no sound to her whisper, but she knew Dirk heard her.

"Be still," he whispered back.

Easy for him to say, she thought as whatever it was brushed up against her leg. This time, she thought she felt the scratch of claws.

She leaned closer to Dirk. "What is it?"

His breath was warm against her cheek when he answered her. "Rat."

Bethany felt the scream well up inside her as she shrank back as far as the shaft would allow. When the rat burrowed between her legs, she let loose with a bloodcurdling yell.

Chapter
24

The vampires immediately zeroed in on the shaft and hurried toward it. Beside her, Dirk swore. Then there was a violent flurry of movement between their bodies, as if the rat was attacking. Dirk struggled beside her and then she felt the brush of fur against her face just before she heard something smack against the far wall of the tunnel.

There was a scurrying sound and then the vampires' excited growls grew fainter.

Bethany felt Dirk squirming beside her and seconds later she was being hauled bodily out of the shaft and into a pair of well-muscled arms. She was vaguely aware of the chains, still wrapped around Dirk's forearms, biting into her. She didn't care.

"Beth, honey. It's okay. They're gone."

She clutched his shirt in her fists and looked around, even though she couldn't see a thing. "Where's the rat?"

"He ran down the tunnel."

"And the vampires?"

She heard the smile in his voice. "Gone for now; chasing after that rat." Then he sobered. "I don't know how long it'll take them to figure out that was a human scream they heard, so we should get moving again. Do you think you can?"

She nodded. "Yes," she whispered.

"That's my girl." He tipped her face up to him and quickly kissed her. Then he took her by the hand and led her down the tunnel.

They walked for what seemed like hours and Bethany had no idea where they were and prayed that Dirk did. Fatigue rode her, but she knew she couldn't be as tired as Dirk. The fights with Patterson and Harris left him weak and with the chains weighing him down, he had to be exhausted. Finally, he stopped so they could rest.

"We can sit here for a while," he said, lowering himself to the ground.

"But for how long?"

"Not very. The vampires are still out there."

Despite her fatigue, Bethany found it difficult to relax. Robbed of sight, every noise seemed amplified. When she first heard the snarls of several vampires echoing off the walls around her, she thought it was her imagination reacting to the recent scare. When she felt Dirk tense beside her, she knew it was far worse. Not only were the sounds real, but there was no echo in the tunnel. They were trapped, with vampires approaching from both directions.

She didn't see any way to avoid a fight and knew if it came to that, in Dirk's weakened state, they'd both die. Unless . . .

"I can help you," she said.

"No. You can't fight them."

"But I can give you the strength and energy *you* need to fight."

He went still beside her. "I'm not going to drink your blood." His tone and refusal were adamant.

She placed her hands on either side of his cheeks and pulled his head down to hers so she could kiss him lightly. "You have to," she whispered. "It's the only way."

"Beth, biting you in the throes of passion is one thing. If I bite you now, it's going to hurt."

"Not as much as those vampires will hurt me if they get hold of me." Still he hesitated and she grew desperate. "We don't have time to argue. Do this, please. I promise, you won't hurt me."

She pulled his head to her neck. "I want you to do this," she whispered, her heart already pounding in anticipation.

The sounds of the vampires were louder and she prayed they had enough time for this to work. She felt Dirk's warm breath on her neck and it was hard not to react. Running her hand up his back, she pulled him close. She felt the prick of his teeth when he bit her, but instead of the sharp pain she'd felt with Patterson's bite, a spear of desire shot through her. Dirk's hands gripped her shoulders and head, holding her while he drank, and she heard the ragged sound of his breathing that told her of his arousal.

A tension built between her legs and she shut her eyes until tiny white lights burst behind her closed eyelids. Dirk was breathing hard when he finally pulled his head away from her neck and a small wave of dizziness hit her, causing her to hold on to him to keep her balance.

Immediately he steadied her. "Are you all right?" he asked, concerned.

"I'm fine. How are you?"

"I feel drunk, I feel so good." She heard the smile in his voice.

"Good."

The vampires were close now, though Bethany still couldn't see them.

"Wait here," Dirk ordered her.

"Be careful." She wouldn't allow herself to think about what would happen if he didn't come back.

The sounds of the fight drifted to her as she leaned against the wall and listened, trying to make out what was happening. She should have been terrified, sitting in the dark, vulnerable, dizzy and weak, but all she felt was tired; bone-weary, mind-numbing fatigue. Gradually, her thoughts grew vague and her eyelids grew heavy.

With no weapon to stab through the vampires' hearts and no way to behead them, Dirk knew his options for killing the vampires were limited. The blood he'd taken from Beth sang in his veins, giving him an energy rush like nothing he'd experienced before. Moving with a speed even faster than normal for him, he rushed the vampires, catching them unawares. He broke the neck of the first one and flung him into a second while he tackled the third. More animal than human now, their fighting skills were minimal and he was able to dispatch them quickly. They still weren't dead and he worried how he might dispose of them.

For now, though, they weren't moving and the vampires on the other side of Beth were coming too close, so Dirk raced back up the tunnel to meet them. When he passed Beth, he saw that she hadn't moved, but sat with her head bent forward. Something about her pose sent alarms pinging in his mind, but there wasn't time to check on her. He had to deal with the remaining vampires first.

These were two of Patterson's more recent recruits. Dirk recognized them as the two who'd held him captive earlier and was glad for a chance to get a little payback. When they saw him, they stopped in their tracks and Dirk used their momentary hesitation to attack.

They were harder to disable, but again, Patterson had been recruiting average citizens and their fighting skills were no match for Dirk's. Limited in options, he broke their legs, making it impossible for them to come after him.

Once he had Beth safe at the mansion, he promised himself that he'd come back with Mac and they'd finish off these creatures.

With the two vampires writhing on the ground, Dirk hurried back to Bethany. She didn't move when he leaned down to wake her. Checking her pulse, he found it faint, but steady. Scooping her up in his arms, Dirk started back down the tunnel and hoped he could remember how to get out of there.

He carried her for as long as he could, traveling a great distance before he finally had to stop and rest. Sitting down, his back against the wall, he cradled Beth in his arms. When he'd rested as long as he dared, he lifted her again and walked on.

His muscles screamed in agony, but he refused to put her down. At some point in the night, her breathing changed and he thought that maybe her body had recovered enough to move from unconsciousness to sleep. At least he hoped so, but he didn't try to wake her.

Once, when he'd heard the snarl of vampires, he stood still and the creatures had gone in the opposite direction. After several wrong turns and what seemed like hours, Dirk reached a dead end. Looking at the side of the wall, he noticed the rungs leading up and saw the faint outline of the round iron plate covering the exit.

He couldn't climb up and open it with Beth in his arms, so he laid her gently on the ground. He stood and stretched, trying to ease his body's aches and pains, and then he tackled the rungs. Each step required greater effort and Dirk knew that the effects of taking Beth's blood had worn off.

Reaching the top, he peeked through the holes in the plate, making sure that in the event this wasn't the park exit, he wasn't about to lift the plate and crawl out into oncoming traffic. All he saw were trees and gave thanks that something, finally, had gone right.

Gritting his teeth, he pushed up on the plate and shoved it to one side. The night sky was now a light smoke-gray and Dirk realized that it had taken all night for them to escape. He also knew that dawn was imminent and as soon as it came, he'd be too tired to move. It was imperative that he get Beth to safety now.

Climbing back down, he went to her side. Placing his hand on her shoulder, he gently shook her. "Beth, honey. Can you hear me?" It took several attempts, but finally her eyelids fluttered open.

"Dirk?" Her voice sounded weak and there was a lost expression on her face as she looked around. Then she reached out and gripped his arm as it all came back to her. "The vampires?"

"Incapacitated."

"What about you—are you hurt?"

He smiled, hearing the concern for him in her voice. "I'll live." Then he grew serious. "Beth, I found the exit but I don't think I can carry you up. Can you climb the rungs by yourself?"

She followed them up with her gaze, then turned to him. "You carried me all this way?" She sounded amazed.

"Piece of cake," he lied.

Her expression turned determined and she held out her hand to him. "Can you help me up?"

He stood and pulled her to her feet. She swayed a little and Dirk was afraid she'd be too weak to climb, but then she steadied herself and let go of his hand. "I'm okay." Her first steps were hesitant, but she made it without needing his help.

Staying behind her, they started up together, Beth trapped between his arms in case she got dizzy and fell.

They'd only climbed a few rungs when something slammed into Dirk from the side, knocking him to the ground. When he looked up, Patterson was staring down at him.

Chapter
25

This time, Adams, I'm going to kill you." Patterson drove his fist into Dirk's jaw, almost knocking him unconscious. In his current state, Dirk had little hope of surviving. As long as Beth got away, Dirk was okay with dying.

As the stars in his head faded, he glanced up the rungs and saw that Beth had stopped climbing. She stood midway, staring down at him, fear and concern etched across her face. "Keep going," he called out to her, afraid she would try to help him. He saw her hesitation and was about to yell at her again when Patterson kicked him.

This time, he tasted blood as his own fangs cut into his lip. From the corner of his eye, he saw Bethany moving and with a feeling of relief realized she was going to escape. All he had to do was keep Patterson busy until she was completely out, then if Patterson killed him, he hadn't died in vain. He only wished he'd told Beth how much he loved her.

Braced for Patterson's next blow, he was surprised when Patterson moved away from him. Then he noticed the direction of Patterson's gaze. Dirk struggled to his feet just as Patterson reached the first rung. He lunged forward, grabbing the Prime by the ankle, and pulled.

They both fell, with Dirk landing on his back. He lay there a second, stunned. Beth, he noticed, had reached the top and was almost out. Behind her, he saw the skies growing lighter. She was safe.

Then suddenly Patterson attacked, falling on Dirk, his mouth going for Dirk's throat.

Dirk twisted his body, knowing that if Patterson bit him, it would be all over. With strength born of desperation, he pushed the vampire away and scrambled to his feet. Patterson jumped up and hit him. The blow knocked Dirk back, but he didn't go down. As he shook off the dizziness, a shadow of movement flickered above him. He realized it was coming from Bethany, standing overhead.

Then Patterson rushed him. His fists pummeling Dirk's face, Patterson drove him back, step by step, until Dirk was trapped against the wall with only Patterson's hand against his throat to hold him up.

The Prime gave Dirk a hideous smile. "It's over, Adams. I win. Does the dying man have any last words?" he goaded.

"Move!" Dirk choked out as loud as he could.

He saw the confusion on Patterson's face. Then Beth stepped aside and the newly risen sun she'd been blocking filled the opening, sending a beam down into the hole to land on the very spot where Patterson stood.

Dirk saw the vampire's eyes open wide as he realized

the implication—and then he froze in place as his body rapidly turned to stone.

Dirk reached up and grabbed the hand still at his throat, crushing it in his fist. Dragging in an unrestricted breath, he pushed away from the wall and shoved the statue, watching it fall to the ground where it exploded on impact into a cloud of dust. Patterson was no more.

"Dirk?" Beth's worried voice floated down to him through the opening.

"It's over," he called up to her as he moved to the rungs. Knowing she waited for him gave Dirk the strength he needed to climb. Nearly blind from the sun's glare in his eyes, he reached the opening and she was there to help him out. It felt good to breathe the clean surface air, instead of the rancid sewage smell, and the brisk cool morning breeze was refreshing. Better than all that, though, was the feel of Beth in his arms as he held her close and kissed the top of her head before laying his cheek against it. He would have stood there for hours, but suddenly she shoved him away.

"Don't you ever do that again," she snapped at him.

"What—?" Her anger surprised him.

"Risk your life for me. Don't ever do it again, do you hear?" She struck him in the chest, though there was little force behind it. "Just what in the hell did you think you were doing?" Her voice cracked and though he could barely see her, he knew she was crying. She raised her fists to hit him again, but he caught them easily and held her.

"Beth?" He spoke her name softly, trying to understand.

"Why would you think I'd want to live if you died?" she choked out between tears.

"Hush," he whispered, pulling her against him. "It's over." He stroked her hair as he spoke. "Patterson is dead. We're safe."

"But there are others."

"We'll take care of them."

Neither of them mentioned Harris. Dirk had been hunting Harris for so long, part of him felt compelled to continue, but he knew he wouldn't. In his mind, Harris had achieved the same status as Dr. Weber. Knowing that there were now two vampires in the world who seemed capable of acting honorably reminded Dirk once again of just how little they knew about vampires.

It was more than he wanted to think about. Right now, he only wanted to rest.

Barely able to see but needing to take care of something before anything else happened, Dirk guided them to a park bench beneath a stand of trees where they could be in the shade. Beth sat down but instead of sitting next to her, he knelt on the ground at her feet. "There's something I need to tell you." Taking both of her hands in his, he gazed into her eyes. "I love you, Beth, with all my heart. I think I fell in love with you the first time I saw you on the street, God, it seems like so long ago." He paused before going on. "I'm sorry, I should have told you before, but I didn't know how. I kept looking for the right words and the right time, and then last night, I was so afraid I'd never see you again and I hadn't said anything—"

He hadn't realized just how afraid he'd been until that moment and he swallowed hard, fighting to keep his emotions in check.

Beth pulled her hands from his and laid them against his cheeks, caressing his bruised and battered face with her gaze as her eyes welled up with tears. "I love you, too." She leaned forward and kissed him carefully, not wanting to hurt him. "Come with me." At his confused expression, she merely smiled as she stood and waited for him to join her. Then she led him to the nearest tree where she sat on the ground with her back against a large trunk and gestured to the ground next to her. "Sit down before you fall down."

As soon as he did, she patted her lap. "The sun is up, the vampires are no threat right now, and you're tired. Rest a bit and then we'll figure out how to get home."

He seemed to hesitate and she knew it was hard for him to trust someone else to watch over him. She didn't push, but let him decide. Finally, he lay down, resting his head in her lap. She ran her fingers through his hair, letting the motion lull him to sleep. She saw him fight to stay awake, but eventually, the rhythmic motion, the events of the night, and the brightness of the day caught up with him.

The admiral and Mac found them an hour later, with Dirk still asleep, his head in Bethany's lap. With some effort, they got the two in the car and drove them home, with Beth explaining as much of the night as she could remember.

Once they reached the mansion, Bethany insisted that they help Dirk to her room and Julia brought her a first aid kit, a large bowl, and extra linens. Then she gave Bethany a quick hug and left the room.

Bethany wasted no time ridding Dirk of his clothes, bathing him, and treating his various wounds. Then, exhausted herself, she took a fast shower, toweled off, and crawled into bed beside him, where they both slept the rest of the day.

Bethany was sitting in the living room when she heard the massive front door of the mansion open early that evening. She looked up from the book she'd pretended to be reading and exchanged quick knowing glances with Lanie and Julia. The men had returned home safely. For the first time since the sun had set, she relaxed.

"Hello, ladies," Admiral Winslow said as they walked into the room. "What have you been doing while we've been out?"

"Charles," Julia scolded him, "you know perfectly well that we've been sitting here on pins and needles worrying about you men. Now, tell us all about it."

The admiral chuckled and, placing a hand at Julia's elbow, leaned forward to kiss her cheek. "Julia, it was exhilarating. We arrived at the entrance well before sunset and went in. The stench was awful. Dirk, Bethany, I don't know how you endured it for so long."

Bethany looked at Dirk and Mac as they moved into the room. Mac walked over to Lanie, who stood up and kissed him. Then they sat on the couch to listen to the admiral recount their adventures.

Bethany listened with half an ear, conscious of Dirk hovering nearby. When she glanced at him, he winked at her and smiled. She couldn't help but smile back as he came over to stand in front of her. Pulling her to her feet, he kissed her soundly in front of everyone. "I missed you," he said softly.

She smiled up at him. "I missed you, too. I'm glad you're safe."

"Takes more than a couple of vampires to bring that boy down," the admiral boasted from across the room.

Dirk smiled down at her, then sat in the chair, pulling her onto his lap.

For the next hour, they listened to the admiral recount how they had gone into the sewers and hunted the vampires. They'd found most of the ones that Dirk had fought the night before.

"There were easily twenty or thirty vampires," the admiral told Julia.

Bethany looked in alarm at Dirk, who grinned and mouthed the word "ten." Leaning against him, she smiled and listened to the rest of the admiral's story. When he was done, her thoughts turned to other things.

"Did you find Harris?" she asked, almost afraid to hear the answer. "Do you think Patterson killed him?"

"No," Mac answered. "To both questions."

"How do *you* know?" Dirk asked. "Just because he wasn't in the tunnels—"

"He's the one who called and told us where to look for you in the park," Mac said. "At first, we thought it was a trap, but we couldn't take the chance it wasn't."

Once again, Bethany found herself feeling grateful to the vampire. Then her thoughts returned to other questions she had. "If Miles was working for Patterson all along, then why was he talking to Santi? And who killed Santi?"

"I think I know the answer to that," Dirk answered. "Patterson had every intention of selling the venom on the black market. Santi was the dealer he chose to work through."

"Then why would he kill him?"

"He didn't," Mac answered. "Neither did Miles. I spoke with John. Santi really was killed in a drug deal."

Bethany took a minute to digest all of that. "I feel like such an idiot for letting Miles take advantage of me like that. I really thought I knew him."

Dirk pulled her close. "Don't be so hard on yourself. It's not your fault. Miles was a master in the art of manipulation. He used people to get what he wanted and when he saw a chance at immortality, he went for it, not caring who paid the price."

"In the end, though, Patterson cheated him out of that as well, didn't he?" Bethany asked. "He never was going to be like Harris or Patterson, retaining a part of his humanity." She turned to Dirk and spoke softly. "He would have killed a lot of innocent people if you hadn't stopped him. Thank you."

Dirk looked at her with surprise and then tender gratitude. She gave him a smile filled with the love she had for him.

"Speaking of Miles," Mac said. "John said that the media found out about Miles being killed by the Exsanguinators and assumed he was somehow working for them. His family's not too happy, from what John's heard."

"That's not good." Bethany knew how influential Miles's family was and worried about what trouble they might start.

"Don't worry," Dirk said, as if reading her mind. "We'll deal with it later, if we have to. For now though, I have other priorities."

He eased her off his lap so they both could stand and then draping his arm across her shoulders, he pulled her close. "I think we're going to call it a night," he said to the others.

"What about dinner?" Julia asked, concerned.

"We'll get something later," Dirk promised her with a smile. "Much later."

"Same here," Mac said as he and Lanie also got to their feet.

"I guess it's just you and me," the admiral said as he stood and offered Julia his hand. "I'm glad you decided to move in," he told her warmly.

She smiled back. "Thank you. Me, too. Oh, before I forget, you had a phone call earlier this evening. A Jessica Winslow?"

The admiral smiled. "She's my cousin's daughter. I haven't heard from her in years." His smile faded. "There's nothing wrong, is there?"

"No, no. Nothing like that. She wanted me to tell you that she's on her way. She's flying in and wanted to know if she could stay here for a few days. I believe she's bringing you something from Gerard as well."

The admiral's excitement grew. "She must be bringing the sword. This is wonderful news. I can hardly wait to see her. She must be in her twenties now." His eyes took on a faraway look. "My, time does fly, doesn't it?"

Then, as if he felt them watching him, he smiled. "Good night, everyone."

Beth and Dirk went upstairs to his room, where they spent a considerable amount of time exploring their love. Much later, they fell asleep wrapped in each other's arms.

It was well after midnight when Bethany woke up feeling hungry. Dirk was fast asleep and not wanting to wake him, she slipped out of bed, pulled on his T-shirt, and padded down to the kitchen for something to eat.

Gem was standing by the back sliding glass door and she turned those large, red eyes on Bethany when she walked in.

"What's the matter, girl?" Busy watching the small creature, she didn't hear Dirk until he spoke.

"What're you doing up?" He came toward her, wearing nothing more than his jeans.

"I was hungry. I'm sorry if I woke you."

"I missed you."

Gem pushed against the door again, distracting Bethany. When she turned back to Dirk, he was leaning against the counter, staring fixedly at the floor.

"Hey, what's the matter?" she asked softly, going to stand beside him, touching his arm. He raised his head and looked so troubled, she was immediately concerned. "Dirk?"

"Marry me."

Her heart stilled as various emotions hit her. Mistaking her silence for hesitation, he hurried on. "I don't want to rush you, and I realize that with everything that happened with Miles—"

She placed her finger against his lips to silence him, then leaned forward and placed a short, sweet kiss where her finger had just been. "Yes."

He looked at her, surprised. "Yes?"

She smiled. "Yes, I'll marry you."

"What I do is dangerous. You heard the admiral. No changeling has lived very long. You could end up a very young widow."

"I'll take my chances."

"I'd want you to be up at night, while I'm awake, and sleep during the day, with me," he warned her.

She trailed a finger down his chest. "Despite the vampires, I've grown rather fond of the nights," she said playfully, lightly kissing each corner of his mouth. "You might say I've been seduced by the night."

He smiled then and the transformation made her heart sing.

"Stay right here," he told her, pushing away from the counter and leaving the kitchen. For a second, she was too stunned by his departure to do more than stand there. Then, as she considered going after him, he returned, strolling toward her with his hands behind his back. "I have something for you." He held the "something" out to her and she gave a small gasp. Sitting in the palm of his hand was the clown doll her grandmother had given her.

Tears filled her eyes as she took it from him. "Where? How?" She'd thought it lost forever. Bringing it close, she hugged it as she had when she was a child.

"I found it at the lair," Dirk explained. "I thought you might like to have it back."

Overwhelmed, she threw herself into his arms and kissed him until the only thing either of them could think about was returning to their bedroom where they could finish what they'd started.

They were halfway to the stairs when a rattling noise stopped them.

"What's the matter with her?" Dirk asked, watching Gem pawing at the sliding glass door. He pulled Bethany after him as he went to investigate.

"What's that?"

Bethany looked at the object lying against the back

door and felt a small chill run along her spine. "It looks like Dr. Weber's journal," she said in awe, recognizing the book. Dirk opened the door to retrieve it and when he did, Gem shot past him.

Bethany and Dirk exchanged worried glances. About to go after her, they both stopped.

Standing at the far end of the yard was the adult chupacabra. Gem ran up to her and they rubbed muzzles in an obvious show of affection. Beside the adult was the lone figure of a man, his red eyes a faint light in the distance.

"Harris," Bethany whispered.

She and Dirk stood watching him. After a moment, Gem ran back to the mansion, brushed past them, and disappeared inside the house. Bethany took the journal from Dirk's hands and held it up so Harris would see that she had found it. She knew why he'd returned it and she wouldn't let him down. She was starting a new life with the man she loved—and now, she had a purpose.

After a moment, Harris raised his hand in farewell. Dirk and Bethany waved back. Then, vampire and chupacabra turned and walked away, disappearing into the still, dark night.

About the Author

Robin T. Popp grew up watching *Star Trek* and reading Nancy Drew, Robert Heinlein, Sharon Green, and Piers Anthony. She loved the daring and romantic exploits of heroic characters on grand adventures in otherworldly places. It wasn't long before she wanted to write such tales to share with others. Though she was forced to take a thirty-year detour through the real world—which certainly wasn't without its share of adventures—armed now with two master's degrees, a full-time job, and a family, she has taken the first steps toward realizing her original dream of becoming an author.

Too Close to the Sun, a futuristic romance published in July 2003, was her first novel. *Out of the Night* was her second novel and represents her first foray into another of her favorite alternate realities—the realm of vampires.

Robin lives southwest of Houston, Texas, with her husband, three kids, three dogs, two frogs, one rabbit, and a mortgage. She is living the American dream.

If you hunger for more
Robin T. Popp,

turn this page for a preview of
her next Night Slayer novel

Tempted in the Night

Available in mass market

early 2007.

Chapter
1

"Tell me, Boehler, just what the fuck were you thinking?" Assistant Chief Gamble's voice was loud enough to rattle the windows in his small office.

Veteran homicide detective John Boehler remained unfazed as he faced his boss across the desk. "I'm sorry, was that a rhetorical question?"

"What the fuck do you think?" Gamble bit out sharply.

John thought it sounded like another rhetorical question, but this time kept his thoughts to himself. He was too tired to sit through much more of this "ass-chewing," not that he had any hope of getting to bed soon.

"Why in the hell would you even approach Simon Brody after the trial? Much less threaten him in front of every reporter in the greater D.C. metro area?"

"I didn't threaten him," John said with as little inflection as he could.

Gamble picked up the TV remote on his desk and aimed it at the small television sitting on a nearby bookcase. Soon, the news footage outside the courthouse was rolling across the screen. John didn't bother to watch. He didn't want to see Simon Brody strolling down the steps of the court-house, a smug, self-satisfied grin plastered across his face. Hearing the little cock-sucker's seemingly heartfelt reaf-firmation of his innocence was harder to ignore, especially when Gamble turned up the volume. As it had before, both the tone and the words ignited a slow, white-hot burn of rage deep inside of him. Today, justice had not been served. The jury may have found Brody innocent, but John knew the truth.

Then John heard himself saying, "Don't get too com-fortable, Brody. You're going to hell—if I have to drag your sorry ass there myself."

Gamble shut off the television and the silence that fol-lowed was deafening, if brief. "Damn it, John, what were you thinking?"

John didn't bother to respond. At the time he'd uttered his threat, the media had been the least of his concerns. Five long months of hard, by-the-book investigative work flushed down the proverbial toilet because someone in the department had managed to "lose" a critical piece of evi-dence. John had no doubt that Franklin Brody and his mil-lions were somehow involved.

Daddy might have saved his spoiled son from death by lethal injection, but who was going to save the young women of the Washington D.C. area? Now that Simon Brody was free, it was just a matter of time before he killed again.

"I want to know what's bothering you, Boehler," the assistant chief continued in a surprisingly sympathetic tone. "You haven't been yourself, lately. You used to be one the best detectives I had. Lately, though . . . I don't know." He studied John's face closely in a fair imitation of the department's psychiatrist trying to see inside his head. "Are you having problems at home? With your wife?"

John wanted to laugh at the absurdity of the question. "I'm not married, remember?" He had been once, fifteen years ago, if one could call a night of drinking, a quick trip to Vegas followed by eleven months of sheer hell a marriage. John didn't.

"Then maybe you need to find someone; settle down; start a family."

Yeah, John thought, because it had worked so well the first time. Gamble's attempt to counsel him was pissing him off. "I'm fine. Just a little tired." He didn't want to continue this particular line of conversation, so he changed the subject. "Sir, I'd like permission to look into how that evidence against Brody disappeared."

"That's not your job."

"I realize that. However—"

Gamble waved him to silence. "Forget that. You have bigger problems to deal with."

"Sir?"

"First, you practically accuse the late Miles Van Horne of being involved with terrorists. Now, you're publicly threatening the son of Washington's *second* most influential man? Is it the rich you hate, Boehler, or are you just tired of being a cop? Because I assure you, you're well on your way to committing career suicide."

John felt himself grow very still. "Van Horne wasn't a random target. The Exsanguinators killed him because he tried to double-cross them. I'd call that being 'involved.'"

Gamble heaved a frustrated sigh. "Well, his mother disagrees. And now Marcie Van Horne has got the D.A. breathing down my neck to reopen the case. I'm having to bring in someone from Internal Affairs to take a second look at the case."

John wasn't stupid. He read between the lines. Gamble was bringing in IA to investigate him as much as the circumstances of Miles Van Horne's death. And if they got too close . . .

John wondered how much time he had to "clean" up his files and was about to make his excuse to leave when Gamble pressed the button on his intercom. "Gail? I want to know when Dresden gets here. He is? Good, send him in."

A moment later, the door to the office opened and a short, stocky man walked in wearing a pressed suit, polished shoes and an attitude that said his shit don't stink. John hated him instantly.

"John, meet Richard Dresden, with Internal Affairs. He'll be handling the investigation into the Exsanguinator cases. I expect you to show him the same respect you'd show me—and give him your full cooperation."

Yeah, John thought, he'd show *Dick* some respect. Count on it. He managed to keep his mouth shut and his face expressionless.

At his boss' dismissive gesture, he stood and headed for the door. He was seconds from a clean getaway when the assistant chief dropped the last bomb on him. "Don't let me catch you anywhere near Simon Brody or anything having to do with him, got it? Right now, you've got two strikes against you. One more and you'll be so far out, not even God can get you back in the game."

A couple of hours later, it was dark and instead of being at home in bed enjoying another sleepless night, John was driving around, scanning the dark streets for . . . he wasn't sure what, exactly. If anyone had asked, he would have told them he was looking for members of a fanatical group of serial killers—a group he, himself, had dubbed The Exsanguinators because of the way they drained their victims' bodies of blood.

Of course, he was more likely to find one of their victims than the actual killers. In over a year of searching, that's all he'd ever found.

His first exposure to The Exsanguinators had come when several Navy SEALS had disappeared under violent and mysterious circumstances. Days later, one of them was found dead in an abandoned building. There had been no obvious wounds and yet, the body had been drained of blood. Later victims would be found also drained of blood, but with the two puncture wounds in their neck that was to become their signature mark.

That case was a first for John and in his search for answers, he had called in the dead SEAL's commanding officer, Admiral Charles Winslow. John had met the older man years earlier, when the admiral had been a guest lecturer for one of John's college classes. They'd instantly struck up a friendship that had survived the years.

To his surprise, the admiral had claimed to be familiar with both *modus operandi* and the group responsible, leading John to believe that the problem was something the government was handling. This wasn't the first time the police and the government had worked on the same case, so John took more of a support role, calling the

admiral or one of the members of his security team whenever he found another victim, but otherwise adopting a
hands-off approach.

He hadn't closed his eyes, though, and what he'd observed had raised a lot of questions. The admiral and his
team had not been exactly forthcoming with information,
leaving John to draw his own conclusions which, he reflected as he parked his car and got out, were almost as
disturbing as the killings themselves.

No one had ever used the word "vampire" around him;
the mere idea should have been absurd. But as a detective,
John could put the clues together and, regardless of how
crazy he thought it sounded, the end result always came
up "vampire."

He'd considered approaching Winslow with his theories, but he hesitated. Even if the killers were actual vampires—and who would believe that?—the nature of the
killings had lately undergone a subtle change.

Over the past couple of months, the victim demo-
graphics had changed. Instead of average citizens, the latest victims had been known criminals; scum of the earth
who had, through power, money or the negligence of the
legal system, managed to escape justice. In a bizarre
sense, The Exsanguinators—or vampires, if that's what
they were—had been performing a community service.
John wasn't sure he wanted that to end.

Getting out of the car, John started walking. The park
loomed like a graveyard, silent and eerie. The shadows
of trees obstructed his view, but he continued forward,
pulling his coat tighter to keep out the stiff January breeze
and wondering if his purpose tonight would still make
sense in the morning.

Last week's snowfall lay in dirty piles of slush along the edges of the street and he had to step over several small puddles to avoid getting his shoes wet. When he reached the park, he stepped onto the paved path. His senses were hyperextended as he strained to pick up even the slightest sound and though he heard nothing, he sensed he wasn't alone.

Moving as silently as he could, he continued on, eyeing the large grouping of bushes ahead to his right. He was less than twenty yards away when a figure suddenly appeared on the path before him.

Time stood still as John stopped to study the man whose features were too shadowed to see clearly. It wasn't unusual to see someone in the park this late and the man could be anyone—or no one in particular. Yet, when he lifted his head, his eyes, glowing with an unnatural red light, caught and held John's attention.

Vampire. The word echoed through his mind, no longer sounding as absurd as it had earlier.

At that moment, John heard a noise, off to the left, and turned to see what it was. From out of the darkness, the lithe figure of a woman came racing toward them, long black hair flapping wildly in the wind behind her. The exact details of her other features were lost in deference to the sword in her hand, which she wielded with apparent confidence and purpose.

Her attention seemed focused solely on the other man and, screaming like a banshee, she raced forward, showing no signs of slowing.

Almost belatedly realizing her intent, John shouted at the man to run. Then, without a thought to himself, he rushed to intercept her, leaping through the air in a flying tackle. He caught hold of her sword arm with one hand and, wrapping his other arm around her body, bore her to the ground.

They landed with a painful jolt that should have knocked the wind out of her, especially with John's added weight on top of her. Amazingly, though, she recovered quickly and immediately began fighting him, trying to buck him off, all the while shouting at the top of her very British lungs.

"I'll kill you, you blood-sucking—"

"Settle down," John ordered her. "I don't want to have to hurt you." His words seemed to have a small effect as the woman ceased her struggling long enough to really look at him. When she did, John saw her eyes open wide in surprise.

"You're human!"

John found her choice of words particularly interesting given his own purpose for being in the park. He took another hard look at her. "That's right. What were you expecting?"

Instead of answering, she started to struggle, so he levered himself up, flipped the woman onto her stomach and shoved a knee into her back to keep her down.

"Oompf! Bloody Hell," the woman swore, twisting her head, trying to look at him. Her dark hair, in wild disarray, enveloped her head like a dark cloud. "What are you doing?"

"I would think it's obvious," he replied, trying to ignore her enticing shape as he ran his hands up and down her body, searching for hidden weapons.

"You're letting him get away! Let me up now before it's too late."

John glanced around and saw that the man had, indeed, disappeared. The observation brought anger and disappointment. He'd never know, now, if that man was the one he'd been searching for.

He turned his attention back to his prisoner and saw that her sword now lay harmlessly off to the side. He picked it up to move it a safer distance away, noticing that there was something familiar about it, but he couldn't remember what. Then he flipped her over and helped her to sit. "You want to tell me why you're running around the park at night with a sword?"

A glare was the only response he got.

"Look, here in the states, we don't go around waving swords and trying to lop off people's heads. And I'm betting over in England—that's where you're from, right?—I'm guessing they don't allow it, either. So, bottom line, you're in serious trouble."

Still, she ignored him.

John cast a furtive glance in the direction that the man had disappeared. "Who was that? Your boyfriend?"

She huffed at him in anger. "Not bloody likely."

He tried to read her expression. Green eyes, darkened to the color of emerald gem, looked up at him from between the twin silken curtains of ebony framing her face. Suddenly, the screaming banshee was gone and in her place was a lost waif.

When she spoke, her words were soft and beseeching. "Please, you have to help me. More people are going to die if we don't stop him. You have to let me go."

She sounded so sincere, he was almost tempted to do as she asked. "I don't think so."

She swore and renewed her struggle to break out of the

cuffs. John let her try, knowing that she wasn't going any-where. Watching her, he was reminded of her strength when she'd fought him and one thing was very apparent. This was no lost waif. This was a deeply disturbed, possi-bly clinically psychotic woman in desperate need of a seventy-two hour lockdown and a Thorazine drip—and he knew just the man to arrange it.

John was jerked from a deep sleep by the sound of his phone ringing. As he lay there debating whether or not to answer it, the ringing stopped. He held his breath, wait-ing to see if it started up again and when it finally seemed like it wouldn't, he closed his eyes and let his mind drift . . .

His cell phone started ringing.

Glancing at the bedside table, he noticed two things. His cell phone wasn't where it should have been and the clock showed it was almost noon, which meant he'd had almost two hours of sleep. Throwing back the covers, he half-rolled, half-fell out of bed, still fully clothed in yes-terday's wrinkled outfit, and stumbled across the room to where his coat lay draped over the back of a chair.

Hauling it up, he dug in the pocket closest to him until his hand reappeared on the other side, having slipped through the hole he hadn't known was there. There was something about that new hole that should have bothered him, but the incessant ringing demanded his immediate attention. Reaching into the other pocket, he dug out his phone and answered it just before it rolled over to voice mail.

"Boehler, here." His voice sounded like wet gravel under rolling tires.

"I want to see you in my office. Now," Gamble ordered.

"Yes, si—" He was speaking to a dead phone. Gamble had already disconnected the call.

John stared at the phone in dumb fascination for a minute. "Good morning to you, too," he mumbled, wondering what he'd done wrong this time.

The events of the prior evening came racing back—the dark figure in the park, the screaming banshee with her sword. With his luck, the man was someone of influence and power and had shown up at the station to press charges against the woman who'd tried to kill him, only discover that she wasn't in custody. Why he hadn't arrested her, John couldn't say. He attributed it to the judicial insanity that seemed to be sweeping the city lately. After all, why should he follow the rules when no one else did? Okay, he knew the answer to that, but chose to ignore it.

John remembered the look of hate and betrayal when he'd dropped the woman off at the psych facility for lockdown. He could keep her there seventy-two hours for observation, after which time, she'd either have to face charges or be admitted for a full psych evaluation. He'd been hoping that twenty-four hours would be enough to convince her to cooperate. His plan to pay her a little visit as soon as he woke would have to wait.

Not bothering to change clothes, John ran his fingers through his hair and put on his shoes. His holster was slung over the bedpost, so he strapped it on and then checked the gun to make sure the safety was on. As he left the bedroom, he grabbed his coat and pulled it on as he walked through the small apartment, checking all his pockets as he went. He was almost to the front door when he froze and rechecked his pockets.

His wallet was there but his ID badge was missing.

He put his hand into the right coat pocket and felt it slide all the way through the fabric. The hole! Great. Just what he needed.

He pulled out his cell phone and called the main desk of the police station. "Hi, Joyce. I need to report a lost ID. Yeah—mine."

The call took about ten minutes and by the time he clicked off, he was in his car, already halfway to the station. Traffic wasn't a problem and fifteen minutes later, he was walking through the building, headed for Gamble's office.

His cell phone rang again and he recognized Joyce's number. Hoping someone had turned in his badge, he answered the call. "Tell me you have good news."

"Sorry, John, not the kind you're hoping for," she replied sympathetically. "Sammy, over at Impound, called. He said to tell you they just brought in a car you might be interested in—a rental."

John knew the Jane Doe from the night before hadn't materialized out of thin air. He figured she'd left her car close enough to walk, so had asked to be notified of any cars being towed in that were picked up inside a two-mile radius of Thompson Park.

He glanced at his watch and saw that it was almost noon. "Joyce, Gamble's expecting me to walk in the door any second. Can you call Sammy back and tell him not to do anything with the car? I'll be there as soon as I can."

"Will do."

"Okay, thanks. I owe you."

Once he reached Gamble's office, he took a bracing breath and then knocked on the closed door.

Gamble's voice erupted from inside, "Come in."

John opened the door, but hadn't even made it to the chair in front of Gamble's desk before the assistant chief started in on him. "Were you in Thompson Park last night? South side?"

Warning bells started pealing inside his head, but he saw no reason not to answer. "Yes."

"What were you doing there?"

"Just taking a walk."

Gamble stared at him, his hard glare boring through him. After a second, he opened his middle desk drawer, reached in to grab something and then tossed it across the desk to John. "Lose something while you were there?"

John stared down at his badge, realizing now it must have dropped out of his pocket when he was wrestling with Jane Doe. That part made sense to him. What didn't make sense was how Gamble came to have it.

Resisting the urge to snatch it up, he held Gamble's steady gaze. "Where'd you find it?"

"Under a bush, about eight inches from Simon Brody's dead body."

Authors Dish

What could an author of historical romances and an author of contemporary vampire fiction possibly have in common? We find out when authors Kathryn Caskie and Robin T. Popp chat online about their books.

Robin T. Popp: Do you know that the hero of *Seduced by the Night,* Dirk Adams, was never intended to be a long-term character and end up with his own story? When I first created him in *Out of the Night,* he was supposed to be like one of the extras on *Star Trek*—killed off in the first fifteen minutes of the show.

Kathryn Caskie: You mean the guy in the red shirt with the landing party, right? Don't tell anyone, but I grew up watching *Star Trek.*

Robin T. Popp: Me, too. I loved that show. So, what about in *Love is in the Heir* (on sale now)? Any "red shirts" turned heroes?

Kathryn Caskie: No red shirts, but over the course of the book my hero did split into two characters. You see, my heroes are usually bad boys, but Griffin, the hero of *Love is in the Heir,* couldn't be. Problem was, no matter how hard I tried to keep him in line, his wicked side kept showing up, making my heroine hate him. Then my heroine thought, it was almost like he was two different men. And that is exactly what he became: two separate people. The good twin, Griffin, and the rakish twin, Garnet, who are both pretending to be the same man.

Robin T. Popp: I foresee many interesting situations.

Kathryn Caskie: It's especially bad when Griffin tells her he loves her and wants to marry her, and they make love. Then the next day, she runs into the rakish twin who acts like it never happened. She thinks she's fallen for the oldest trick in a rake's book.

Robin T. Popp: Why are Griffin and Garnet pretending to be the same man?

Kathryn Caskie: There is this law called primogeniture. The eldest inherits everything—titles, houses, money—but if no one knows which twin was born first, meaning no clear heir, the Crown can reclaim it all. The ailing earl in my story doesn't want that to happen when he dies so he makes a deal with the twins. The twin to marry a woman of quality first will be named "firstborn." This is all pretty illegal, so the bride hunt has to remain a secret.

Robin T. Popp: Ah, secrets, lies, and deceptions. In *Seduced by the Night,* I have a similar situation when Beth (the heroine) believes Dirk is something he isn't. She's a biochemist and vampires are trying to kidnap her because they want her to duplicate the chupacabra venom that turns humans into vampires—they plan to sell "immortality" on the black market. So Dirk, as her bodyguard, is trying to protect her without her knowing that he, himself, is a changeling—half-human and half-vampire.

Kathryn Caskie: Griffin's dilemma is that he wants to tell the heroine everything, but he can't because he doesn't want to betray his brother's trust. It's a case of honor and integrity versus love.

Robin T. Popp: Dirk faces a similar choice. If Beth discovered the truth, she'd be terrified of him. This is further complicated because Beth is engaged to another man and while honor dictates that Dirk keep his emotional distance from her, his heart demands otherwise.

Kathryn Caskie: I wouldn't have thought our stories could be so different and yet share so much common ground—two books about deception and dual identities.

Robin T. Popp: Tough issues to overcome, especially in a romance story.

Kathryn Caskie: But as you say, our books are romances, so our characters will live happily ever after.

www.kathryncaskie.com   www.robintpopp.com

Want to know more about romances at
Warner Books and Warner Forever?
Get the scoop online!

WARNER'S ROMANCE HOMEPAGE

Visit us at www.warnerforever.com for all the
latest news, reviews, and chapter excerpts!

NEW AND UPCOMING TITLES

Each month we feature our new titles
and reader favorites.

CONTESTS AND GIVEAWAYS

We give away galleys, autographed copies,
and all kinds of fun stuff.

AUTHOR INFO

You'll find bios, articles, and links to personal
Web sites for all your favorite authors—and
so much more!

THE BUZZ

Sign up for our monthly romance newsletter,
and be the first to read all about it!